These delightful romantic classics have been specially reprinted under Fawcett's new Coventry line.

They represent the best of the genre, proven authors who have become immensely popular over the years.

For those who have long loved tales of the Regency period as well as those newly enamored of them, these enduring romances represent a rich reading experience.

Look for new and enthralling titles available each month from Fawcett Coventry.

Also by Joan Smith:

AUNT SOPHIE'S DIAMONDS	50015	$1.75
BABE	50023	$1.75
ESCAPADE	23232	$1.50
LA COMTESSE	23490	$1.50

Buy them at your local bookstore or use this handy coupon for ordering.

COLUMBIA BOOK SERVICE (a CBS Publications Co.)
32275 Mally Road, P.O. Box FB, Madison Heights, MI 48071

Please send me the books I have checked above. Orders for less than 5 books must include 75¢ for the first book and 25¢ for each additional book to cover postage and handling. Orders for 5 books or more postage is FREE. Send check or money order only.

Cost $_____   Name _____

Postage_____   Address _____

Sales tax*_____   City _____

Total $_____   State _____ Zip _____

*The government requires us to collect sales tax in all states except AK, DE, MT, NH and OR.

An Affair of the Heart

A NOVEL BY

Joan Smith

FAWCETT COVENTRY • NEW YORK

AN AFFAIR OF THE HEART

Published by Fawcett Coventry Books, a unit of CBS Publications, the Consumer Publishing Division of CBS Inc.

Copyright © 1977 by Fawcett Publications, Inc.

ISBN: 0-449-50061-6

Printed in the United States of America

First Fawcett printing: February 1977

13   12   11   10   9   8   7   6   5   4   3

Chapter One

Lord Claymore's handsome brow wore a frown as he pelted down the steps of the mansion on Tiburn Lane and leapt into his curricle. His tiger, Black Cat, was too wise to make reference to the danger of springing the grays in the middle of town. Be lucky you didn't get the crop across your shoulders, saying a word when he was in this mood. Anyway, there was no one to speak of in the park at this unfashionable hour of the morning, and they would be on the Chelsea Road in next to no time, the way he was springing 'em. There he might run his bits o' blood into the ground without killing anyone save themselves.

So, Black Cat thought with a smug smile, she'd turned him down, and thank God for it! To be carting that China doll round town, going no more than five miles an hour and stopping at every carriage with a crest on the side of it, was not Blackie's idea of driving at all. A nifty piece she were, to be sure. Pretty as could stare, with her blond curls and blue glass eyes. The carriage hit a rut in the road, and its occupants were lifted six inches from their seats. Milord's curled beaver left his head and went whirling down the road behind them.

"Eh, you've lost your lid," Blackie informed his master.

"Shut your face," was his reply.

"A new one it were," he continued, undaunted.

Milord was obviously paying no heed, for Blackie escaped scot free for his impudence. The carriage continued bolting down the road at its dangerous pace, but its driver's heart remained behind at Tiburn Lane with *her,* Gloria Golden.

She had been the acknowledged queen of the season just closing. Beau Brummell himself had hardly more power than Miss Golden where it counted—in society. Every buck and beau in town had been at her dainty feet, heart in extended hand. It was one of the *on dits* that she'd had to hire a secretary to answer her invitations, and it was *said,* though the lady was too modest to confirm the rumor, that she had every week a box of trinkets received from her admirers hauled off to be sold, and the proceeds sent to her favorite charity, the London Orphans. She did blushingly admit, however, that the overflow of floral tributes was sent daily to St. Bartholomew's to be admired by the patients there. It was not within her power to deny Lord Cushington's having bred and named a yellow rose for her—the Golden Rose it was called—when everyone knew it had taken first prize at the Hampshire Flower Show. Inspired by the incident, Brummell had concocted a perfume for her sole use, and called it Rose d'Or. Lord Petersham had offered to make her up a batch of her own snuff, and though she was gratified, she had declined, having no desire to mar either her nose or her gown by this dirty habit. The Golden Rose bonnet, worn by her at an *al fresco* party given by the Prince Regent, had been an immediate success, and shamelessly copied by every lady with any pretension to fame or fashion. Her gowns, pelisses, coiffures, reticules, even her faint and enchanting lisp were similarly copied, till it seemed all of fashionable London was inhabited by a hundred Golden Roses. But always the original, unique, incomparable Golden Rose herself was at the lead.

It was not to be imagined that a connoisseur like Lord Claymore would be tardy in recognizing such an Incomparable, and be among the first to attach himself to the comet's train. Nor did it ever occur to him that his attentions were unwanted. *His* offerings—floral or otherwise—were never carted off with the others, for she frequently wore the corsage sent by himself, and had used every flummery bit of stuff he had ever conferred on her. Fans, satin roses (golden, of course), perfume bottle—all were displayed to the eyes of her goggling public, and their donor acknowledged. Such encouragement gave him no cause to expect his offer of marriage would be unwelcome. In fact, he had even more explicit reason than this to think himself *the one*. Unbeknownst to any except himself and the Rose, she had *twice* allowed him to touch her rosebud lips. Once fleetingly behind the pillar at Lady Castlereagh's ball, when Fate had conspired to give them a moment alone, and once in her garden just at dusk, behind the fountain her great-grandpapa had imported whole from Italy. And on that occasion it had been more than a touch. He had felt it as good as an acceptance. Had, in fact, from that moment on considered her his own.

He smiled secretly to hear the odds at the clubs were running two to one in favor of Everleigh, the Duke. As if the Golden Rose would attach herself to that black thorn, old enough to be her father. Leading comments that the Duke was a great friend of her papa, and had besides twenty-five thousand a year, were shrugged off. Even if he had three estates, besides his London residence and hunting lodge in the Cottsmore Hills, he had also a nose as long as a parsnip, and gray hair, to counterbalance those material advantages. Rose actually *laughed* at him behind his back, and called him "the old goat." Others, who were on Claymore's side, contented themselves with the banal reference to Beauty and the Beast. Obviously there would be no match between that mismated pair.

Yet she had not a quarter of an hour ago informed him that a marriage had been arranged between herself and the Duke of Everleigh, to take place a month hence. She had besides pokered up and pouted at him when he reminded her of those stolen kisses and her numerous slurs on his grace. Even his impassioned plea that he be al-

lowed to rescue her and spirit her off to the Border had
been shunted aside.

"I don't want to *escape*, silly," she had said, tapping
him on the wrist with her fan—the ivory fan with painted
lace covering he had given her only a week ago.

"Miss Golden, you cannot mean you entered *willingly*
into this match?" Lord Claymore asked, aghast.

"Of course I did. I must marry thomone," she lisped.
"He is a duke, and I should like very much to be a
ducheth."

"But—but I can make you a marchioness," Claymore
reminded her.

"Yes, but a ducheth rates higher than a marchioneth,"
she had retaliated happily.

"Is that all our relationship has meant to you? You will
turn your back on me only because of a greater title?"

"Oh, it is not only the title," she said pettishly, arising
and pacing about the Green Saloon (which Mama had refused to have redone in gold) where she was receiving his
offer. She was exquisitely aware that her perambulations
showed off her figure and her Italian silk gown to advantage. "Our families have been connected forever, and
besides, I am ever so fond of Iggy. He will deny me nothing."

Claymore was too overcome to argue further. It was
plain as a pikestaff she was *selling* herself to the highest
bidder. Pride overcame chagrin long enough for his
youthful visage to assume a sneer, and he congratulated
her on her conquest.

"Now don't be like that, Clay," she said, dimpling
adorably. "Let uth still be friends." She had come and
laid her hand on his arm. He felt that if he tried to kiss
her again, he would not be repulsed. Almost those
pouting lips seemed to invite.

He was not to be won over. "You might have told me
you had accepted Everleigh and saved me the bother of
making an offer in form," he said stiffly.

"Oh, but I wanted to see if I couldn't bring *you* up to
the mark too," she returned pertly.

"You are to be twice congratulated in one day,

ma'am," Clay said. "Good day, Miss Golden." Turning, he fled the room.

The remainder of that morning was never entirely clear to Claymore. He remembered only the wind whistling in his ears, and green fields whipping past him. He did not recall at what point Blackie had taken over the reins, but at noon he was being deposited at his own house on the corner of Curzon and Half Moon Street, and walking up the steps in a sort of daze. He was heartbroken, incredulous still, mortified, and extremely ill-tempered. He rounded on his innocent butler and demanded of him if it was not possible to ever be greeted by a *smile* when he came home, and why was it his house must smell of fish? Decaying fish.

His friend, Rex Homberly, was awaiting him in his study, sipping a glass of ale and tossing cards into his hat, which he had placed on the floor halfway across the room.

"Why have you been put in *this* room?" Clay demanded. Rex looked at him in astonishment as it was in this cozy if shabby little study that they regularly conversed.

Rex did not consider himself a knowing one, but figured he knew at least what this fit of pique was all about. "Heard the news," he said by way of commiseration. "In the *Morning Observer*. Brought it over. Thought you might not have read it, but I see by your face you have."

Clay wordlessly accepted a glass of ale which a servant had been hurriedly sent off to get him. His domestic menials were not always so alert, but when his lordship came in lambasting a body for not grinning like a hyena when he went to the door, something special was called for.

"Thing is," Rex continued, tossing a card a foot wide of his hat, "no point in offering for her now. Good thing we found out before you went making a cake of yourself."

"I made an offer this morning," Clay admitted, and colored under the look his friend bestowed on him.

"What! She let you. . . ? Oughtn't to have done that. Not the thing to be receiving you alone when she'd already accepted Everleigh. Dashed loose way for a young lady to be acting. And *you* shouldn't have gone dashing off without reading the paper. Ought to have looked at the Social Column first, Clay. Told you it would be published any day. Everybody knew it. Pity to give her the satisfaction." He whizzed another card, and it landed by accident in the hat. It was the last, and he arose to his full five feet six inches and looked up at his miserable friend. There was ready sympathy in his bright blue eyes, and on his childish face.

Clay was not in the mood for sympathy. "No harm done," he said nonchalantly, willing down the urge to rant and rave.

"No, but she'll blab it all over town. Make you look a terrible fool. Oh well, you would have looked that anyway, the way you've been dangling after her all Season, showering her with flowers and cheap junk."

"As to looking the fool, who will look wise in *this* affair? Everleigh marrying a girl young enough to be his daughter, Miss Golden latching onto a title and a fortune, and me, 'making a cake of myself' over her, as you so kindly pointed out. Fools all!"

"I wouldn't call the Rose a fool," Rex said consideringly. "Not by any manner of means. As shrewd as she can hold together, if you want my opinion. Everleigh was the pick of the Season's beaux, not a doubt of that. The only duke in the race, and all those estates and what not. Quite a catch."

"An ugly old man in his forties!" This seemed an advanced state of decrepitude indeed to one who was not yet twenty-five himself.

"Thirty-nine," Rex corrected unhesitatingly. "Born within two hours of my Aunt Marjorie. They was neighbors, and it used to be talked up at home that she'd nab him, but then she developed that squint. Unfortunate."

"He is old enough to be her father in any case."

"He'd have had to marry awful young, and the Everleighs don't. His younger brother only got hitched last year, and *he's* thirty-seven. Anyway, he *ain't* her father, that's the thing."

"I trust they will not try to palm this off as a love

match," Clay said, leaning against an old desk, much battered and strewn with debris.

"Easy to love twenty-five thousand a year," Rex replied in an attempt at lightness. He heartily disliked seeing his friend in such a fit of the sullens. Wouldn't be up for any sport all day if he carried on in this fashion.

"They're all alike," Clay said in disgust. "Money and titles, that's all women think of. Everleigh has *bought* Gloria with his twenty-five thousand a year and his coronet, and she has sold herself to become a duchess. A man may buy anything or anyone if he is rich enough."

"That's true," Rex admitted, assuming his "wise" face, which is to say he wrinkled his brow and pursed his lips. He then proceeded to mar the effect by sticking the head of his cane in his mouth and sucking it. Finding the flavor not to his liking, for the cane was tipped in silver and had a metallic taste, he removed it and added sagely, "Daresay I could attach Miss Simpson if I had a title, and a quarter of your fortune."

"Certainly. I shouldn't be surprised to see her have her legs amputated to please you, if only you had a handle to your name."

Miss Simpson was of a build currently described as Junoesque. She was close to half a head taller than Rex, and a more foolish sight than Mr. Homberly partnering her on the floor, his neck arched back to look up at her, was seldom to be seen.

"Yes, if I had a handle, like you," Rex replied. "No reason for *you* to fret, dear boy. You ain't a duke, but you're a marquis, next best thing to it, and your blunt must nearly match Everleigh's. Figures, if he gets first prize—the Rose—you ought to pick off the next plum, for you're second in title and fortune."

But there was an unbridgeable chasm between Miss Golden and the second plum. There was no one who came near her. "Whom do you have in mind?" Clay asked, with little interest.

"Miss Sitwell, say."

"That mousey little thing." Clay waved a hand in dismissal of this unexceptional lady.

"Ain't mousey. Got nice teeth."

This only served to call up the bewitching smile of Miss Golden, who had, naturally, a set of matched pearls in her mouth.

"Or Miss Danfers. Striking woman."

"I don't recall Miss Danfers."

"That would be because you wasted the whole Season trailing after the Rose. Miss Danfers is a brunette. You like brunettes."

Clay scanned his mind for an attractive brunette. "I *do* seem to remember seeing a pretty dark-haired girl, early on in the Season. But she just—disappeared."

"Well, Miss Danfers didn't disappear, for you stood up with her at Marston's ball two nights ago."

"Did I?"

"Course you did. So did I. Wore a flowered gown, with pink roses in her hair."

"Oh, that one," Clay said, already dismissing the girl from his mind. A plain, platter-faced woman. "That wasn't the one I meant."

"Don't know who you could have meant then."

"She was some connection of the Siderows, I believe. Looked a little like Lady Siderow."

"Ah now, there's a smashing-looking woman, or must have been five years ago. One of the Wanderleys, you know, neighbors of mine. Fine-looking women, the whole bunch of them. Lady Tameson was one of them too. Four girls in a row. Have a son now, though, the last born."

"Well, and was one of these Wanderleys presented this year?"

The cane not being to his liking, Rex stuck his thumb in his mouth and worried it a while, as he pondered this weighty matter. "Wanda," he announced at last.

"Wanda Wanderley?"

"Yes, she was brought out by her sisters, Lady Siderow and Lady Tameson. That is, the mother was here, certainly, but I think it was the Siderow house that was used as a base of operations, for old Adam don't have a townhouse. Well, stands to reason you couldn't be growing orchids in a townhouse."

"Orchids?" Clay asked. He was accustomed to his friend's elliptical manner of speech, and felt secure that some sense would eventually emerge from his natterings.

"Yes, the father, Adam Wanderley, grows exotic flowers, you see. Has an orangery a couple of acres in size, full of the grandest flowers you ever saw, Clay, and not an orange in it. Has one in there that *eats* you."

"Indeed!"

"Yessir, or eats flies and midges and such things anyway. A vicious-looking little plant, all spikey around the edges. Showed it to me once. Put a fly in front of it, and it just snaps and eats it up whole. Ain't that terrible? A curst rum touch, old Adam."

"But a breeder of beautiful daughters, as well as flowers?"

"Four of them, before his good woman finally gave him a son. Must have been a vast relief to them, eh? Just goes to show you—if at first you don't succeed, try, try, try again. I got the right number of trys in there? Four daughters, then a son comes along. Called him Abel. Papa's name is Adam, you see, and of course they wouldn't want to call the boy Cain, because of the mark and all, so they called him Abel. A good chap is Abel, but only seventeen."

With singular tenacity, Claymore recalled his friend to the main thread of the conversation. "And this Wanda Wanderley, would she be the dark-haired girl I saw early on in the Season, I wonder?"

"Very likely. Certainly she'd stand out in any room. Would have given the Rose a run for her money if she'd stuck around."

"But what happened to her? I don't remember seeing her but once or twice."

"Yes, I'm coming to that. The pox, was it? No, she'd have got over that in time to come back for the rest of the Season. Ah, I've got it now. She broke her leg."

His patience rewarded, Clay continued. "Will she be returning in the Little Season, then, in the fall?"

"Might be, if she ain't buckled by then."

"Ah, already been sold, has she?"

"Sold? No such a thing! Adam may be a fool, but he don't *sell* his girls."

"Lets them do the bargaining, does he? They must be singularly capable, for both Lady Siderow and Lady Tameson have made creditable matches."

"Yes, and with no dowry to speak of either, for old Adam squanders every cent he can get his hands on for his flowers. Paid five hundred pounds for a stupid old flower Abel was showing me. From Brazil it was, growing right out of a tree stump. Had the stump and all shipped in from Brazil."

"And what bargain has this Wanda struck? She can't have had had much time to look about her, for she wasn't at more than two or three balls, I think."

"Wouldn't take her that long. The fact is, though, she was as well as buckled to the squire's son before ever she came to London, and once she had to go home, he'd be forever hanging around. Crazy about her. The mama had hoped for a title, which is why she presented her."

"Only a squire's son? Come, come, Rex. You must know my title and fortune take precedence over a *squire's* son. I shall attach Miss Wanda before the month is out."

"Don't be such a sap-skull, Clay. You're only saying that because you want to put the Rose's pretty nose out of joint. I know you. Too proud by half. Think she'll be boasting about her offer from you, and you want to saunter in with a pretty chick on your wing to show her how little you're suffering."

Clay concealed his sheepish smile behind his ale glass, and feigned deafness. "I was extremely taken with the young lady, I promise you," he replied blandly when he had drained the glass. In point of fact, he would not have recognized Wanda had she walked into the room that minute. He vaguely recalled a pretty dark-haired girl who had been around, then suddenly vanished. But as his obtuse friend had surmised, his reason for interest in Miss Wanda was to put the Rose's nose out of joint. Make a laughingstock of him, would she? And lead him to declare himself when she was already promised. His pride stung, he was determined to have the last laugh yet. If Miss Wanda was half so pretty as her sisters, she would be just the one to help him. Squire's son, indeed. He of all people knew the efficacy of a title and fortune!

"I daresay you were, and it's a pity she couldn't have stuck around to give the Rose some fair competition. Really nobody else worth a second look brought out this year. Just like the Wanderleys, though, to go breaking their legs. Hoydens, Clay, the whole lot of them. Joan rode astride till she was into her teens—that's Lady Siderow. And Caroline—"

"About Wanda," Claymore interrupted impatiently. "Took a tumble from her horse, I suppose?"

"No such a thing. She don't ride much, actually. She was climbing a tree, not to be outdone by Ellie, you know."

"Another sister?"

"The fourth of the Wanderley beauties. No, or is it third now? Yes, she was born a little before Wanda." He had to nurse his thumb after the strain of delivering this news.

"Some nine or ten months before, I must presume."

"No, it wasn't nearly that long." Claymore stared at this miracle, and Rex rambled on. "They was twins, you see, that's how it was."

"I see. And why was not Miss Ellie presented this year, then, being, er, older. Broke her head climbing a tree, did she?"

In spite of considerable thumb-sucking and ear-rubbing, Rex could not explain the mystery, though he assured his friend there must have been a good reason for it. Even if Ellie wasn't quite as pretty as the others, she would certainly get her crack at the London beaux; her mama and her married sisters would see to that.

"Well then, my friend, you must present me to these wonderful Wanderleys," Clay declared magnanimously.

"Can't do it, Clay. For one thing, the Season's over, or next to it, and they ain't in town. As I said, Wanda's as well as hitched. Wouldn't be surprised to read the announcement any day."

"I have not read it yet, and I'll wager a pony we will not read any such thing once *I* have offered for her."

"Lord, you haven't even *met* her! You might not care for Wanda at all. *I* don't. Like her the least of the batch, and that's a fact. You'd do better to have Ellie, though of course she ain't so handsome, and wouldn't square you with the Rose at all."

"It is Wanda I have decided on."

"Well, if you ain't a loose fish, Clay. Getting yourself buckled to a girl you don't even know, just to spite the Rose."

"What does a man ever know of the girl he marries?" Does Everleigh know, for example, that his bride called him 'the old goat' behind his back, and showered her kisses on anyone who bothered to reach out and take them? No, indeed, all you *knew* was what you could see, and if Miss Wanda proved attractive to the eye, he would have her.

"You know Wanda don't love you, for I'm telling you she's powerful fond of George Hibbard."

"We'll see if she isn't powerful fond of a title and a fortune as well. I think, Rex, I shall do you the honor of accepting your kind offer to pass a few weeks at the Abbey."

"What offer?"

"The offer you are about to extend."

"I was thinking of going to Bath, Clay."

"Think again. You are about to go home and visit your mama."

"*She's* going to Bath too."

"Not till July, I think?"

"Yes, but dash it, Clay, I want to get there before her, and have a bit of time to enjoy myself, for you know once she and my sister, Missie, get there, I shall be pressed into service taking them to Pump Rooms and libraries and such dull stuff."

"It is only early June, Rex. I shan't burden you with my presence for more than two weeks. That should be sufficient time to reach an understanding with Miss Wanda."

"I wouldn't wish that woman on my worst enemy, let alone my best friend. Just such a spoiled beauty as the Rose."

"That is precisely the sort of beauty I require," Clay returned firmly, even grimly.

"Yes, to flaunt in Miss Golden's face, and pretend you ain't all cut to ribbons by her having Everleigh."

"Just so."

"Well, we'll go to the Abbey, but Wanda won't have you, and I'm glad of it, for you two wouldn't suit in the least."

"We shall deal exceedingly," his friend replied. Then he walked to the center of the room, dumped the three cards that were in the hat on the floor, handed the hat to Rex, and ushered him to the door.

Once alone, Claymore felt very much like bawling, but he called for his housekeeper instead, and in a fierce tone demanded to know why he had not been handed the *Morning Observer* with his breakfast, and felt very foolish when she pointed out that it had been put on the table and he had not picked it up.

"Well, see that it doesn't happen again," he said.

His poor servant hardly knew whether she was to refrain from having it in the breakfast room at all, or to personally place it in his hands, and she frowned at him in perplexity.

"That will be all," his lordship said in a voice nearer normal, which did not enlighten her very much, but at least informed her that he "was getting over his snit."

Chapter Two

It was arranged that the two would set out early for the Abbey, Homberly's ancestral home in Surrey, just north of the Sussex border. But somehow it was very late in the morning before they eventually got away, and between stopping for luncheon and wasting the better part of an hour on a wager to determine which of the two could down a glass of ale faster, it was just turning dark when they tooled their curricles into the drive that led to the Abbey. They were both a trifle foxed, as it had taken some six bottles to ascertain that Rex could consume his drink nineteen seconds faster than his friend. Rex, however, was not so foxed as to fail to welcome the news that his parents were dining out. Cut up devilish stiff would his mama if he landed home anything but cold stone sober. He was wonderfully happy to know he need not curtail his drinking, for the parents were at Ashton Manor, five miles away, and were as well staying for a game of cards, so it was unlikely he would see them before midnight.

Therefore, he and Clay might have as many bottles of wine as they pleased cracked open, lift their hessian-clad feet to the table (no need even to change for dinner), and proceed to become as drunk as wheelbarrows. This pastime was engaged in, upon this occasion, to drown Clay's sorrow at losing the Rose. He had scarcely been sober since her refusal the day before. The preceding evening they had dined alone at Claymore House in London, as Clay was feeling too disgraced to visit any party when it was four pence to a groat Miss Golden would be there, decorating the arm of her old goat.

By the time they had finished the second bottle of claret, Lord Claymore had the marvelous idea of presenting himself that very night to his new beloved, Miss Wanda Wanderley.

"Not the thing, Clay," Rex was still sober enough to reply. "Too late. Damme, it's ten o'clock."

"Damme yourself, she wouldn't be in bed at ten o'clock. Nobody goes to bed at ten o'clock."

"Yes, but we ain't *there*," Rex argued. "They live in Sussex, you know. This is Surrey."

"You said they live next door. Remember distinctly," Clay pronounced, not very distinctly.

"That's because Surrey turns into Sussex about a quarter of a mile down the road. Another foot of land and Papa could boast he had estates in two counties. Don't though. We stop at the border, and Wanderley owns Sussex."

"Must be devilish rich. I never knew Wanderley owned Sussex. East *and* West Sussex?"

"Dash it, Clay, you're bosky. I didn't say he owned Sussex."

"Dash it, Rex, you're foxed yourself. Course you did. Just said it. Ask anyone."

Rex looked around the table obediently. "Know what, Clay? Ain't nobody here to ask. We're all alone."

"The devil you say!" Clay answered, also looking around. "By Jove, you're right. All alone. All alone," he repeated forlornly. "I'm sick of being all alone, Rex. Going to meet Miss Wanderley."

"No, are you though?" Rex asked with interest, as the fumes rose to his head. "Know where she lives? Sussex. That's where she lives. Sussex."

"Papa *owns* Sussex," Clay told his friend sagely.

"Don't say. I didn't know that. Never told me nothing about it. Bought it, did he? Be trying to buy up Surrey next thing you know. Be planting his old dendrons from Brazil, cluttering the place up with trees and flowers. Well, he won't get the Abbey. Been in the family forever, ever since Henry the Eighth stole it from the Papists anyway. Devilish long time."

"You a Papist, Rex? I didn't know that."

"No such a thing! *You* a Papist, Clay?"

"Nope. Miss Wanda a Papist?"

"No, no. Know what, Clay? I think she'll have you. Devilish sly girl. She'll throw Hibbard overboard and snatch your title."

"Course she'll have me. Marquis of Claymore. Twenty thousand a year. Course she'll have me, old goat."

"No, really! Not a goat at all. Pretty little puss, but mind she's got claws."

"Not *her*. Him."

"Oh, *him*." Rex tipped the bottle and stared blankly as two drops fell onto the linen tablecloth. "All gone, Clay. This bottle is empty."

"All gone," Clay agreed, shaking his head in misery.

"Know what, Clay?"

"What?"

"Let's go and see Miss Wanderley."

"That's a good idea, Rex. Let's go and see Miss Wanderley."

They lurched to their feet, and ordered a worried footman to have their mounts brought around. "I don't have a hack here," Clay reminded his friend.

"What, no hack? Deuce take it, Clay. What did you do with all your cattle?"

Clay looked puzzled, but the matter defied memory. "You got a hack to spare, Rex?"

"Stable full of horses. Take your pick, old friend. If I can't mount my best friend, what the devil's the world coming to? Take your pick, Clay."

But it was their grooms who carefully chose two ancient nags for them, upon hearing of their condition, and assured each other the buckoes would be lucky to get beyond the gates on these glue pots.

"You call this a horse?" Clay asked, insulted to be presented with such a sack of bones. "Ready for the tanning factory, 'pon my word. Wouldn't have believed you kept such nags."

"Gone downhill something dreadful," Rex said sadly, shaking his head. "I'll speak to Papa. Oughtn't to offer an earl a nag like this."

"*Marquis*, Rex," his friend reminded him in a tone that tried to be haughty.

"By Jove, that's right. Marquis of Claymore."

"Yessir, Marquis of Claymore. Going to buy a girl, Rex. Prettiest girl in the whole damned countryside. Miss Wanda Wander-er-er-erley."

"Who?"

"*Her*, you know."

"She might have you, Clay. She just might have you."

"Where does she live?"

"Sussex. This way," Rex replied, turning his dispirited nag down the road to the Wanderley home.

"Is it far to Sussex?"

"Not far, if Adam didn't move it. Wouldn't put it past him, the clunch. Devilish loose screw. Know what he did? Bought Sussex. Somebody told me."

"Must be a nabob. Wonder if he'll sell Wanda."

"Wouldn't be surprised. He'll be wanting to get a toe into the next county. Need the money. Might very well sell her, but it won't be for no old song. You'll have to come down heavy."

They meandered down the road, sometimes talking, sometimes singing in loud, carrying voices, till they came to the entrance to the Wanderley house. It was an old brick home, and presented a charming view in the daylight, but at night it formed a dark hulk of a shadow on the hill, and looked eerie in the moonlight, for by the time the gentlemen reached their destination it was after eleven, and the family had retired.

"Ain't nobody home," Rex said.

"What, after we've come all the way from Surrey! I call that shabby treatment. I don't like it, Rex."

"Something damned smokey here. Why ain't they home? Never told me nothing about leaving home. Out buying up Hampshire or Kent, no doubt."

"Which room is hers?" Clay asked, scanning the windows that glinted white and ghostly in the moonlight.

"Dash it, how would I know? I don't go creeping in her window. Don't like Wanda above half. Told you so. Ellie now . . ."

"I have the gift, Rex. I ever tell you that?" Clay asked in a voice laden with meaning.

"Eh? What gift is that then? You didn't say nothing about buying a gift."

"*The* gift. You know. I can tell things. Strange, supernatural things. A spirit will tell me where abides my love."

"Tiburn Road. We both know that."

"Hah! Not her. I'm speaking of Miss Wanda. It's that room," and he pointed to a window no different from any other, except that it was open six inches at the bottom.

"That one, eh? Well, she ain't there. There ain't nobody home. They've all slipped off to buy up Kent."

"The spirit tells me she's home. See, she has her window open to welcome me."

"Ought to warn her to close that window, old fellow. Take her death of cold."

They dismounted, tethered their nags to a tree, and walked softly, so as not to disturb the empty house.

"I'm going in," Clay announced firmly.

"Can't do that. They ain't home."

"She's home. I can hear her heart calling me across the miles."

"What miles?" Rex demanded sharply. "She ain't ten yards away, if she *is* home." They were now directly under the window designated by his lordship as being *hers*.

At his words the window was raised another foot, and a head peeped out. In the dim moonlight only an oval of white was visible, with a cloud of a dark hair billowing

about it. "Rex, is that you?" a lady's voice asked in a
lowered voice.

"Damme, now see what you've done," Rex complained
to his buddy.

"Give me a lift up," Clay demanded.

"You can't go in there! 'Pon my word. Not the thing,
to be sneaking into a lady's chamber in the dead of night.
Adam'd have your skin."

"What is going on?" the voice asked. "Rex, are you
drunk? Is that Abel with you?"

Executing an elegant if slightly wobbly bow, the Marquis of Claymore made himself known. His introduction
was acknowledged with a nervous giggle. "You *are* drunk,
both of you," the voice chided. "Go away, Rex, and take
your friend with you."

It was only the Marquis who went away, while Homberly remained behind to inform the lady they were both
as sober as judges. Within minutes Claymore was back
with a ladder, which he had espied on the ground on his
way in. He leaned it against the house, and proceeded to
climb it, till he was as close as he could manage to get to
the face that leaned toward him. It was, however, a short
ladder, one that had been used that afternoon to retrieve
Pudding, a foolish kitten, from a tree, and it did not reach
milady's chamber window. By balancing himself on the
second rung from the top, Claymore could nearly reach
her. He thought he could even reach her lips if she would
lean over farther.

"I am come to make you an offer in form, Miss Wanderley," the Marquis said, with hardly a slur in his voice at
all. Miss Wanderley looked down into his face, and
thought she had never seen anyone so dashing and handsome in her life. It was all so dreadfully exciting and romantic, and the fear that Mama might at any moment
come in and discover her, and very likely kill her, made it
the more piquant.

"Oh, my lord, you are *foxed*." She laughed tremulously.

"Drunk with love for you, my pretty," he returned gallantly, and jiggled so precariously that she feared he

might fall at any moment and break his leg. She involuntarily reached down her two hands and grabbed his shoulders, and as she did so, the upper part of her body was projected out the window, revealing a pair of shapely arms, and the outlines of an equally entrancing bosom beneath her nightdress.

"Do pray get down, before you kill yourself," she implored. Claymore looked up into her worried little face, then allowed his eyes to travel down to her body, and he made no motion to get down.

"I am going in and closing this window," she said severely. Then she let go of his shoulders, but did not pull her head in, for she had never so enjoyed herself in her entire sheltered life.

"Not till you accept my offer."

"Go away," she implored. Looking out, she addressed herself to Homberly. "Do take him home, Rex, before he takes a tumble and hurts himself."

"I am a marquis, with twenty thousand pounds a year," Clay boasted.

"You are drunk," she said, and she regretfully pulled her head inside, and finally closed the window. Sound was not entirely eliminated, however, as she kept her ear to the glass. She heard quite distinctly the scrape of the ladder against the side of the house, and the thud as the Marquis hit the ground. She put her fingers to her mouth, and giggled softly into the darkness. So handsome, she thought, and never even remembered his title, nor the exact sum of his fortune.

Picking himself up, Claymore brushed himself off and said to his friend, "I told you it was her room. I told you I heard her calling me. Gad, but she's a beauty, Rex."

"Well, if you ain't a gudgeon, Clay. That wasn't Wanda at all. It was only Ellie."

Chapter Three

Somehow the gentlemen managed to get safely to the Abbey. They even found their chambers, and were in bed before the return of the Homberlys from their evening out. They did not, however, arise early after their libations and nocturnal ramblings. The sun was midway across the sky before they sat down to a steak and ale, which gave Mrs. Homberly (informed of their arrival by her servants) time to get Missie decked out in her best sprigged muslin gown and herself time to wonder and wonder again *why he* was come. *He,* of course, was not her beloved son, but his guest. Missie might be only sixteen, but she was large for her age, and with the Marquis not a day over twenty-five, if that, there was no saying. . . . As soon as her son told her they were off to the Wanderleys, though, her hopes plunged. Not only had that wretch of a Wanda nabbed the squire's son, now here was Ellie about to snap up this very eligible parti. At least that would be the last of the Wanderley girls to worry about. Thank God they had finally had a son, so that they might quit breeding those damned beautiful girls every few years.

The gentlemen were a good deal more circumspect in

their selection of horses in the daytime than they had been the night before, and made a decent showing on the bays they rode on this occasion. This was their first chance for private discourse since their evening's orgy, and it was Clay who raised the subject.

"Do you happen to recall, Rex, did we do something foolish last night?"

"Not *we, you.*"

"I rather feared it might be me. I have a devilish sore arm this morning. All bruised."

"That'd be from falling off the ladder."

"On a ladder, was I? Dear me. What could I have been doing there?"

"Trying to get into Miss Wanda's room."

"I didn't make it, did I?" Clay asked, with a worried frown.

"Nope, you fell off."

"Good. Did I like Wanda?"

"Didn't see her. Got the wrong room."

"Good again. Whose room did I get?"

"Only Ellie's. It don't matter. She won't cut up."

"I hope she won't tell Wanda."

"Shouldn't think so. Funny little creature, the shy one of the family. Didn't tell a soul when I accidentally broke her mama's Sèvres vase, throwing it at Abel."

"Accidentally?"

"Accidentally picked up a good one. Thought it was only a cheap one. He went and told Wanda I'd been seeing Millie Winters."

"You were dangling after Wanda yourself, I take it. Is that why you dislike her now, because she jilted you?"

"Didn't jilt me. Never cared for her except for about two weeks when I was fourteen or so. Too conceited. Well, you know the way pretty girls are. Not like Ellie at all."

They crossed the border from Surrey into Sussex, without either of them recalling who was purported to have bought up the county, and before long were cantering up the road to the Wanderley house. It was now early afternoon, and the brick house was revealed as a picturesque home, three stories high, with a slate roof and a general appearance of prosperity, in spite of Adam's squandering of his money on flowers. They were admitted by the butler, and Mrs. Wanderley came into the drawing room, bringing with her her youngest daughter, Miss Wanda.

The girl was quickly judged by the Marquis, and decided to be beauty enough to pit against Miss Golden. She had fine raven hair, blue eyes, a suitably modest expression, and a figure that would not show to disadvantage beside the Rose. She conversed agreeably, and before ten minutes were up, Claymore was picturing her in her bridal gown, and also in various ball gowns, trailing on his arm, and turning every head in the room by her stunning appearance.

Wine and biscuits were served. Rex, divining his duty, drew Mrs. Wanderley aside to discuss local matters, leaving Clay free to further his suit with Miss Wanda. Mrs. Wanderley was only minimally interested to hear Rex's mother had been to dinner at Ashton Manor, having heard it already from his mother, yet she was not loath to give the other two young people a moment to become acquainted. Quite the contrary, she led Rex on with a million questions he could not answer, and even favored him with a recital of her sister's daughter's friend's latest romance. He had never received such condescension from her before.

Claymore smiled inwardly as he absorbed the charms of his new beloved. The very one to set the Rose down a peg, and to refute the foolish rumors that were no doubt going the rounds about his being all cut to shreds by her rejection.

"I understand your first Season was cut short by an unfortunate accident," Clay said.

"Yes, so foolish of me. I took a tumble from my horse at a fence. She was frightened by a mole, else it would never have happened."

"It was London's loss," he told her gallantly, while remembering quite distinctly Rex's comment that she had fallen from a tree. Beauties were notoriously proud, of course, and naturally she would not own up to such conduct as climbing trees. What puzzled him slightly was *where* she had been climbing a tree in London. While these thoughts flashed through his mind, he continued with his conversation. "I hope we may have the pleasure of your company for the Little Season."

"I am not sure," she said vaguely. Certainly no comment was issued to the effect that she might be married by then to a squire's son.

"Come, Miss Wanderley, you must give us bachelors who failed to make your acquaintance during your short visit a chance to impress you favorably." He smiled. She blushed, and looked up at him modestly from beneath her long lashes in the approved manner.

"Such plain girls as myself cannot hope to impress favorably when there are true beauties like Miss Golden around," she replied coyly. So she knew about that episode. With Ladies Siderow and Tameson to keep her informed, he could not have hoped to keep his affair to himself.

"Some gentlemen like that pastel sort of beauty, but I must own I have always preferred brunettes," he said. Now that is not even a lie, he congratulated himself silently. Till he had clapped an eye on the Golden Rose, he *had* preferred brunettes.

"Such a whisker, my lord," she teased gently. "You must know everyone expected you to offer for her."

He swallowed his ire. No doubt everyone would also know shortly that he *had* offered for her, and been refused. That would do him no good in his conquest of this proud beauty.

"You must not believe everything you hear, Miss Wanda," he returned grimly. Seeking for a means to turn the conversation from this topic, he said, "How does your broken leg go on? I notice you do not have a limp."

"It was not actually broken, but merely a slight crack the doctor thinks. In any case, I can walk very well now, and even begin to dance again."

"That is good news. I hope I may soon have an opportunity to see how well you can dance."

"Oh, as to that, I daresay there will be any number of

assemblies and balls soon. With all the families coming
back from London again, things will pick up here. It has
been so very boring to be stuck out in the country these
months." She sighed wearily, and Claymore thought it a
little odd that she should find it boring, when it was the
only life she had known but for that week or two in London. Besides, spring was the prettiest time of the year to
be at one's country seat, and he personally found the
London Season was held at the worst possible time.

"In any case, I hear your papa has a very interesting
hobby, which must have helped you pass the time."

"What, his flowers? I do not interest myself in them."

"Ah, that is a pity. They might have been a diversion
for you when you were not able to get about much."

"Yes, well, I am better now, thank heavens."

They chatted on for fifteen minutes more, giving Clay
ample time to discover that Miss Wanda was very much
like other young ladies of her years and class. She liked
dancing above anything, she *adored* Byron, she read
gothic novels, she sketched a little, played a little, spoke a
little French, and was ready to flirt with and be prodigiously amused by a handsome marquis with twenty thousand a year, though in justice she could hardly know the
exact total of his fortune. He thought that he could win
her favor in a week's concentrated assault. From the
gracious smiles her mama was bestowing on them, he
foresaw no difficulty from that quarter. She was, he
thought critically, just as pretty as Miss Golden, and he
had no reason to think he could not send a notice in to
the papers well ahead of Miss Golden's nuptials.

After the prescribed half-hour allotted to a social call,
the gentlemen arose to leave. They were invited, not to
say pressed, to return for dinner the very next evening.
Rex was reminded to drop by and see Abel, who had a
new hunter he would like to show his friend, to show
Lord Claymore the conservatory, and in general to make
the place their own.

At the door Rex said, "Where's Ellie today?"

"She is with her papa, I expect," the lady of the house
replied. "She gives him a hand with his orchids."

"No, she's spraying the roses, Mama," Wanda contradicted.

"Such a quaint little creature," the mother explained deprecatingly. "As though we had not two gardeners to do such things. I am sure I don't know why she bothers her head, for she might much better be practicing her pianoforte. She is an abominable player, I promise you, in spite of years of lessons." Turning to her daughter, she added, "I hope she is wearing her bonnet, or she will be all tanned. Was she wearing a bonnet, Wanda?"

"I didn't notice, Mama."

"Well, never mind that. Tomorrow evening then, my lord. Come early, and my husband will show you his plants before it comes on dark. I am sure you will be greatly interested in them. I'll tell Abel you're home, Rex."

They were shown to the door, and escaped into the sunlight. "What did you think of her?" Rex inquired directly.

"Charming. I liked her exceedingly."

"She was putting her best foot forward to impress you."

"I hope she may continue to do so."

"She will till you're caught anyway. Then the tune will change."

"I am firmly caught already, dear boy. I have quite decided to offer for Miss Wanda."

"Hsst! Rex!" a sound came from round the corner of the house.

"You hear anything, Clay?"

"Here. Come here, Rex. I want to speak to you." A large floppy straw hat peeped round the corner, and a beckoning hand urged them come. On the hand was a very dirty twilled cotton glove, several sizes larger than the hand within.

"Oh, Ellie. There you are," Rex said good-naturedly. "Was asking for you. They thought you was with your papa."

"No, I was spraying the rose bushes, but I am finished that. Come around here. I don't want Mama to see me

talking to you in all my dirt, or she'll scold." A trim little
figure, tall and straight, led the way to an area at the side
of the house that was sheltered by a cantilevered roof,
and on a work table beneath it various pots, humus,
bulbs, trowels, and plants were spread out. The destination reached, Ellie turned around and faced her followers.

They looked, and Claymore could not believe this was
a daughter of the house, for her soiled apron, bedraggled
hat, wispy and disheveled hair proclaimed a very under-
ling of the domestic staff.

"Clay, this is Ellie," Rex explained, and considered
that sufficient introduction.

"Your servant, ma'am," Claymore said, bowing stiffly.

Ellie performed half a curtsy, then changed her mind
and proffered her gloved hand. Looking at it, she swished
it back behind her back with a grimace. She had been in
the potting shed when the guests arrived, and so did not
know of their presence in time to get cleaned up. Alice, a
kitchen maid who happened by, mentioned that Mr.
Homberly was here, with a *lord* from Lunnon. Ellie immediately knew it to be her moonlight visitor, and stood
by to hear their departure. She was eager to see the newcomer in the clear light of day to determine if he was
really as grand as she had thought last night. He was. He
looked a positive Apollo beside poor stubby little Rex.
His dark green riding jacket fit his shoulders without a
wrinkle, and his fawn trousers hadn't a spot on them. His
top boots, too, were unmarred. As the Apollo's brown
eyes raked her own awful garments, she realized too late
her mistake in appearing before him in such an unbecom-
ing guise. She slipped off her gloves, and tucked a few
stray strands of hair up under her sun hat. She then made
the error of wiping the perspiration from her brow, and a
long streak of mud was trailed across her forehead. Now
that they were here, she was uncertain what she had
meant to say.

"You look the very devil, Ellie," Rex said kindly. "I
don't believe even Missie goes about in such rags as
you're wearing. 'Pon my word, I don't know what your
mama's thinking of."

"I have been working—potting these bulbs Papa has received from America," she explained, while Claymore continued to look. There were some distinguishable traces of the Wanderley beauty there under the mud, he thought. The eyes were fine—like Lady Siderow's. Maybe even bigger than Wanda's, though not so cunningly used, with batting lashes and coy glances. A direct, forward gaze. They were gray eyes; Wanda's were blue.

"You ought to let one of the gardeners do it," Rex continued.

"We only have one, and he only comes three days a week," Ellie said, thus revealing her mama's proud lie that they had two.

"Well, what did you call us for?" Rex demanded impatiently.

"I was just wondering about last night."

"What about it?"

"You were here, perhaps you don't recall, for I think you were both tipsy," she said stiffly, quite overcome with embarrassment as Claymore's brown eyes continued to take in details of her awful toilette.

"I pray you will accept our apologies, ma'am," Claymore said. "I fear we may have been a trifle tipsy."

"Ape drunk," she shot back, goaded on by embarrassment to anger. "Climbing up a ladder, and saying all manner of foolish things."

"Shut up, Ellie," Rex said bluntly, stealing a quick look around, lest they were being overheard.

"I hope you will be kind enough to disregard any foolish utterances I may have made," Clay broke in. Even if the girl was a hoyden, one did not tell a lady to shut up.

"Naturally I paid no heed. Did you hurt yourself, my lord? I feared you may have done yourself an injury when the ladder slipped, for it seemed to me you hit the ground very hard."

"Nothing to signify."

"What is it you want anyway?" Rex insisted. "Haven't got all day, Ellie."

"I was only curious to know if you were both all right after your night's activities," she said, and blushed at her forwardness at having accosted them at all, but as she was already rosy from her work, the blush went undetected.

"Of course we are, and don't go blabbing about last night to your mama—or Wanda either," he threw in for good measure.

"As if I would."

"Come on then, Clay," Rex turned to his friend.

"Delighted to have made your acquaintance, Miss Ellie," Clay said, bowed politely, and smiled. He had a very cold smile, she thought. He hadn't looked like that last night. It was the wine that had done it, she supposed. Quite obviously it was the wine that had induced his passion for her as well, for he was certainly not impressed with her today. Had seemed to take her in disgust.

When she resumed her activities, an occasional thought of a declaration of love by moonlight intruded itself, but she was not desolate at having it come to nothing. She worked fast, as she wanted to have a ride before dinner and had to be home in time to prepare herself for Mama's company, even if it was only Magistrate Maherne and his wife. The wife would pound the pianoforte for hours, she supposed, and her husband sing "Blue-Eyed Mary" offkey. No matter, she would slip away to the library and work on the family history. It had been kept for nearly three hundred years. The family was an old one, but her mama had not kept it up, and Ellie was now endeavoring to add to it what she knew or could discover of recent import. The marriages of her two elder sisters had to be recorded, and some notes of the Siderow and Tameson connections. Uncle Gerald, too, had distinguished himself in Wellington's Peninsular campaign, and she had to write to him and discover what battles he had taken part in. With both of her sisters increasing, there would soon be births to record as well. Maybe even another wedding this year, if Wanda decided to have George Hibbard. Someday she would be recording her own marriage, she supposed. It seemed to her something in the infinitely removed future.

Chapter Four

The intervening day passed with no occurrence of note. Mrs. Homberly induced Rex and his friend to take Missie to the village for some embroidery cottons, hoping to put her a little in Claymore's way. He found her to be very much in his way, but it gave him not the least pleasure. Wanda, too, was sent to the village in hopes of encountering the Marquis. Her errand was to stop at the Vicarage and leave off some flowers for the church, as her mama thought it would be a suitably romantic chore should she *happen* to encounter Rex and his friend. However, she missed them by a quarter of an hour, and when Mrs. Wanderley in desperation had the gig put to to transport herself and Wanda to visit Mrs. Homberly, she was again too late. The gentlemen had taken their fishing rods to the trout stream, so she returned home to prepare the evening's attack.

Late Wednesday afternoon Rex and Claymore presented themselves at the Wanderley residence, to be regaled with a stroll through a damnably hot greenhouse, and a lecture on orchids, humus, temperatures and the difficulty of maintaining them at the proper level, bugs, slugs, and other matters of a horticultural and unappetizing nature. Finally, their brows moist, their collars entirely wilted, and their shirts clinging to their backs, they escaped and gulped in the fresh evening air before going to the Green Saloon, where the family was impatiently passing its time with a glass of sherry while awaiting their arrival. Both guests would have preferred a tall, cool glass of ale, but had the sherry pressed on them, and preferred it to a burning throat. Clay felt he could break Rex's record at that moment, if only he could get his hands on a glass of ale.

He cast a quick glance around the room as he sipped his drink, and discovered Wanda on a settee, conveniently apart from the rest of the family. After making his bows to everyone, he strolled to her side and sat down.

She had her hair dressed à la Méduse, with a riot of soft curls setting off her exquisite face to advantage. A pink gown in the Empire style covered without quite concealing her corporeal charms. She looked so striking that for a full minute Clay forgot to compare her to the Golden Rose, and when he did remember, the comparison was all in favor of the lady present. When he had taken in the full grandeur of her toilette, he said, "You are looking particularly lovely this evening, Miss Wanda, if I may say so."

"As to that," she said archly, "I fear developments in London have given you a dislike of fair-haired girls." She had that afternoon read in the *Gazette*, which they received late from London, of the engagement between the Duke of Everleigh and Miss Gloria Golden. She was both miffed and happy. The Rose's betrothal meant that Claymore was definitely free, yet it took the edge off her own success. She was second choice, and being sought out on the rebound, too, as it were.

"I am afraid I don't understand you, Miss Wanda," he said obtusely, being only too sure that he understood her perfectly.

He was shortly made to understand, with coy glances and bold smiles, that Miss Wanda was not seven years old, and knew why he was rusticating. Without a doubt she would shortly know as well that he had actually offered for the Rose, as soon as Lady Siderow or Lady Tameson had time to take pen in hand. He must work quickly and gain her acceptance before that event took place.

"Is the engagement finally announced then?" he asked smoothly. "I have known of it for some time, for the Rose was a good friend of my family."

"A *very* good friend of one member of your family, if I am not mistaken, my lord?" she teased.

"A very good friend of Mama's," he returned, without so much as a blush at his mendacity. His mama had not set a toe in London during the last Season, and had never clapped an eye on the Rose.

Across the room, Ellie regarded this rencontre going forward in a corner. Wanda, the cunning creature, had sat off there by herself on purpose, just to get Clay away from the others. She was flirting outrageously—look at the way she was batting her lashes and simpering. Ellie felt a pronounced desire to go over and shake her. Why, she was all but engaged to George Hibbard, and had begged Mama not to invite him this evening, too. She was setting her cap for Claymore, that was the thing. Yes, and would very likely nab him. The worm of discontent in Ellie's breast was not entirely caused by Wanda's shabby treatment of George Hibbard. How lovely Wanda looked, with her hair all curled and teased, and that little pink bow perched over her left ear. If only one had not to endure such bother from the papers to get those bouncing curls, Ellie thought she would like to try the style herself. Her hair was, as usual, pulled back from her forehead and tumbling down behind her in a basket of curls. It was very effective from the *rear*, but after all, it was the front of the head a gentleman saw when he was flirting.

Wanda may say what she liked about Claymore's being jilted by the Rose, he did not act in the least like a brokenhearted gentleman. Quite the contrary, he was already ensnared in Wanda's net. How warm his smile was for her, not in the least like the stiff little smirk he had honored herself with the day before. No indeed, it was the smile he had worn the first night, when he had offered for her in the moonlight, balanced on a ladder. Drunk as a

wheelbarrow, of course, and not in the least aware of
what he was saying. Still not aware that he had ever said
it. But he was not drunk now.

The group went in for dinner, with Wanda latching
onto Claymore's arm, when he had ought to have taken in
Mama. There, Papa and Abel were taking in her mother,
one on either side, which left Rex for herself. Homberly
entertained Ellie during dinner with comments on Clay's
ardor for Wanda. He hardly needed to tell her, for she
could see perfectly well across the table that he was en-
chanted with her. It was always the same, any time a new
gentleman came to call. He would end up with Wanda,
that same glowing smile on his face that Claymore was
wearing. It was very lowering to be a common variety of
flower among Adam's exotic blooms.

In fact, Clay's enchantment did not last through the
neck of venison. There were only so many witty remarks
she could make about Roses having thorns, and a limited
number of compliments he could devise on sapphire eyes
and raven curls. Both were exhausted during the turtle
soup. They had very few friends in common, and the
news that Claymore was acquainted with Ladies Siderow
and Tameson and liked them tremendously did not take
long to impart. Was over well before the turbot and
smelts were even served. He already knew she adored Byron, though he heard it again during the neck of venison.
By the time the sweet was before him, he was looking
around the table for a fresh topic. His eyes lit on Ellie,
who sat directly opposite him. She was imparting to Rex
the information that her great-great-uncle Horace had
been secretly betrothed to his great-great-aunt Cybil, only
the families did not allow the match, because Cybil had
been mistress to some prince or other. He thought Rex
did very poorly to reply only, "Pooh, no such a thing."
He could have done with some of that conversation Ellie
exhibited, and regretted it was impolite to speak across
the table.

"Well, it's true, and she was very pretty, too. I found a
little ivory miniature of her amongst Uncle Horace's papers, which I was going through last night. She looked

rather like Missie. Perhaps you would like to have the picture for Missie? Papa would not mind, I think."

"What for? She's dead, ain't she?"

"Of course she is dead. She was *born* in 1700."

Clay could not speak across the table, but at least he could listen, and find fresh fruit for talk with his partner. "Your family is a very old one, I believe," he ventured to Wanda.

"Oh no," she replied, offended. "Lady Siderow is only thirty. She is the oldest, and Lady Tameson is just turned twenty-eight."

He stared at her ignorance, and said, "I see." Still one could not give up this easily, and he forged on. "I understand you and Miss Ellie are twins."

"She is the elder."

A situation that had been puzzling him was called to mind, and he inquired, "Why was she not presented this year?"

"Ellie is rather immature. Joan—Lady Siderow, that is—thought she would improve with a year's aging."

"I see." Yet a second glance across the table assured him that she did not *look* immature. With her hair pulled back severely in that old-fashioned style, the lovely contours of her face, which had been concealed yesterday by her straw hat and disheveled locks, were accentuated. The eyes were magnificent—great stormy pools, with lashes a yard long. "Was she content to remain behind and let her younger sister go off before her?" he said lightly.

Wanda hunched her entrancing shoulders, not in the least amused by this interest in anyone save herself. "Oh, Ellie is the shy one of the family. She was happy enough to stay home. To tell the truth, I don't think she wanted to take her bows with *me*."

"Why not?" Clay asked, giving his dinner companion a very poor opinion of his common sense. It must be obvious to the meanest capacity that Ellie would show to great disadvantage beside herself. In about two seconds he caught the full import of her remark, and said, "It would have been something quite out of the ordinary to have two such beautiful sisters make their bows together."

He laid down his fork and looked frankly at Wanda to see how she would take this lack of praise.

She took it very ill indeed, but was too cagey to show it. "I can't imagine what the reason could be," she replied sweetly.

Glancing across the table again, Clay could see no trace of this vaunted shyness of Miss Ellie's. She was making valiant efforts to draw that uncouth lout of a Rex into conversation. Truth to tell, she had been catapulted into animation by the awareness of those penetrating brown eyes trained on her.

"Useless things," Rex was saying. The first part of the conversation was missed by the eavesdropper.

"They are not useless, for besides being very pretty, orchids give us the vanilla flavoring. In fact, you are eating it right now, in this cream cake."

"That so?" Rex asked. "Well, I *do* like vanilla."

Even a four-course meal is over eventually, and at last the ladies went into the drawing room, and the port was served to the gentlemen, who remained behind at table to have a cigar.

Adam Wanderley's mind was never far from his greenhouse. "I was thinking whether I couldn't grow my own tobacco plants in my conservatory and make up my own cigars," he commented. as he lit up a cheroot and blew a puff of smoke. He was a big, homely man, an unlikely sire to the Wanderley beauties.

"West Indies," Abel replied. "The best tobacco for cigars comes from Cuba, Papa." He had his father's form, with some saving refinement of features from his mother.

"I know that. These are Cuban cigars we're smoking. I'll look into it."

"Don't know where you'll put the plants. The place is jam-packed already. They're big plants."

"I'm planning to expand," Papa told his son.

"What are you planning to use for blunt? Mama says she's getting new curtains for the three drawing rooms out of this year's revenues, or she's moving out. And there'll be Wanda's wedding—" A sharp rap in the ribs from Rex's elbow brought Abel to a halt. He looked guiltily at

Claymore, and mumbled on, "Not that there's anything definite about Wanda."

"Aye, but look at the saving on cigars," Adam continued, unaware of the little scene.

"They'd end up costing you a guinea a piece the first year," Abel said, and they continued discussing the feasibility of the scheme for half an hour, when the gentlemen removed to the Green Saloon with the tatty curtains. Wanda was soon prevailed upon to take a turn at the pianoforte, while Abel sang "Green Grow the Rushes, Ho" in a creditable baritone. This was followed by "Blowzy Bella" and other country songs. During the "Fleuve du Tage" Ellie rose and slipped silently from the room, unobserved by anyone except Rex. Looking around a little later, though, Claymore remarked upon her absence to his friend.

"Ellie always slips out when the going gets rough. She's heard Wanda strum them tunes a hundred times. Always plays the same things. Heard them a score of times myself."

"Where does she slip out to?"

"Library. She's working up the family history. Well, stands to reason, if she don't do it, it won't get done, for Adam has his head full of his plants, and the mama ain't literary at all."

Before long, Adam as well headed for the door, and went to check up on his cattleya, which was showing a sad tendency to wilt, and he had paid two hundred pounds for it not a month ago. A table of piquet was got up, with Abel the odd man out. After half an hour it was suggested that Abel sit in, and Claymore was the first to offer to give up his seat, which irked Rex, who was desirous of slipping out to blow a cloud himself. Dead bore, playing for these chicken stakes.

Wanda had every expectation that Claymore would take up a seat where he might admire her beauty without the diversion of playing cards. Indeed he did so, for three full minutes, before he said offhandedly that he believed he would stroll across to the library and pick out a book.

Entering the library, a large square room lined with

oaken bookshelves, and with two large tables placed end
to end in the middle of the room, he noticed it was well
lit, but apparently unoccupied. Books and writing materials were laid out on one of the tables, but no one was
about to use them. He strolled in and looked around.
Then he heard a scrabbling sound behind him, and turning, he saw Ellie balanced on a short ladder, reaching
above her head for a book.

"Allow me, Miss Ellie," he said, and rushed to her aid.

"Oh, you scared the life out of me," she said bluntly.
"I didn't hear you come in, for since Mama has had this
carpet laid, the room is nearly noiseproof."

"You appear to have a well-stocked library," Clay said,
by way of making polite conversation.

"Yes, loads of books, but all as old as the hills. Papa
has not kept it up as he ought to have."

"I collect I will find the works of Byron here at least,"
he said lightly. No lady of fashion dared to be behind in
her reading of Byron. He already knew Wanda to be an
aficionada.

"No, not even the illustrious Byron, I'm afraid," she
confessed.

"Ah, I thought Wanda said—"

"Very likely Joan has a copy. Lady Siderow, you
know."

"Very likely." He carried the heavy tome to the table
for her. "What is this weighty matter you are looking
into?" he asked.

"Harold—Lord Tameson—told me I might find an account of his ancestors in here. It is Rutledge's *History of
Dorset*. That is where he is from."

Clay dutifully volunteered the information that he was
acquainted with both her married sisters, and liked them
prodigiously. He waited for her "indeed" or "how delightful" or some such banality.

He was surprised to hear her say, "I like Joan and
Bunny, but Harold is quite hopeless."

"Who, Tameson?"

"Yes, he is so top lofty and *boring*."

It was himself who said, "Indeed."

"You cannot know him well, or you would not be surprised. No one likes him. None of *us,* I mean. Always prosing on about his ancestors, who are supposed to be something special only because he can trace them back to Norman and Saxon times. Well, it is very foolish. Everyone's ancestors go back forever, back to Adam and Eve, and I don't see that it ought to lend any extra cachet if they happened to be living in England, or if you can find them mentioned in some book. And it is not as though the family has distinguished itself in the least. They have gone downhill dreadfully, if you want my opinion." He blinked in surprise, and she added, "But I don't think you do want my opinion, and I hope he is not a great bosom-bow of yours."

"Not in the least. Merely I am surprised to hear you profess such views, when it is yourself who are keeping up your own family history."

"Well, I don't enjoy it, except for the *human* side that comes out occasionally. All those lists of properties exchanged, and families connected, of court appointments and titles and battles engaged in is very dull stuff. But once in a while some item of interest comes up. A great-great-ancestor of mine—she was an Egerton, born in 1650, imagine only a few years after Shakespeare died— kept a diary, and I have enjoyed dipping into it immensely, for we have so few accounts of anything written by women at that time. You could not imagine, my lord, how she was treated. Her husband *beat* her, and locked her in her room. And indeed she never wished to marry him at all, for she loved another, but he was rich you see—the husband—and very likely her family forced the match on her. The night before her wedding she made a long entry. Oh, I must show it to you, all tear-stained, and the brown marks still there after all these years. Only it is in my room, and I shall show it to you another time, if you are interested."

"I am. Interesting what you said—about so few women having written anything at that time, when it seems every woman of my acquaintance is scribbling her memoirs now."

"The Countess of Winchilsea is the only female writer I have found, and then only the merest little dabs of verse. Now, of course, it is different, since we are educated. In a way that is, though of course we are not well educated, and I don't know why we must spend hours practicing the harp or pianoforte when we have no aptitude for it, and had much rather be doing something else."

"What would you rather be doing, Miss Ellie?"

"Nearly anything," she replied. They sat down at the table, and Ellie closed the book in which she had been writing, then fell silent. Clay did not force conversation; he was thinking about what she had said, and found a good deal of sense in it.

"Is the card game over already?" she asked.

"No, they are still playing. I am taking a turn out."

"Would you care for a glass of wine?"

"No, I am happy just as I am. That diary you mentioned—it sounds a valuable document, for students of social history."

"Yes, I have been after Papa to give it to a university, or to see about having it published. Surely many women must feel as I do, that they would like to know something about life in those days, from a woman's point of view. They cannot all have been greenheads, for Shakespeare portrays very active and vital women in his plays."

"But not in his sonnets," Clay mentioned. He was only familiar with these poems from using them as models for his own poetic offerings to Miss Golden.

"Yes, that is true," she said consideringly. "He is always holding out the lure that if they become his lovers, he will immortalize them, otherwise they will sink into total obscurity. They must have been the silliest things in nature to fall for such a story."

"This ancestor of yours, Egerton was it?" Clay asked, wishing to divert the topic, since his companion had obviously a more thorough acquaintance than he had himself with the sonnets of the Bard.

"Yes, Mary Egerton. She was in love with her neighbor; his name was Tom. She doesn't describe him at all, only to say he is very kind. She spells it k-y-n-d-e. I don't know whether she was a poor speller, or that was the spelling of it in those days. Spelling has changed greatly, of course. I can scarcely make any sense of Chaucer at all."

"You read Chaucer? I thought young ladies of your class contented themselves with Byron and Mrs. Radcliffe."

"As I have told you, Papa is really shocking in the way he has let the library fall out of date, and we have no lending library in the village. But I daresay when I get to London next year, I shall catch up on all the latest works."

"You won't have time for that, Miss Ellie," he answered with a smile. "Balls and breakfasts and routs and drives in the park—no time at all for reading."

She looked quite alarmed. "Is it so bad as that?"

"Bad? It is considered good by most ladies, I believe. In fact, the more engagements you can crowd into one day, the more successful the Season is considered to be."

A flicker of a smile came and went so quickly on her face it was hard to be sure whether it had ever existed. "It is the beauties that you are speaking of, I collect. A plain girl will not be so rushed off her feet."

"What, fishing for compliments, Miss Ellie? And I am now to assure you that you are by no means a plain girl, I suppose?"

"Save yourself the trouble. I know I am plain compared to my sisters."

"Well, you are not," he told her gallantly. "You bear a strong resemblance to Lady Siderow, and when you are fixed up—that is, when you have mastered all the tricks of flirting and what not, you will go on famously."

"Yes, Joan felt I was not ready to make my debut this year. I daresay she was right, even if I am the elder."

"A whole ten minutes older! You are not much alike, for twins."

"No, we are not the sort of twins that are exactly alike. Wanda has more confidence. If *she* were the elder, she would be called Miss Wanderley, as the elder should be,

but somehow we are called Miss Ellie and Miss Wanda. It
started, I suppose, before the other girls were married."

"Wanda tells me you are the shy one," he said, and
smiled. She was gratified to see it was his nice, warm
smile, not the chilly parting of the lips she had received
the other morning.

"I am not *shy,* precisely. I can converse well enough
with one or two persons, like now. It is only that I clam
up like a lobster in a large crowd. Joan says I have not
the gift of small talk, but she thinks it can be acquired."

"Well, don't change, Miss Ellie, for shy beauties are all
the rage." He regarded her shy blush, despite her small
audience, and considered his blatant lie. Shy beauties
were not at all the rage. The Rose set the tone, and a less
shy creature than that brazen hussy had never seen the
light of day. But even if Miss Ellie were shy, she had
countenance, and considerable charm and vivacity. She
was not exactly a beauty. Wanda was the beauty of the
two—no doubt of that. With a little confidence, however,
and town bronze, Ellie would hold her own. At least she
was conversable, which Wanda, for all her looks and
wiles, was not. He did not much look forward to returning
to the Green Saloon, but could not make the selection of
a book last forever, so he grabbed any old book from the
shelf (it happened to be Guthrie's *Geography*) and returned, just in time to replace Rex, who promptly vanished out the door, one of Adam's cheroots in his pocket.

The game did not last much longer, and the gentlemen
were soon heading back to the Abbey. "Still set in your
decision to have her?" Rex asked.

"Certainly. She looked very well this evening, did she
not?"

"Rigged to the nines. And Hibbard wasn't there, I noticed. I guess it ain't as well settled between them as I
thought. I asked about him while you was out, and she
said, 'This isn't the only house Mr. Hibbard calls at. Pray
don't go giving anyone that idea.' I guess I know what
'anyone' she had in mind, eh? You was gone a deuced long
time, Clay. What kept you? You ain't usually one to shove

your nose into a book. Not the musty old books you'll find in Adam's stacks anyway."

"I was having a chat with Miss Ellie."

"That'd be a rare treat," Rex offered ironically.

"Yes, she is an intelligent girl."

"Not in your style."

"Funny, Rex, you said the other day I should do better to offer for Ellie."

"I wasn't thinking when I said that. She wouldn't do for you at all, though she's *nicer* than Wanda. What you want is a beauty to set the Rose down a notch, and Wanda is the one to do it right enough. Looking very fine this evening."

"Lovely. I am taking her out in my curricle tomorrow afternoon. Her mama threw no rub in my way. I thought she might find it a trifle fast."

"No, not in the country. Where you taking her?"

"I don't know. What do you suggest?"

"There's Needford, about ten miles away. Got an old church there you might have a look at."

"That wouldn't amuse Wanda."

"It'd be up to *you* to provide the amusement yourself. Stop at some inn for tea. Buy her a trinket, Clay, that's the thing to do. Then after you go home she has it to look at, and remember you."

"Yes, a good plan. What will you do?"

"I'll think of something. Maybe I'll go with you."

"Now really, Rex. Little romance that will add to the atmosphere."

"I could take Ellie. A bit off-putting for her, seeing Wanda jaunter off with her beau, while she sits home like Cinderella."

"If you do that, take her in your own curricle, and don't be suggesting we all go together in a carriage. It is privacy with the young lady I require."

"Don't worry. I ain't that fond of Wanda's company that I'd put myself forward to share your trap. Course I daresay Ellie'd prose my ear off about saints and martyrs and what not—going to a church, you know. Maybe I'll take Missie instead. That'd please Mama."

"Yes, that's a good idea."

"Or I could take 'em both, and let 'em rattle on to each other, and slip off for an ale while they go to church."

"Any they end up trailing after Wanda and me! No, my friend. If you take them, you conduct them to this curst church yourself."

"Shouldn't ought to call a church curst, Clay. Not the thing. A shocking loose fish you're becoming."

"Shocking."

Chapter Five

After the gentlemen departed, Mrs. Wanderley called for a fresh pot of tea, and the three ladies commenced to rehash the evening in the time-honored fashion, while Abel slid out the door to indulge in another time-honored custom pertaining to gentlemen. This particular entertainment was named Effie; she was a poacher's daughter who entertained many young gentlemen in the neighborhood.

"It went well, I think," Mrs. Wanderley began, addressing her speech to Wanda. Mrs. Wanderley smiled fondly at her beauty as she spoke, and remarked, as she so frequently did, that of all her lovely daughters, it was Wanda who most closely resembled herself at that age. Yes, and she was still a good-looking woman too, even if she had passed that hateful half-century mark on her last birthday.

"You should have had a few more guests, Mama," Ellie suggested. "You are making it too obvious you mean to nab him for Wanda. Besides, it is very bad to throw poor George over, when he was as well as accepted."

"And who said anything about throwing him over?" Wanda demanded. "Surely we may entertain another guest if we choose. Besides, he called on Nora Langdon last Sunday. I heard it from her brother."

"That was only because you were flirting with that ugly old Elmer Rountree after church," Ellie reminded her sister.

"I was not flirting with him! In fact, I told him I would be busy Sunday evening, and then George didn't even call, but went slipping off to the Langdons'."

"Children, children! No wrangling, please. Remember you are *ladies*. It is *this* evening's entertainment we are discussing. I thought the cream cake had an odd flavor. I wonder if cook used cream that was going bad in it."

"No, Mama," Ellie explained. "It was Papa's vanilla beans that lent it that odd taste, though I did not mind it, and Rex said it was very good."

"It is not *Rex's* opinion we are interested in, my love. Did Claymore comment on it, Wanda?"

"No, Mama. I wonder where he means to take me tomorrow afternoon."

"What, are you walking out with him tomorrow?" Ellie asked, as this was the first she had heard of it.

"No, *driving* out with him in his curricle. I suppose we might drive over to Langdon's. How I should love to see Nora's face—"

"Are you mad?" her mother interposed hotly. "Let that sassy chit of a Nora get her talons into him, when she has already whisked young Hibbard right out from under your nose! Don't be such a goose, Wanda. Take him over to Needford. There is that old church there you might show him."

"He won't care about a church. But they have a rather good inn, and I expect we will be stopping for tea."

"It sounds very fast to me," Ellie objected, but in such an obvious pique of jealousy that no one heeded her.

"Invite him for dinner after," Mrs. Wanderley suggested. "Never mind that he will not be dressed. It will be only a potluck thing, quite *en famille*. We can send word over to the Homberlys' not to expect him back."

"You are going a deal too fast, Mama," Ellie warned

again. "Joan always says to play hard to get, especially when it is perfectly clear that the gentleman is smitten."

"It is not perfectly clear yet, Ellie, for he did not stay in the room when he was odd man out at the card game, but went shabbing off to the library or some such thing. I daresay he slipped out for a cigar, for he was gone a long time."

Ellie kept quiet, and did not reveal where he had gone. She might not receive a scold for her part in his absence, but she would be given to understand she had erred.

"He was dangling after Gloria Golden all Season. Everyone knows that," Wanda sniffed. "He is only making up to me to pretend he wasn't jilted. I am not at all sure I shall oblige him by being his new flirt."

"Flirt indeed!" Mrs. Wanderley said in a shocked voice. "I should say not. If he is not serious in his intentions, he may take himself off. But Gloria is engaged, my love, so he is quite free, you know. Quite something to be a marchioness. Neither Joan nor Caroline did so well as that. Plain Mrs. Hibbard is nothing in comparison to it."

"We'll see," Wanda replied, with a very smug smile. Pooh for Nora Langdon. George Hibbard would see what happened if he chose to ignore her. Not only had he called on Nora Langdon on Sunday evening, but here it was Wednesday, and she had not heard from him since Saturday. She was not so unnatural as to dislike the idea of becoming a marchioness and outdoing all her sisters, but the thing was, she *loved* George. She would be plain Mrs. Hibbard—not even a baronetcy or a knighthood. But George was wildly handsome, with the most melting brown eyes—much nicer than Claymore's. His had a bored, glazed look in them when he spoke to her. She saw very clearly why the Rose preferred Everleigh. Something about Claymore gave the impression that he was insincere. All his compliments and pleasantries had a strained sound to them, as though it were just some dull game he was playing. Without ever for one moment underestimating her own considerable charms, she thought the Marquis of Claymore did not love her. Still, he would be extremely useful in bringing George to heel.

"Wear your yellow gown, Wanda, and that lovely green crocheted shawl that Caroline got you in London, in case it becomes chilly. And don't dress your hair in that style you are wearing tonight, for in a curricle it will be windy. Wear a close-fitting bonnet, and perhaps you might slip it off in the inn to show off your hair. You will be in a private parlor, and you might say it makes you warm."

Wanda nodded, and yawned, and very soon excused herself and went off to bed. Her mother, too, arose and said to her other daughter, "Don't stay up all night, Ellie. And for goodness' sake, can't you do something else with your hair besides scraping it all back like a washerwoman? It is not at all attractive, love. Next year I shall take you in hand, and see if we can't nab a title for you, too. Hah! How I laugh every time I think how Marie Homberly and her set used to pity me, having four daughters. A title and a fortune for every one of them, and then Abel, too, at last, to secure the estate."

She pranced off in high good humor, and actually hummed as she mounted the stairs to her room. The hum died on her lips as she noticed the threadbare carpeting beneath her feet. Nuisance of a man, with his expensive flowers. Drapes for the three drawing rooms this year, or she would go to London and stay with Joan till he came around.

Once Rex was so indiscreet as to indicate to Missie that he *might* take her for a spin in his curricle, his fate was sealed. Not only did she rag the life out of him herself, but she also told her mama, who promptly added her solicitations to those of her daughter. Actually, Rex was rather fond of his little sister, and showed it in the usual manner of elder brothers by forgetting her existence nine-tenths of the time, teasing her occasionally, and bristling at any slight offered to her by anyone but himself. In any case, by midmorning it was firmly established that Missie was to go to Needford with Rex.

Missie and her mother were both of the opinion that it was Miss *Ellie* Wanderley who was to accompany Lord Claymore in his curricle. Wanda, after all, was as well as engaged. So Missie was happy in the knowledge that she would have a famous outing. She and Ellie were bosom-bows in spite of the two years that separated them. It was largely Missie's approval, in fact, that led Rex to consider her such a right 'un. At the last moment Mrs. Homberly was hit with the marvelous notion of Missie going in Claymore's carriage as far as the Wanderleys'. Claymore was not caught in the parson's mousetrap yet, and who was to say he wouldn't as lief have Missie as Ellie. Obviously he was not looking about for a lady of fashion. Unaware of the reason for this slight modification of plan, Missie hopped happily into the curricle, and proceeded to amuse Claymore with a recital of how she planned to be an actress when she grew up, which whiled away the time very gaily for both. Clay congratulated her on her inter-esting choice of career, and asked nonchalantly if her mama knew of it.

"No, no one but Miss Ellie knows, for we are very good friends. I had hoped she might come to London with me, but I suppose now . . ."

"Has Miss Ellie different plans then?"

"But of course she has. That is . . . well, she very likely will have, if you make her an offer."

A startled brown eye was lifted from the road long enough to show Clay's astonishment. "Make her an offer!"

"That is why you're here, isn't it? At least Mama thinks it is, and I must say, I don't know why else you would come to the Abbey, for there is nothing here to amuse an out-and-outer like you. Yes, and I am *sure* Rex said you came to make an offer to Miss Wanderley. Ellie is Miss Wanderley, even if no one calls her that. Besides, it can't be Wanda, for she is practically engaged, because, of course, she is so much prettier."

"No, you exaggerate the matter. She has said nothing to me about being on the verge of an engagement."

"Why should she? It is Ellie you're dangling after."

"No, it is not."

"Oh." Missie looked moderately surprised. "But it *can't* be Wanda. And why are you taking Ellie to Needford if it is Wanda you fancy?"

"You misunderstand the matter. It is Wanda I am taking to Needford."

"What?" Missie demanded, deeply offended at this trick. "You mean Ellie is not coming? If I'd known that, I should have stayed at home. It won't be any fun with Wanda."

Clay heard the blunt exclamation with outward calm, and asked on what that assumption was based.

"I hoped we might have a curricle race. Rex says he has sixteen-mile-an-hour horses, and I was sure we would have a race. But if Wanda is along, she will not want to go fast, for it will ruin her hair, or give her freckles, or some such thing."

"Your mama would not appreciate our racing with ladies in the curricle," he comforted her. "Not quite the thing, you know."

"No, but *I* wouldn't care, and neither would Ellie. So Ellie is not to come at all, then? I wonder if Rex would mind if I stayed behind at the Wanderleys'. Then he needn't go dragging off to Needford at all, and *you* can take me back to the Abbey with you, which will please Mama."

Clay bit back a smile at her artlessness. "A pity you hadn't sent a note ahead asking Ellie to come with you. Your brother mentioned it last night, and there would be room in his curricle, I think."

"Did Rex mention it? Well then, I shall ask her when we get there."

"She won't be ready."

"Pooh! How long will it take her to throw on a hat and a pelisse?"

"Quite a while, if she is in the state she was in the other day, covered with mud and messing around in flower pots."

"That's true. I hadn't thought of that. But if she is *clean,* I shall ask her to come."

The young lady's physical state of readiness was not immediately evident upon their arrival, for she was nowhere to be seen. Was, in fact, sulking in her room, determined not to be hanging about like an unwanted dog when Claymore arrived for Wanda. But upon the breathless entry of Missie into her chamber, and a hasty explanation of the situation, she had on her little buff straw bonnet and a paisley shawl that clashed dreadfully with her sprigged muslin in the twinkling of a bedpost. There was really no need for such haste, for the gentlemen arrived at the appointed hour, and naturally Wanda the Wonderful had to keep them waiting for a quarter of an hour while she put the finishing touches on her toilette. She was not such a flat as to be ready and waiting! A protective layer of Gowland's Lotion was carefully applied to her charming visage, for wind and sun wreaked havoc with a delicate complexion. Then she had to try on the mauve silk pelisse and see whether it didn't go better with the yellow gown, but it looked gaudy, so she exchanged it for the green crocheted shawl, as Mama had suggested. By the time she had got a fresh hankie and transferred all her essential items to her yellow and green beaded reticule and descended the staircase, the party were all chomping at the bit to get going, and it was only the grandness of her getup that put Claymore back into good humor. Even that did not quite restore the others.

Clay's curricle headed off first, and as his grays were fresh as rain it was not long before he put a few hundred yards between his carriage and his friend's. Missie's suggestion of a race appealed strongly to him, but he noticed that Wanda was already holding tightly to the edge of the seat, and not even trying to make conversation as it took all her efforts to just remain seated.

"Shall I slow down?" he asked.

"Oh no. Such fun! Very exhilarating to be jolting along at this rate. It makes me quite giddy with pleasure." Clay smiled at her, and thought how the girl was traduced by her jealous detractors. She would have loved a race. But within a half-hour her giddy pleasure had given over to plain giddiness, and she had to beg him to slacken the pace, just a little, as her hands were quite cramped from holding on for dear life. At their reduced speed it was not long before they were caught up by Rex and his party, and when Wanda risked a glance over her shoulder, she

said, "Perhaps you had ought to slow down just a trifle
more, and let them pass." He did so, and the ladies in the
other carriage had obviously great powers of balance, for
their hands were free to wave merrily as they shot by.

"There is no great hurry, is there?" Wanda asked apologetically.

"Certainly not. The day is so fine, and the scenery so
beautiful, that we shall just poke along at a nice slow trot
and enjoy ourselves."

Conversation was possible at the five miles an hour to
which they were reduced, and Wanda undertook to amuse
her driver by pointing out the various farms they passed,
and mentioned the names of the owners, and something
of their condition. After a few miles she said, "It is very
hot, it is not?"

"You might take off your shawl," Claymore pointed
out.

"Oh no, my *shoulders* are freezing. It is only my face
that is hot. It is that sun, beating right in my eyes. We
ought to have remembered the sun would be in our eyes
if we drove west in the afternoon. I hope I don't become
all splotched." She bent her head, so that the rim of her
bonnet might protect her from the sun's blasts. Short of
turning the carriage around and heading home, Claymore
was at a loss as to how he might protect his precious
charge from the elements.

"The sun will be behind us on the way home," he said
hopefully.

"We should have brought a closed carriage," she replied. But she rallied after this exchange, just when he
was sure she was going to sink into the sulks. She even
raised her head from its bent position, and pointed out
that the little farm there, rather falling apart, belonged to
Tom Langdon. He had a daughter, Nora. A very nice
girl. She further forgot herself so far as to crane her neck
around after they were past, to determine whether Nora
was about, and perhaps to determine as well whether she
had a caller.

A little farther along, a fine home appeared, in the
Tudor half-timber style, with a view of cultivated fields

stretching behind it, and a large herd of cattle grazing in the pasture. "That's a fine-looking place," Clay said. "Who lives there?"

"That is Squire Hibbard's place," Wanda answered curtly, and volunteered no further comment. She showed an amazing lack of interest in it, and in fact never so much as glanced to the left as they passed. Clay waited for any more information she might have to impart, but her conversation was at an end. She was silent for the better part of the rest of the trip. The poking pace he was obliged to keep, coupled with his companion's sullen silence, was putting Claymore into a bad humor. This outing had been a mistake. With fashionable young beauties, the thing to do was entertain them with balls and routs and parties, where you didn't have to endure long stretches of their company all alone. He considered that other beauty whose company he had recently been enjoying, and he observed with surprise that he had never been so long alone in her company as he was today with Miss Wanda. The whole affair had been an attempt to get her alone for a moment or two, for she was always surrounded by her court. Even the dullest rattle must appear gay with a dozen men offering her compliments. If she had nothing to say, it was hardly noticed, for she would be smiling, and batting her fan, and listening.

When they eventually reached Needford, it was not difficult to find the ancient church. It was the largest building in the village, yet not so large either, a squat stone affair, with Norman doorway and windows. Outside it, Rex's curricle was being walked by a local urchin, stiff with dignity at the responsibility placed on his ragged shoulders. Another boy shot forward to claim the job of walking the newly arrived vehicle. Clay flipped him a coin for his trouble, and escorted his wilting companion inside. A cool dampness greeted them.

Wanda said in a dying voice, "I shall just sit here at the back and let you join the others. I have seen this old church a dozen times, and I am so tired." Clay made offers to remain with her, but she insisted that he leave. She was determined to be alone, for she had private matters to consider. She had, unbeknownst to her escort, espied *him* walking along the street of the village. He was with Robert Langdon, Nora's brother, which boded ill. What was George doing here, and why was he with Robert Langdon? It bespoke a friendliness with the family that she could not trust. He might have asked Abel to accompany him, if he wanted to come to Needford. He might have called for Robert—though actually *he* lived closer to the village—and if he had called for Robert, there was not a doubt in her mind that Nora had been present. It was now Thursday—five whole days that he had not called on her. He usually came every single day, rain or shine. It was *not* because she had befriended Elmer Rountree either, on Sunday after church. She had only done that because he had danced twice with Nora at the assembly on Saturday evening. He was tired of her, that was the thing. Well, she hoped he might see her on the arm of the Marquis of Claymore. She was very sorry she had turned her head away when she saw him coming. If she heard he was playing up to Nora Langdon, she would have the Marquis, so there.

Clay deserted his charge, feeling rather guilty about it, but determined to have at least a glimpse of the building after dragging all this way in the heat to see it. Silly not to do that much, and she said she wanted to be alone.

"Don't seem right to me, a dog in church," Rex was announcing, and the group were standing around a tomb where a martyr or crusader or some such old fellow was interred. Carved in stone on the tomb was a small pup, curled up at the man's feet, his nose resting on his forepaws, looking as natural as if he might wake up at any moment and wag his tail.

"I don't see why not," Ellie returned. "They are God's creatures too, and I daresay He likes dogs and cats as well as the rest of us do."

"Yes, but dash it, Ellie, not in church. It ain't fitting."

"It is only a statue," Missie pointed out.

"They should at least put wings or a halo on it, to make it look a little holy."

Ellie's sense of humor overcame her at this proposal,

and she gurgled, "Or give it a harp, and pretend it is an angel. You are too nonsensical for words, Rex." Then she spotted Claymore, and asked, "Why, where is Wanda?"

"She is resting there at the back," he indicated, with a toss of head.

"Resting again?" Missie teased. "It seemed to us that you two rested all the way here. We have been looking at the church for an age, and are about ready to leave."

"She is not overcome by the heat, I hope?" Ellie inquired.

"I think not. Merely a little tired."

"Take her to the inn and get her a glass of something wet," Rex recommended.

"It is a shame you do not have a chance to look over the church while you are here," Ellie said to Claymore. "*I* could stay with Wanda. The church is very old, you know, and I don't know whether Wanda pointed it out to you, but there are some rather fine carvings outside at the main doorway."

"I didn't notice. I'll have a look on the way out, but I believe Miss Wanda wants to be alone, so don't feel you must cut your visit short."

"Let us go on," Missie said to her brother, being no more interested in ancient architecture than he was himself.

"Tell you what, Clay," Rex decided, "you stick around and let Ellie show you the place. Knows all about them old brass plaques and what not, for she's always taking rubbins of them. I'll take the ladies along to the inn. You join us there when you're finished it."

"Oh no," Ellie said. As Rex intercepted a surprised glance from his friend, he remembered that he was by no means to separate Clay from his love of life, and he changed his tactics. "Well, there's nothing here but an old pile of stones anyway. Come along and we'll all have a bite to eat. Be just the thing to get Wanda's crest back up."

It was agreed, and they all four strolled back to the back of the church, where Wanda was sufficiently recovered to go along to the inn. No mention was made of the

fine carvings on the doorway as they left, without so much
as a glance at them. A private parlor was procured at the
inn, but not before Wanda had a fleeting glimpse of Hibbard, accompanied by not only Robert Langdon, but also
his hateful sister. Nora was wearing a new bonnet, with
darling little roses on it, and a *pink* pelisse that clashed
dreadfully with her orange hair. Silly girl, just like her to
go thinking she could wear pink, only because she had
seen herself in a stunning rose gown at the assembly. If
that was the taste George Hibbard had, she was well rid
of him.

"I'll tell you what," Rex said, suddenly inspired. "You
and Miss Wanda stay here in this stuffy old parlor, Clay,
and I'll take Missie and Ellie into the common room."

"I wish you would," Missie replied. "It will be ever so
much more amusing than cooped up in here, with no one
to see."

"No!" Clay said in a very loud voice, which startled
Rex no end, as he thought he had hit on a very sly plan
to throw them alone together, to get on with their court-
ing.

"Why not?" Rex asked.

Claymore was too well bred to admit he was bored to
flinders with his lovely companion, and suggested that for
propriety's sake they ought to remain together.

"Didn't think about that when you asked her in the
first place then," Rex reminded him. "Didn't know then I
was to bring the other girls along."

Clay cringed at this loud recital, but Ellie replied to
Rex. "Mama would not like Wanda to be alone with
Claymore, when we are all here at the same inn. It would
look so very odd."

"Let us all go into the common room," Wanda suggested. She was by no means sure George had seen her, and
certainly he had no way of knowing her escort was a
titled gentleman, unless she could call him "my lord"
within that other party's earshot.

Clay was not accustomed to dining in a public room
when he chaperoned ladies, but he was broad-minded
enough to submit to the plan, even though he had no idea

why they found it so desirable. In general, ladies desired all the consequence of private parlors and any other nicety that money could procure. He was not long in the dark as to why the common room was preferred.

"Why, there is George Hibbard," Missie announced in her trumpeting young voice, immediately audible throughout the entire room. "And with the Langdons. I shall drop over and say hello to them." She dashed off, while Wanda examined the white tablecloth with great interest, and asked whether Ellie did not find the room very pleasant.

"Yes, very pleasant," Ellie agreed, wondering at her sister's mood. If she had decided not to have George, she ought to be happy he was leaving her alone. But she was not happy. That wan smile and martyred expression might be indicative of many things, but certainly not of joy. Secure that Missie would impart the identity of her escort, Wanda became quite lively during the meal. After a glass of wine she even said she was looking forward to the return trip in the curricle. Such fun driving the open carriage, and the sun would be behind them.

This animation from his erstwhile lover, and even more the knowledge that her escort was a marquis, loaded with blunt, as Missie had happily told him, so enraged George Hibbard that he bent over backward to show Wanda how little he cared. This was made very easy by the presence of Nora Langdon, who was more than willing to flirt outrageously, pop morsels from her plate into his mouth, roll her eyes at him, and in general behave in a manner designed to inflame Wanda the Wonderful with a terrible jealousy. Not to be outdone, Wanda turned a beaming face on the Marquis, and playfully proposed a toast to the Golden Rose. In a loud aside to Ellie she added it was a pity they were both dark-haired, for London gentlemen would look at nothing but blondes.

Heated denials of this, and a toast in turn from Lord Claymore to the Wanderley Flowers confirmed Hibbard's suspicion that he had been jilted for a title, and before long he and his party took themselves off. A strange listlessness fell upon Wanda when they were gone. She asked offhandedly of Missie what the Langdons had had to say.

"They said they were surprised to know a marquis ate in the common room," Missie replied.

"How did they know who I am?" Clay asked.

"Why, I told them, of course," Missie replied, nonplussed at his stupidity.

By the time the second party left the inn, it had begun to cloud up slightly, and they decided to return home immediately. Clay didn't even remember to purchase a trinket for Wanda. "Lord, let us get home before it starts to pour," Wanda whined. "That's all it needs to make this day complete."

Such a leveler as this left Claymore in no doubt that she had enjoyed the outing as little as he had himself. Once home, no offer was extended to remain for dinner, nor would it have been accepted if it had. Claymore's temper, never calm, was about at its breaking point. Definitely the excursion had been a deplorable idea. A delicate girl like Wanda required a completely different sort of background to show to advantage. The theatre, the opera, a ball—that is where she would shine. He would soon have an opportunity to judge if he were not right, for there was an assembly to be held that coming Saturday. Mrs. Wanderley told them about it, and determined as well that Rex should take Claymore to it. That gave both discomfited parties a whole day—Friday—to recover from the fiasco of the expedition to Needford.

Chapter Six

On Tuesday evening Mrs. Wanderley had written to Lady Siderow regarding the arrival of the Marquis of Claymore at the Abbey, among other less important matters. As Lady Siderow's usual gay round of activities was curtailed by the closing of the Season, her mama had her answer on Saturday morning. She wrote a good clear hand, and didn't stoop to crossing her pages as her husband might frank her letters for her, saving the recipient the expense. "C's arrival," she wrote, "would be the result of his having been turned down by Miss G. It is one of the *on dits* of London that she had an offer from him. He even tried to get her to dash for the Border. What a hulabaloo that would have been! Well, he is free, Mama, and I wish Wanda luck, if that is what you have in mind. Keep a sharp eye, though, or your little girl might be fleeing off to Gretna Green—a high price to pay, even for the title of marchioness." The epistle continued for two pages of lesser news, but it was only the part concerning Claymore that was conveyed to Wanda.

"There will be none of this Gretna Green for you, milady," her mother adjured strictly.

"Pooh. He doesn't even like me. He is still in love with Miss Golden, and only trying to forget her."

"That shows a streak of common sense that I find particularly pleasing. You will wear your white spangled gown to the assembly, love. And I think a more demure hair style might be better than that Méduse thing you wore the other night. Pulled back, with ringlets over your shoulder, and perhaps a rosebud entwined around the knot. If your papa were not such an old skint with his blooms, he might let us have one of his curst orchids for a corsage, but there is no point in asking him."

Wanda took some interest in this discussion, though it was not Claymore she was hoping to impress with her toilette. George would naturally be there too—with old redhead Langdon, like as not, wearing a pink gown.

Receiving no parental help in the matter, Ellie decided to adopt Wanda's Méduse hair style, and spent a miserable Saturday afternoon with her hair done up in papers. She selected a pale green Italian crepe gown that had been given her by Lady Tameson on her last visit, and while it fit like a glove, it was of a more daring décolletage than she normally chose. She was in some trepidation when she entered the Green Saloon, for she was not at all sure Mama would approve. But it was no such a thing.

"Why Ellie!" her mother said, looking with pleasure at the fashionable picture her daughter presented. "How charming you look. Doesn't she look nice, Wanda? The hair style suits you very well. I told you that washerwoman way you wore it was ugly. Only see what an improvement the papers have made. And the gown—Caroline's old green, is it? Very dashing. Fits to a nicety, love. You ought to have some bit of jewelry with it. I'll get my little pearls." She intercepted the butler in the hall, and sent him to ask a maid to fetch her seed pearls. They were duly fastened around Ellie's neck, and her outfit was ready. Even Wanda, Mrs. Wanderley thought in surprise, did not look so very much finer than Ellie when she was dolled up a bit. No problem with little Ellie, after all. Next Season she would do very well for herself. Another title—not a doubt of it. How Marie Homberly would *writhe* in envy.

There was no question of Adam leaving his flowers long enough to accompany them. He was in the process of crossing an epidendrum with his cattleya, and must remain on the premises, like a midwife at a cross-birth. Abel, however, was more than happy to oblige them, and at an hour deemed suitably late to make a grande entrance, Mrs. Wanderley shepherded her charges in, and had the exquisite pleasure of seeing every female eye in the room turn green. A veritable rush of black-coated gentlemen converged on the new arrivals, as the first dance was just over, and the serious business of accepting escorts for their first dance was begun. Unfortunately Claymore was at the punch bowl at the time, so he was not among the first crush. Nor was George Hibbard in the throng, though he was certainly present, and, yes, sitting with Nora Langdon. Wanda's spine stiffened, as she pinned a glittering smile on her face. She accepted the most persistent of her admirers—it happened to be Elmer Rountree. A dead bore, but Wanda thought it was he who had made George jealous on Sunday, and in any case he would do for the time being. Claymore was around somewhere, for there was Rex.

Poor Ellie! Now why had she stood up with Rex? He was impossibly short—in her heeled shoes she was a good two inches taller than he was. Why did short gentlemen not realize what a ridiculous figure they cut when they danced with a tall girl? Rex had been dangling after her once, till she hinted him gently away by saying she did not like stooping to her partner, for it ruined her posture. Foolish little runt. He had held her in dislike ever since, not that she cared. Ah, there was Claymore now, with Mrs. Homberly. Nothing to fear there.

Claymore's practiced eye soon singled out his prey, and he watched in approval as Miss Wanda wheeled around the floor. Very well got up, in that spangled gown, and with a new hair style. He didn't like it quite so well as that tousled do she had worn the other evening. And there was Rex. Now who the devil was the pretty young lady with him? Why, it couldn't be Ellie! Looking as stylish as an actress, and nearly as lovely as her sister. Beauties, the whole family. Yessir, one of them would be the very girl to take the shine out of the Rose. Wanda, of course. Really, though, he thought, as his glance swung from one sister to the other, there was little to choose between them. Wanda had perhaps the more perfect face, but Ellie carried herself with more dignity. From this little distance, Ellie made the more distinguished appearance. Mrs. Homberly kindly pointed out a butter-toothed girl who had no partner, and Claymore went to her rescue. Before long, he was at the side of Wanda, claiming her company for the next dance.

"Beautiful, as usual, Miss Wanda," he pronounced, which won him a smile. He noticed with relief that she made no comment about the Golden Rose tonight. Usually his compliments were met by some playful comparison of their charms, with herself on the bad end, of course, so that he had to contradict her. It was becoming a bit of a bore.

He soon realized he had been overly hasty in congratulating himself on his escape. "I thought you might like the coiffure, for it was one favored in London this past Season, though, of course, it looked more becoming on a *blonde.*"

"I am becoming just a trifle tired of that joke, Miss Wanda," he said, and surprised even himself at the ennui in his voice.

"Well, I didn't ask you to stand up with me," she shot back angrily. Poor Claymore. It was not him she was angry with at all, but George Hibbard, who had gone to stand beside Robert Langdon at the end of the first dance, when Nora had been claimed by another buck. He had eyes for no one but that freckle-faced girl.

"I'm sorry," he said hastily. "That was uncommonly rude of me."

"Yes, it was. And furthermore you needn't think we don't know why you are come to the Abbey, for Mama had a letter of Joan this morning, and she told us about your trying to get Miss Golden to run off with you. That

was very bad of you, and you needn't think I will do anything so stupid."

"I had no notion of asking it of you," he replied stiffly,
a cold anger shaking him at the Rose's disclosure of his
folly. So it was out—the whole thing. Not content with
bragging of his offer, she must reveal as well his insane
suggestion that they run off to Gretna Green.

Miss Wanda was soon full of remorse for her wayward-
ness, and of fear for what her mama would say if she
found out. "I am sure you didn't mean it," she said in
a conciliating voice. "Anyone might say a foolish thing in
the heat of the moment, as I just did myself."

"Pray, it is not worth your consideration."

"Well, I am sorry. I shouldn't have said it, only I have
the most ripping headache." She said this in such a weak
voice that he believed her, and in fact it was no more
than the truth.

He offered to take her out for a breath of air. She
would normally not have accepted his offer, but it
chanced that at that precise moment she glanced toward
Hibbard, and both her and Robert Langdon looked at her
and laughed. In a spasm of fury she accepted Clay's offer—and just let's see what Mr. Hibbard said when he
saw her leave the ballroom on the arm of a marquis. She
had never been so obliging as to bestow the same honor
on George.

Mr. Hibbard said not a word to anyone, but with great
haste and in the most unconcerned manner in the world,
he dashed right out after them. Wanda leaned weakly on
her escort's arm. When a surreptitious peep toward the
door determined that George was in hot pursuit, she allowed herself to be led into the garden.

"I cannot think what came over me. I am not usually
subject to the headache," she confided to her companion.

"It is the heat and noise inside. It is enough to give
anyone the migraine," he commiserated.

"I usually like it very well, but tonight I am not feeling
quite the thing." She looked up through her lashes, in a
manner very like that adopted by the Rose, and lan-

guished, till he was forced to put an arm around her, to prevent her from slumping off the bench entirely.

Thus bolstered, she leaned against him, sensing in every fiber that George was not far behind, seeing the whole thing. There, she heard a twig snap! She would let Claymore kiss her. That for Mr. Hibbard and old redhead! She mentally snapped her fingers. "This is so very comfortable. I wish we did not have to go back in at all." Her head fell back against the Marquis' black shoulder.

Thus led on, Claymore tightened his hold on Wanda. She leaned back harder, and turned her neck, lifting her face toward his. Had she seen the look of utter incredulity on his face, she might have stopped, but she could see no more than the corner of his chin. He was shocked at her fast behavior. Obviously she expected him to kiss her. It was distinctly strange that he felt no inclination whatever to do so. Was there not a woman of virtue left in England? Wanda waited for the next step in her seduction, but as it was not forthcoming, she had to take it herself.

"I ought not to be out here with you, *alone,*" she said leadingly. Surely he would divine her helpless state, and take advantage of it.

"We shall go back inside as soon as you feel sufficiently recovered."

"If Mama saw me, she would be very angry. She always feels that a gentleman will try to take advantage, if I am alone with him for a moment." There now, was he a gentleman or not?

"I hope you are not often allowed to be alone with gentlemen?"

"No, I hardly ever get the chance," she said pertly. Then she craned her neck backward to its utter limit, closed her eyes, and puckered her lips for a kiss.

Claymore was trapped. It would be a positive insult to refuse to kiss those waiting lips. The slow top finally inclined his head, and touched the infamous lips gently, in a fleeting manner.

Before she felt obliged to protest, there was a rush toward them, and Mr. Hibbard dashed in and grabbed her hand.

"So this is the way you carry on behind my back!" he shouted, his voice shaken with anger. Wanda's spirits soared. That voice! He was livid with rage.

Damping down her joy, she replied, "Pray, what business is it of *yours*, Mr. Hibbard?"

"You would never come outside with *me*!" was his childish rejoinder.

At the intruder's arrival, Claymore had jumped up to protect the lady's honor. There flashed through his mind the horrible thought that he might be required to protect it with cold steel. To forestall this contingency, he said, "Miss Wanda was overcome by the heat," in quite a civil tone.

"A likely story," Hibbard shot back.

"I was so, and don't you dare to call me a liar," she retaliated.

"Well, I ain't, but you was never overcome by the heat in your life, Wanda, and don't try to bamboozle me you were tonight, for you just wanted to be alone with your lord."

As the likelihood of a duel subsided, Claymore relaxed somewhat. "Shall we go back inside, Miss Wanda?" he asked, ignoring the newcomer.

"*I'll* take Wanda back inside," George informed him angrily.

"I am not in the habit of abandoning ladies to raving lunatics," Clay told Hibbard amiably.

"Well, if that don't beat all!"

"Oh, pray leave us, Lord Claymore," Wanda said to him, hardly aware of what she said. "I will come in directly."

"I'll take her in," George insisted.

"I think not," Clay replied, taking Wanda by the arm and piloting her protesting body to the door. But as Hibbard made no motion of leaving her other side, Claymore bowed and took his leave of the pair as soon as she was safely inside. Across the room, a little later, he noted that George and Wanda were sufficiently reconciled to stand up together for the dance. She was positively glowing with joy, or victory, and he mumbling something into her ears.

Claymore looked about for a partner. Before he had time to choose one for himself, Mrs. Homberly was at his side, leading him to a "delightful girl, and so pretty behaved." She was unfortunately less pretty of face than of behavior, but no matter. She danced well enough, and did not more than twice tramp on his feet. At the dance's end, he slipped off to the refreshment room to have a glass of wine. Ellie was there, chatting in a corner with Missie.

"What, not dancing?" Clay asked.

"We are not yet allowed to waltz," Ellie explained. "Until I have made my debut, Mama forbids it, and Missie is only sixteen. I think it is very stupid, especially as the waltz is becoming so popular, and they play ever so many of them."

"Yes, and you waltz very well too, Ellie," Missie threw in. "I can't waltz at all, but I have seen you do it at home, and you waltz nicely. Well, as Nora Langdon will be sitting out too, I shall take this chance to have a chat with her." Saying this, Missie walked away from a perfect opportunity of attaching Lord Claymore, a mistake for which her mother would later berate her, when she happened to mention it.

"Actually, I don't mind," Ellie explained to Claymore. "I don't think I should be comfortable waltzing with anyone but Abel anyway. I learned with him, you see, at home."

"Shy?" Clay teased.

"I guess so." She strolled to the edge of the room and sat down, and began to fan herself.

"If you are feeling warm, we might go out in the garden for a breath of air," he suggested.

"Oh no," she looked at him, shocked. "That would not be quite the thing."

"You are right. I ought not to have suggested it." She agreed silently. "You know, Miss Ellie, when I first saw you this evening, I didn't recognize you."

"I am wearing my hair differently," she admitted.

"Getting practiced up for London?"

"Yes," she told him in a matter-of-fact voice, looking

at him frankly with her clear gray eyes. "Taking your advice, and getting myself fixed up."

"No, surely I didn't say anything so rude as that."

"Yes, you did, but I didn't consider it rude. The truth cannot be rude." He looked quite stricken at his supposed rudeness, and to rally him, she said, "Wanda is allowed to waltz, because of being out, you know."

"Is she? Yes, of course she is, for she was waltzing with Hibbard just now."

"What, with George?" Ellie exclaimed.

"Yes, I think they have patched it up."

"Oh! Oh dear," she said, looking at him a little doubtfully.

"They are on pretty good terms, I take it?"

"Yes. I confess that before you came along, we all expected there would be an announcement made any day."

"I think there will still be an announcement made. Any day," he said, and he sighed deeply. He minded much less than he had thought he would. Was a bit relieved, actually. It rankled that he would be the butt of jokes when he went back to London, but somehow Wanda, in spite of her beauty, did not quite please him. Too coy, too many jokes about the Rose, too easily discomposed, as on the trip to Needford, and too fast. Letting, even encouraging, him to kiss her, when he hardly knew her.

"You cannot have had time to fall so very much in love with her," Ellie said prosaically, "so I shan't offer any condolences."

"No, they are not called for in the least," he agreed. His tongue bit on the nearly-expressed thought that she ought to offer congratulations instead on his near escape.

"I really don't think you and she would have suited," Ellie said bluntly. "Wanda is the sort of girl who needs a deal of pampering, and I don't think you are the one to give it."

"Where did you get such a poor reading of my character? I can pamper with the best of them, I promise you."

"No, I think you are too sensible," she replied, and arising, she pulled her shawl about her and said, "I am returning to the ballroom. Do you come?"

He walked behind her, and when the next dance began, he asked her to stand up with him. She danced well, making polite conversation during the occasions when the steps of the dance permitted. Later, he saw her moving about the floor with various partners. His attention diverted from Wanda, he began to think Ellie was quite pretty, in a different style. No posing or flirting, but a directness that was a pleasant change, and rather exciting in its way. Other gentlemen appeared to share his view, for she never lacked for partners.

At dinner Wanda went in with George Hibbard. As Claymore found himself without a partner, he joined Rex, Ellie and Missie.

"I see Wanda has got George back from Nora Langdon," Missie said.

Rex looked at Claymore with a question in his eyes, and said, "Seems so. Been close as peas in a pod all night. Mrs. Wanderley wouldn't have allowed it unless Wanda said something to her. Think there'll be an announcement soon, Ellie?"

"Very likely," Ellie replied, with a glance at her sister's table.

"We'll be getting on to Bath tomorrow then, shall we, Clay?" Rex asked hopefully.

"I understood my invitation was for two weeks, Rex. Trying to get rid of me already?"

"Stands to reason. No point in sticking around now. Engaged."

Ellie darted a quick eye at Claymore to see how this shot was received, and was disconcerted to discover he was regarding her closely.

"But I find the neighborhood enchanting," Clay said, continuing to look at Ellie in a most marked fashion, so that she spilt her ice all over Lady Tameson's Italian crepe, and had to blot at it with a napkin.

"Eh? Ellie do you mean?" Rex asked, with no consideration whatsoever for anyone's feelings.

"This is a terrible fellow," Clay said to Ellie, quite as though Rex were a mile away. "No refinement at all. No thought for a lady's feelings."

"The same might be said for yourself, my lord," Ellie told him stiffly. She was as red as a beet, being unaccustomed to such trifling.

"Eh, that's a good one, Ellie," Rex cheered. "No use trying your conning tactics on Ellie, Clay. She ain't the sort you can go on flattering and buttering up. If you mean to have her instead of Wanda, you'd do better to just come out and ask her. She likes plain speaking, does Ellie."

"Not quite so plain as that, I thank you," Ellie said, glaring at poor Rex, while still blushing furiously. "Besides, it is nonsensical to think anyone would be making an offer to a virtual stranger."

"Don't bother Clay. All he cares about is the looks. You look good tonight, Ellie. 'Pon my word, you don't look bad at all. Darned near as good as Wanda. Ought to rig yourself out like that more often."

"Better than Wanda," Clay threw in, and watched in amusement as Ellie directed her glare toward him, as though he had just insulted her.

"Well, I don't, and it is very bad of you both to roast me, only because I have done my hair up, and worn a different dress."

"Very nice dress," Rex complimented her. "Funny thing, you know, I do believe Lady Tameson has one just like it. At the opera I saw it. Well, sisters. You would have the same sort of taste. Stands to reason."

As Missie was snickering into her fist, Ellie was forced to admit her shame. "Lady Tameson gave me the gown. I would not wear it in London, of course, and if I had known you were familiar with it, I would not have worn it here either."

"Be a waste of a good dress then," Rex told her. "Looks very nice on you. Better than them white things you usually wear. Gives you a bit of dash, you know."

"Lady Tameson is well thought of for her gowns," Clay said, his eyes dancing.

Ellie, who was pretending she was not there, was surprised to receive a jostling of her arm. "Are you sick, or what is it?" Rex hissed. "Here am I bending over backward to puff you up a bit, and you just go on looking into that empty bowl as if it was alive. Wake up and chatter a bit, and *you* might nab Claymore."

Being neither deaf nor blind, Claymore was a witness to this gentle hint, which was delivered in a carrying tone. He was a witness as well to the reply. "I don't want to *nab* anyone, and I wish you would stop embarrassing me with your foolishness." The poor girl seemed on the verge of tears, Clay thought, and could not understand it. Just a little teasing and flattering of a sort that usually sat very well with young ladies, in his experience.

It was the farthest thing from his mind to have embarrassed her, and he looked about for a change of subject, "You are looking very grown up this evening, Missie," he said, feigning admiration of her curls, which had been pinned up for the occasion, and had a sad tendency to spring loose from their moorings and tumble about her ears.

"Missie won't do you no good at all, Clay," Rex warned. "She's too young, and besides she don't hold a candle to the"—a killing grimace from Clay, accompanied by a resounding boot on the shin under the table brought him to a halt—"to—er—to Ellie," he finished up, pleased with his quick-wittedness.

"I must speak to Mama. Pardon me," Ellie said, dashing off as a tear glistened, half-formed, in her gray eyes.

"Now, see what you've done, clodpole," Clay adjured severely.

"Dash it, what did *I* do? Just paying a compliment. Nothing to come the weepy over. Deuced strange business, Clay. Never knew Ellie to act so silly before. What ails her anyway, Missie?"

"She was embarrassed because you told Claymore she was wearing Caroline's gown, I suppose. You ought not to have said anything."

"Nothing wrong in that. You're wearing your cousin Elizabeth's. There, I've told Clay, and I don't see you busting into tears." He did, however, see her burst into anger. Before she could say anything, he continued. "Didn't tumble to it it was Caroline's till I'd blurted it out.

Too late then. *Tried* to cover it up. Daresay she wasn't taken in. Too sharp."

"And," Missie broke into his story, "she was ready to *die* when you said about Clay meaning to have her. It was very bad of you to make fun of her in that way. She is older than Wanda, and will get razzing enough when Wanda's engagement is announced as it is. It must be very trying to have such a beautiful sister. Dozens of them, in fact."

"Only three," Rex corrected.

"Ellie is as pretty as the others," Clay said, to no one in particular.

"I wasn't making fun of her," Rex said, apologetically.

"You were so," his little sister contradicted badly, "for naturally Claymore would never offer for Ellie."

"That is odd you should say so," Clay turned to Missie. "The other day you seemed to think I had come to the Abbey for that very purpose."

"Mama thought so, but she really couldn't believe it either, and she said it was much more like it when I told her it was Wanda you were after."

"He ain't after Wanda now, at any rate," Rex said, and dipped into the plate of strawberry tarts, his favorite of all sweets.

Looking around the room, Clay discovered that Ellie was not with her mama, who was chatting with Mrs. Hibbard, George, and Wanda, in such a jolly fashion that one could imagine they were all one happy family already. Wanda was positively radiant with happiness, the headache miraculously cured. He arose and strolled around the room, determining in the process that Ellie was nowhere present, then went outside.

He set about locating her, which involved walking along a few yards, and going through an arbor into a sequestered garden.

Ellie was there, pretty well concealed in a dark corner, weeping into her hankie. "Is there something wrong, Miss Ellie?" he asked tentatively.

A sound of sniffling stopped abruptly, and a quick movement of the handkerchief tried to erase the evidence of her tears. "No. No, indeed. Merely I wished for a breath of air," she lied promptly, in a voice very close to normal.

He came forward and sat beside her. She averted her head, which made conversation difficult. "I'm sorry if I offended you," he said. The head turned to the front, not toward him, but no longer entirely away either.

"No, you didn't," she replied, in a flat voice

"Well, I think I did, and I am very sorry. Come, let us go back inside. Your mama will think it odd if you are missing when she begins looking about for you." He reached out and tried to take one of her hands, the two of which were squeezed together in her lap, a soggy handkerchief between them. She held them even tighter, and pulled them away a little.

"You go back in," she said evenly. "I—I have got something in my eye, and wish to remain a moment, till it goes away, for it is watering a bit."

"Ellie." It was a soft, cajoling tone. He reached out and with one finger tilted her face toward him, but in the concealing shadows he could see nothing but a white oval, with a cloud of dark hair around it, and a sparkle that might have been eyes. It stirred some vague memory, excited him. She made no move to pull away, and he said nothing more, but just sat looking, not even thinking, but feeling something very moving. The sweet, persuasive scent of the roses all about them hung heavy on the air. Suddenly a soft, hiccoughing sound, as of a swallowed sob, escaped her. He was overcome with a compelling emotion to reach out and take her in his arms, to cradle her, and protect her from whatever was hurting her. He did reach out, but she pulled back so violently that she very nearly fell off the seat, and he was left with his two hands extended into empty space, looking and feeling extremely gauche indeed. "I wasn't about to strangle you," he said sharply, though once the words were out, it didn't sound a bad idea.

"Go away. Please go away," she said in a choked voice.

"I don't see why you are making such a to-do of nothing," he complained, angry at the sudden break in mood. "I have never seen a girl act so foolishly only because someone tries to compliment her."

"You were not complimenting me," she shot back. "I am not so stupid as not to realize when I am being laughed at, and right to my face too. You would never have behaved so rudely to Wanda, or anyone else, I daresay. And I am not trying to *nab* you, so don't think it."

"You will never nab anyone if you go on in this childish fashion when you get to London. I should think that with three sisters you would have more—more sense," he finished up lamely.

"I am not going to London. I have decided tonight. *You* have decided me. If this is the way gentlemen behave in London, I have no desire to meet them."

"What, only because I have said you were looking pretty!"

"Laughing at me! You think because you are a marquis with twenty thousand pounds a year you may act as you please."

"News certainly travels fast," he said ironically. God, he might as well wear a sign.

"Yes, particularly when you go bragging about it, as if that made you something special, only because you were *born* into a title and fortune, and have never done the least thing to merit it."

"Bragging! I hope I am not so crude as that."

"Well, you are, for the very first time I ever saw you, you told me you were the Marquis of Claymore, with twenty thousand a year."

"Strange I have no recollection of the occasion."

"You were so disguised you don't remember," she retaliated.

He didn't believe her, and thought she had the story from someone else, Lady Siderow perhaps, and was only trying to cover up her error in letting it slip out. "Unwise of you to antagonize me, wasn't it?" he asked coolly. "You won't meet many marquises, with twenty thousand a year."

"I hope I don't meet *any* more, if they are all as odious as you."

"You will find they are. The dukes with twenty-five thousand are even worse, but it doesn't prevent their marrying the prettiest girls in town."

"You are insufferably conceited and arrogant and—"

"And rich," he finished for her, as she appeared to have run out of compliments. He was in such ill humor at this calling down that he had to return the blow in some manner. "You know, Ellie, you are pretty stupid yourself. Before our little . . . *chat*, it had been my intention to offer for you." The idea had occurred to him, fleetingly.

She heard it and gasped. "You have saved us both an unnecessary embarrassment then," she replied in a chill tone, "by not doing so."

"So it seems. If you are quite sure you are in no need of help, I shall return to the ballroom."

"Why should I need help from you?" she snapped, which had the effect of getting his lordship to his feet and on his stiff-legged way back to the ball, and leaving her alone to sniffle into her wet hankie with renewed vigor.

Chapter Seven

The next morning Rex Homberly was surprised and delighted when his friend suggested an early remove to Bath. "Not going to make a pitch for Ellie, then?" Rex asked.

"No, it was Wanda I preferred. Perhaps the whole thing was madness."

"Always thought so m'self," Rex said sagely, nibbling his thumb. "Whole thing will be forgotten by the fall. Silly to go shackling yourself for life to a pretty widgeon like Wanda only because the Rose broke your heart. Well, Wanda is to have Hibbard, after all. Mama had it of Mrs. Wanderley last night, so if you don't fancy Ellie, we might as well leave for Bath this afternoon."

"Let us go this morning."

"Thought I'd ride over and congratulate Miss Wanda on the announcement. Mama says I should. You ought to come too, Clay. No point in letting her think she's got you all cut to shreds. Wouldn't satisfy her. Let her see you're merry as a grig before you go."

"Very well," Clay agreed readily, and felt a stirring of anticipation that had nothing to do with seeing Wanda.

They rode out around ten. During the trip Rex asked, "Wonder if she'll go to London next year."

"She says not," Clay replied.

"That so? Well, Hibbards don't have a London residence, but I'm surprised she don't try to talk him into renting one."

"Hibbards? Did you think she would stay with Wanda? I thought it more likely she would go to Lady Siderow's."

"Eh? What the devil are you talking about, Clay? Why would Wanda go to Lady Siderow's?"

"Wanda? I was speaking of Ellie."

"Oh, *Ellie*. She'll go to London, certainly. Next year is to be her year. That was always understood. Can't see why they didn't take her this year. Looked very well last night. If they'd got her rigged out like that earlier, she could be getting married this year as well as Wanda."

"She said she wouldn't go to London."

"She will, though. Won't have a thing to say about it. Why'd she say she wouldn't?"

Clay squirmed uncomfortably in the seat of the curricle and prevaricated. "She doesn't care much for the social whirl, I believe."

"Pooh. What's that got to do with it? Got to go to London. How else will she make a decent match? Wanda got Hibbard. Ain't anyone else around here except me, and *I* don't mean to have her."

"I suppose she will go when the time comes." A soft smile curved his mouth. A frightful temper the girl had. Ripping up at him only because he had tried to compliment her. There would be some burning ears next Season, for she would come in the way of a good many compliments if he knew anything of London beaux.

Wanda and her mama sat in state in the Green Saloon, awaiting congratulatory callers. Wanda was exquisite in a white gown with a blue satin sash, a pert blue bow tucked into her coiffure. She began demurely batting her lashes and smiling smugly when Claymore offered his congratulations.

"Fortunately for me, George does not prefer blondes," she said to him, flirting still in spite of her new status as a betrothed lady, and with the same tired old joke. The girl was incorrigible. *She* would never fly into the boughs and rip up at you only because you praised her a little, nor ever mistake a genuine compliment for an insult.

"Where is your sister this morning?" Clay asked.

"She has the headache," Wanda replied, still smiling smugly. "Very odd that *my* becoming engaged before her should bring on the migraine," and she laughed, showing her even little white teeth. He felt a strong desire to box her pink ears.

"Yes, particularly as it was *you* who had the Season in London," he could not refrain from reminding her.

"I was only there for two weeks," she replied angrily.

Later he overheard her say in a stage whisper to Rex that she was afraid she had hurt Claymore more than she thought, and she hoped he would soon get over it. He could barely keep his tongue between his teeth, and arose after only ten minutes, excusing himself and Rex on the pretext of their imminent departure for Bath.

Strangely enough, Ellie's headache cleared up immediately she heard their curricle pull down the drive, in spite of her younger sister's engagement. She joined the others in the Green Saloon.

"What had Rex to say?" Ellie asked, meaning what had Claymore to say.

"They didn't stay above a minute," Wanda told her. "Claymore was very blue, but trying to hide it, you know."

"I still think you would have done better to have taken Claymore," Mrs. Wanderley repined, for perhaps the tenth, but certainly not the last, time that day. Wanda tossed her black curls and pouted.

"He only wanted me to parade in front of Miss Golden. I do not see why I should oblige him."

"She could not very well have taken him, Mama, when he didn't make her an offer," Ellie pointed out.

"Pooh! I could have had an offer any time these last days if I'd given him the least encouragement," Wanda boasted.

"He wasn't lacking any encouragement all week," Ellie returned.

"Jealous." Wanda sneered, and even stuck out her tongue, child that she was.

"Next Season *you* might make a push to attract him," Mrs. Wanderley said to Ellie. "I notice he dined with you last night. Did he say anything of interest at all?"

"No, nothing of interest," Ellie replied, so grimly that her sister was quite restored to good humor.

"Ellie is not in Claymore's style, Mama. He prefers beauties." Wanda smiled.

It had been my intention to offer for you. . . . Ellie sniffed, and dashed from the room.

"No need to rub it in, love," Mrs. Wanderley chided gently. "And Ellie really looked very nice last night, though I notice she's got the hair yanked back again today. Claymore seemed quite taken with her when they were dancing, and he chose her to dine with too."

"*I* was dining with George, Mama."

"Yes, love, but there were plenty of other pretty girls about. And he was paying marked attention to her over dinner. Several times I remarked him smiling at her, only she is such a silly little goose that she wasn't encouraging him at all. In fact, she got right up in the middle of it and went off somewhere."

"There is the door knocker," Wanda broke in. "Oh, I *hope* it is the Langdons."

Homberly and Claymore left early in the afternoon for Bath, and by the next afternoon they had attended to such duties as entering their names in the subscription books at the Lower and New Assembly Rooms, and had strolled through Sydney Gardens to ogle the beauties. A considerable number of persons had already arrived, and when they entered the Pump Room, they were accosted by a pair of London bucks who formed part of their London set.

It was Rodney Lucknow who initiated the conversation. "So this is where you are slunk off to, Clay, with your tail between your legs."

Clay looked at him with a quizzical frown on his brow. "Slunk off to? What do you mean by that, Lucknow?"

"As if all London don't know about the blow the Rose dealt you, thumbing her nose at you after letting you dangle after her all Season. Well, I don't blame you for ducking out, my friend. Can't be much fun to be the subject of common gossip. Making a great story of it, the Rose. How you tried to get her to dash for Gretna Green and all."

"How does Everleigh take it?" Clay asked, forcing down the ire that rose and burned his throat. "I am surprised he lets her make such a cake of herself."

"Can't do much till the knot's tied. Daresay he'll come down heavy then. On the other hand, though, *he* was spreading the story himself. Well, it would please a homely old fellow like him, I suppose, to know the Rose chose him over a young chap like you."

The other fellow, Ivor Milthrong, added his two cents' worth. "I thought you'd go into rustication at your country place till this blows over. Your mama's at Claymore Hall, ain't she?"

"Yes, she didn't come to London at all this year."

"You wouldn't be any better off there then, for she's as bad as any to turn the screw when the cards are stacked against you," Ivor opined, with a quite careless mixing of his metaphors.

This slur on his parent would not have been borne but for the fact that Ivor was his cousin, and a special friend of his mama. Besides, it was true enough. Sometimes Clay thought he must have the most unnatural mother in the world. Nothing so pleased her as to have something to hold over your head, and pester you with. Did she commiserate if you lost a bundle, or took a degrading tumble from your horse, or lost a girl? No such a thing! She was tickled pink to be able to rag you. It was the reason he was so assiduously avoiding his own home at this time. Mama would have the whole story from her London cronies; even if she didn't much bother with coming to town herself anymore, she took an overweening interest in city happenings, particularly, of course, as they related to her son.

"Bath is as good a place to hide out as any," Rex took

it up. "Nobody here but a batch of old ladies. Wouldn't be here myself but for the fact that Mama has that old falling-apart house at Laura Place."

"You putting up at your mother's house at Laura Place?" Ivor asked, hoping, perhaps, to exchange his barracks at Lucknow's old falling-apart house for a superior dwelling in the same district.

"Yes, but there's only the one servant there, and we're eating out."

"Oh, I see." Better a tumble-down house with meals than a mansion without.

"You'd have to face the public several times a day then," Lucknow said, hoping to get a rise out of his friend. "Pity, that."

Rex, belatedly, sprang to his friend's defense. "Just goes to show you how little you know about it. Why, Clay has been on the verge of offering for another girl since that Golden Rose business. Got over her in no time. Always preferred brunettes. Just a passing fancy, you might say."

"Who's that, then?" Rodney asked, his interest quickening, not that he believed a word of it.

"One of the Wanderley girls," Rex told him.

"The Wanderleys—oh, one of *them*," Ivor butted in. "I suppose you must mean Miss Wanda. . . ?"

"That's it," Rex replied with satisfaction. "And she's got the Rose beat all hollow for looks too. Only a passing fancy, that's all it was."

Clay's spirits sank even further as he remembered that Wanda, too, was about to announce her betrothal. It might appear in the papers today—yet another blow to his dignity. "It wasn't Wanda, Rex," he said helplessly.

"Ellie, then," Rex obediently changed his opinion.

"Ellie? Which one is she?" Ivor asked.

"Why, she's the best of the lot," Rex answered promptly. "Wonderfully taken with her, was Clay."

"I don't recall a Miss Ellie," Rodney said. "Surely the girl's name was Wanda."

"There is a Wanda, but she ain't the one Clay fancies," Rex explained with great condescension.

"A beauty, is she?" Rodney persisted.

"An Incomparable," Rex returned.

"I am looking forward to meeting her," Rodney said, and he looked so smug that there was every reason to doubt he believed the story.

"And so you will, next Season," Rex said.

"Stealing a march on us, you sly old dog," Ivor chided his cousin. "Trying to get this one tied up before ever she hits the market."

"You've learned something from your experience with the Rose," Rodney added. "Not taking any chances. A hard teacher, experience, but an effective one."

They continued in this bantering spirit for some time, till Claymore felt he could decently leave without appearing to run away.

"Hell and damnation," he cursed softly when they were beyond earshot. "It is just as I feared. Everyone is talking about it, laughing at me. I wish I *had* offered for Wanda."

"Wouldn't have done you no good, Clay. She was three-quarters engaged to Hibbard before ever we got there. Pity you hadn't tumbled for Ellie, for she'd have done as well when you got her dolled up a bit."

"That wouldn't have done me any good either. She hates me."

Rex looked at him, dumbfounded. "No, what do you mean, Clay? Ellie don't hate you. Don't hate anyone. Not that sort of a girl. Wanda now, *she's* a hater. Fact, Clay. Hates me only because I happen to be an inch or so shorter than she is."

"Forget about Wanda."

"Forgot about her years ago. Haven't had a bit of use for her ever since—well, never mind that."

"Let's get out of here." Clay arose and dragged his companion from the Pump Room within two minutes of having taken a seat.

A dismal two weeks ensued. This was by no means because of the lack of amenities, for even if Bath had been eclipsed by Brighton, it still offered card parties, balls, concerts, assemblies, parks, pleasant drives, and plenty of company. A surfeit of company, it seemed, all of it full of two subjects: Rose's jilting of himself, and her approaching nuptials. The town was buzzing with it. If they dined at the York Inn, they met the older set, who smiled pityingly; and if, to avoid them, they tried the White Hart, they met their own friends, which was even worse. Even the Pelican was not safe, for there would always be a few fellows with their pockets to let putting up at the cheaper establishment. Clay couldn't eat a bite, and Rex was getting chubbier from eating for two.

While his male acquaintances made not the slightest demur in roasting him over his jilting, the females were even worse. Not that they roasted, but they were so commiserating. They looked at him as an object of pity. Every time he passed a pair of them, he heard whispers behind fans or raised fingers—"Rose," "Miss Golden," "jilted," "Gretna Green," till his head spinned with it. He was of a proud disposition, but even the most humble soul would have been cast into despair at being so openly scorned and pitied.

Through it all there was the unsettling thought that he really could have been quite happy with Ellie. Never once had she mentioned the name of Miss Golden to him. She was damnably attractive, in her sister's gown. Especially that night in the garden, at the assembly. She was not a forward girl like Miss Golden, or Wanda. No stolen kisses for her. She had very nearly knocked him off the seat when he had tried to take her hand. A violent temper the girl had. He could handle that. It was all an academic matter, however, as she had stated quite categorically that she loathed him, and was glad he had saved her the bother of rejecting his offer. Knew about his fortune and title too. Even that had not induced her to be conciliating toward him.

He was on the verge of going to Claymore Hall in Somerset and enduring his mother's disparaging comments for a few weeks, till Rose's wedding should be over, when it happened. He was walking down Milsom Street with Rex one afternoon, looking desultorily in a few shop windows, when he saw approaching Everleigh's cousin, Aubrey Hansom. The sort of a fellow you hated on sight, and there had been a good deal more than mere sight between them over the years. Suffered through Eton and Oxford with the curst fellow, and met him every time you set foot in your club, or the park, or at a ball. He was everywhere, smiling snidely and being condescending, and ready to knife you in the back if you so much as blinked.

"Ah, Claymore, heard you was here," Hansom said, smiling in his hateful way, with mockery lurking behind those old yellow eyes, like a tiger's. Naturally he pulled up for a chat.

"And Rumor, for once, was correct," Claymore informed him, with a barely civil nod.

"Ah yes, Rumor," Hansom replied, in a sardonic way. "But it is perhaps a subject best avoided at this time, *n'est-ce pas?*"

"There is no subject you need avoid in my presence," Clay said, anger gripping him.

"Recovering, old boy? You don't look too chipper to me, but there, it will soon be all over, and society will find something else to chatter about. A nine days' wonder— well, say nineteen." He laughed teasingly.

"What will soon be over?" Clay asked, just as though he didn't know the answer.

"Why, the Rose's wedding to Everleigh. What else is anyone talking about?"

"I thought perhaps you alluded to my own wedding." Fool, fool, fool! He knew while the words were being uttered that he had gone too far.

"*Your* wedding?" The tiger eyes popped. For one exquisite moment the difficulties looming ahead were worth the price, to have had the pleasure of routing this antagonist.

"Not official, old chap. Pray, keep it under your hat."

"But what is this? Whom are you marrying?"

Rex was looking as curious as Hansom, and Claymore cleared his throat nervously. "Not official yet. You'll hear of it soon enough."

"It's the Wanderley girl, that's who it is," Hansom challenged. "Had it of Lucknow, but I thought it was all a hum. So you really mean to have her. It can't be the one who came out this past Season, for she's engaged to someone else, Siderow was telling me. It must be the twin."

Aware that he was slipping into deeper waters than he cared to, Clay began backing off. "Nothing official. I daresay I ought not to have mentioned it yet."

He was not to be let off so easily. "Pretty, is she?" Hansom asked eagerly. "As pretty as Wanda?"

"Prettier," Rex removed his cane from his mouth long enough to answer. "Twins, but Ellie's prettier. And older."

"Well, by Jove." Hansom smiled. One victim had escaped him, but his malice was pretty evenly distributed, and he would not mind giving the Rose's nose a tweak. "Then she must be prettier than Miss Golden too, for I thought she and Wanda Wanderley were evenly matched."

"The announcement is not to be made yet," Claymore reminded him in desperation. "The lady is not even out."

"Ho, you've got the jump on us all this time. She must be something special if you are getting her locked up before anyone else gets a look in. Mum's the word, old chap. Mum's the word." Then he dashed off to tell, in the greatest secrecy, several persons the news that Claymore was as well as hitched to one of the Wanderley Beauties.

"What did you say that for?" Rex asked flatly, as soon as they were alone.

"Because I'm a damned fool, that's why. And I'm sick and tired of being pitied by every school miss and Bath quiz in town. Yes, and I'm sick and tired of hearing whispers behind my back about Miss Golden. I wish I had never met the girl."

"Yes, but the thing is—said Ellie hated you. Don't think she does, but you oughtn't to have said you was engaged, Clay. Not the thing."

"You don't have to tell me! I hope Hansom keeps his face shut."

"Half of Bath knows it already, if I know Hansom. Yes, and the Rose will know before many hours too. He'll make the trip to London special to tell her. Spiteful fellow. Pity you told this Banbury tale to *him*, of all people."

"It was almost worth it, to see him stare."

"His jaw fell an inch."

"There's only one thing to do now, Rex. We'll go back to the Abbey, and I will offer for Ellie."

"That don't solve nothing. Not if she hates you. Don't know why you think so, Clay."

"Because she *told* me so, that's why," he explained in exasperation.

"The devil you say! Came right out with it? Don't sound like Ellie. On the other hand, though, she talks plain. Well, I'll tell you, Clay, there's no point in going. She ain't going to have you if she hates you. Stands to reason. Even I can see that."

"But does she hate my title and fortune?"

"No, she ain't that dumb, but she has to take *you* to get her hands on them, and Ellie won't marry you if she hates you. I mean, even Wanda wouldn't have you, so that goes to show you they ain't the kind that goes marrying for money, whatever you may say."

"I don't know why she should hate me. I never did her any harm." This was a point that had bothered Claymore considerably over the past weeks. Ellie had seemed to like him well enough till that night in the garden, or perhaps in the dining hall before they had gone into the garden she had already been glaring at him. But why? All he had done was to tease and flirt a little. Lord, what was there in that to give her a disgust of him, and to go saying that if London beaux were like him, she didn't want to meet any of them. A very unnatural girl was what she was. But the more he thought of her, seated in the garden, hiccoughing into her hankie, the more he longed to see her.

"Thing is," Rex advised, assuming his wise face, "you can just deny it flat. Say it was all a misunderstanding, and you can be sure the Wanderleys will say the same thing. Who's to believe it, when you both deny it flat?"

"I can't take any more humiliation, Rex. Everyone will think I've been ditched again. I'm going back to the Abbey, and I'll *make* her marry me."

Chapter Eight

The gentlemen arrived back at the Abbey on the very day chosen by Mrs. Homberly for leaving for Bath. She was excessively cross with her son for not being prepared to accompany her on the trip. No lessening of her anger occurred when she learned that he was not only not to accompany her, but had plans to entertain in her house, with half its servants gone and the drawing room in Holland covers, a very eligible young Marquis (who was excessively fond of Missie). Rex accepted her tirade calmly, told her not to worry, he and Clay would do fine with the Ruxteds, the couple who were staying behind to look after the house. Finally, to appease her wrath, he told her they would join her at Bath later, though he was pretty sure this formed no part of Claymore's plans. The Marquis was spared her abuse, as he was upstairs directing his valet to get him some clean linens and press a coat, as he was going to make a call directly.

Within ten minutes of the family's quarrelsome departure he was downstairs in the Rose Saloon, sitting on a Holland cover that had been placed over the "good" rose cut velvet chair, to prevent its becoming dusty. He was rubbing his chin, and rehearsing words designed to soften the heart of a woman who hated him. Unfortunately it was the words "marquis" and "twenty thousand a year" that kept recurring, and he was by no means sure they were the right ones. In his own mind they were the sole advantages he had to offer, for at this moment of truth he was only too aware of his own ugly person, his extravagance, and generally worthless character.

Rex entered, eating a ham sandwich he had procured from Mrs. Ruxted in the kitchen. "You're all cleaned up," he said accusingly.

"I can't make an offer in form in dirty linens and dusty top boots," Clay returned angrily.

"You're never going to do it *today*! I thought you'd wait a bit. Soften her up first. Flatter her and so on. Maybe take her for a spin in your curricle."

"She hates flattery. That is precisely when she began to hate me, when I told her she was prettier than Wanda. I have been reconsidering that whole night, and that is when she first began to glare at me. Yes, and rides in the curricle don't work either. It was the curricle that turned Wanda on me, the day I took her to Needford. We'll forget the flattery and curricle rides and get on with making the offer."

"Can't do it on an empty stomach. I'll have Mrs. Ruxted fix you some bread and meat."

"I don't want food. My stomach is churning already. What should I say, Rex?"

"What did you say to Rose?"

"Whatever I said, it was not efficacious. As you may just happen to recall, she turned me down."

"That's true," Rex said, licking a blob of mustard from his thumb. "I'll tell you what, Clay. Tell her you love her. That ought to do it. You wouldn't stick at one little white lie, would you? Shouldn't think so anyway. Been telling enough of 'em, all over Bath any time this fortnight. Only thing to do. Daresay you'll come to love her in time. A nice little thing, Ellie."

"I *do* love her," Clay said, scowling harder than ever at Rex, who was looking at him in amazement.

"Eh? Love Ellie? Since when?"

"Since . . . oh, devil take it, how should I know? But I do love her, Rex. That's why I don't know what to say. It was no problem with the Rose, for I don't think I really cared a hoot whether she had me or not, except for my pride. But I *love* Ellie."

"Tell her then. That'll turn the trick. See if it don't."

"It won't if she hates me," Clay said gloomily.

"Write her a poem," Rex said, marveling at his ingenuity.

"I don't know how to write a poem."

"Used to scribble 'em off to the Rose. Seen you do it a score of times."

"Just changing a word here or there in a *real* poem. That won't work with Ellie. She *reads*." He arose and said staunchly, "I'm off. The worst she can do is refuse me. She can't kill me."

"No, no. Not violent at all. Besides, you're bigger than she is." Rex's reassurance went unheard, as Clay was already heading for the door.

Mrs. Wanderley and Wanda were in the village selecting materials for lingerie—the bride's clothes proper would be purchased in London, but they had to buy something to entertain themselves. The butler informed Claymore that Mr. Wanderley was in the conservatory. With sinking heart, Clay made his way to the overheated building and found Adam poking his fingers into black soil around a strange-looking plant with thick spreading stems covered with large spines.

"Grandicornis," Adam told him. "Of the Euphorbia family, all the way from Africa. This soil is too moist. It's a succulent plant, like cactus. Abel must have watered it. It's going soft around the roots."

"That's very interesting, sir," Claymore told him. "Er, I wish to speak to you on a matter of some importance. . . ."

"Yes, go ahead. I'm listening," Adam said over his shoulder. If he could hear over the clatter of pots and watering jugs, it would be a miracle.

"About your daughter, sir. . . ."

"Too late. She took Hibbard," Adam replied offhandedly.

"Not Miss Wanda, sir. It is Ellie I hope to offer for, if you don't dislike the connection."

"Ellie?" The clatter stopped, and the head came up to attention. "No. Ellie ain't out yet."

"Well, I know that, sir, but she *is* eighteen."

"What do you want her for?" Adam asked bluntly. His suspicious eye seemed to suggest the reason could not possibly be a good one.

"Well, I *love* her."

"How does she feel about you?" Claymore felt no eyes had ever looked so deeply into his soul as those blue eyes that were trained on him now. Almost as if they could read the truth—that Ellie hated him.

"I—I don't know, exactly. I haven't spoken to her, you see. Sir."

"Ho, don't try to gull me you haven't been making up to her on the sly. Will she have you?"

"I don't know." Clay felt his shirt stick to his back, with the combined heat of discomfort and the conservatory.

"All alike, you London beaux. Young Siderow slithering around behind trees with Joan, saying he didn't know if she'd have him too, never knowing she told me I was to give my permission two days before. Well, Ellie hasn't said anything to me. It's up to her. She has no fortune to speak of, you know. You'll have to do something handsome for her."

"I am prepared to do that. I have twenty thousand a year."

"I know that. Know all about it. Thought it was Wanda you were after, or I'd have hinted you away."

Claymore looked at him in perplexity. The objection obviously was not to himself, if he was considered good enough for Wanda. Nor did he quite forget, in his state of alarm, that he was a marquis, with twenty thousand a year. "I'm afraid I don't understand you, sir."

"I'll make it clear then. Ever since Wanda was two years old she's had an eye for the fellows. The only thing for a girl like that is to get her buckled up young, and I'm not too fussy who gets her. He'll have his hands full, and no bargain either. Well, the Hibbards are settling ten thousand on Wanda. Ellie is a different matter. She's young—young-thinking, I mean—not in any hurry to get riveted. She'll improve with age, as Joanie did. She might have whom she pleases when she gets to town, and I'm in no hurry to give her away."

"I have agreed to make a settlement."

"It's no paltry ten thousand. You understand that?"

"Paltry!"

"Paltry." The eagle eye glared, and Claymore felt his own eyes fall.

"How much?" he asked.

Adam considered the most prohibitive figure that would still be within the realm of reason, and said in a firm voice, "Twenty-five thousand."

"Good God!" Clay exclaimed. "I don't have that much in cash."

"Get it then. Come back when you have it."

"It would take years."

"Haven't you got any saved up? You get twenty thousand a year. Surely you don't run through that sum."

"With my estate in Somerset, and the London residence . . . I haven't more than ten thousand in cash. Bonds that is, and Consols."

"Set up some arrangement with your man of business. You can cut back your expenses to ten a year and pay off the rest over the next couple of years. Set up a trust fund. I mean to see that Ellie gets twenty-five thousand. That's what Joan got." (Or was supposed to get, he said to himself, though after ten years it was still not paid off, and never would be.) "Caroline now, she was like Wanda. Tameson gave her fifteen, and we'd have taken ten. Who's to say you won't die young, without a male heir, and there is Ellie out in the cold, with some cousin of yours taking over the estate and leaving her cooped up in some little Dower House. She's not the type who would be marrying another man in the space of a year or two. Not like that. Someone has to look after her. Twenty-five thousand is the price, take it or leave it." Adam turned away, and began pouring some green liquid into a watering pot. He hadn't a doubt in the world he had gotten rid of Claymore. No one in his right head would fork over twenty-five thousand. The lad didn't care a hoot for Ellie; had been dangling after Wanda two weeks ago. Still, you couldn't very well tell a marquis to go take a leap. Let Ellie come out in the usual way. Another year or two she'd know her own mind.

Claymore swallowed twice, during which time the thought flashed through his mind that, as he had suspected all along, the girls were for sale, and at no bargain prices either. "Very well. Twenty-five thousand it is," he answered hollowly.

Adam jerked around to look at him, his face incredulous. The man was a fool. "You have my permission," Adam said curtly. "Mind, I bring no pressure to bear on the girl. It's up to her."

"I understand," Claymore said. He reached out and shook hands with Adam, then, brushing the mud from his right hand, he left, in a daze.

He was trembling when he got outdoors in the fresh air. Twenty-five thousand pounds, by God. He'd been mad to accept it. Where the devil was he to get his hands on twenty-five thousand pounds? He was angry, offended, and not in the least triumphant at the bargain he had struck. That he, the Marquis of Claymore, should be groveling for the hand of a country gentleman's daughter, and paying a preposterous sum for her. Twenty-five thousand! What had come over him? If his mother ever found out, she'd kill him. He bet Everleigh hadn't settled anything like that sum on the Rose, and *he* was old enough he might go popping off any day. He was in no mood to make an offer to Ellie, but he supposed he must now. He was actually relieved when he was told, back at the house, that she was out visiting an aunt in the village. He left a message that he would return the next morning. He wanted a night to consider his folly.

Dinner at the Wanderleys was not attended by any guests that evening, but the table was a lively one for all that. Wanda's wedding date had been set for the autumn, giving her a whole spring and summer to arrange her bride's clothes and enjoy her role as the fiancée. She was enjoying it to the hilt. Even more would she enjoy the trip to London for shopping. She and her mama would go very soon, so as to get home before the paralyzing heat of summer struck the city. The date of mid-October for the wedding had been chosen with the convenience of the married sisters in mind, for they were both increasing, and would be delivered in late August. By October they would be able to travel home and take part in the festivities. The mother and daughters were all full of plans. Ellie was to be bridesmaid, so that she, too, had to participate in the selection of gowns, and as she had not been present for the shopping, she was treated to a long list of necessary items that could very well be purchased right in Needford, and save hauling them from London.

Her papa supposed Ellie's lack of enthusiasm to be due to pique at being left behind when Wanda married, and he smiled at the news he had for her. He made no mention of it in front of his wife, for if she got ahold of it, Ellie would be bound to have Claymore whether she wanted him or no. He would tell her in private, and if she didn't want him, he wouldn't say a word. Twenty-five thousand, though—you could have bowled him over when the lad agreed to it. Must be devilish fond of Ellie to have swallowed such a sum. But a strange turn it was, when he'd made no bones about dangling after Wanda not two weeks before. Something off there. He'd speak to Joan about it. She was the one who was up to every rig in London. If there was something amiss with the fellow, she'd be the one to know.

A smile of contentment settled on his face as he considered Joan. She was his favorite of all his daughters, closely followed by Ellie. He used to worry about that Siderow she married—Polish, and lord only knew whether he was a count or not, as he said he was. But Esterhazy knew him, and he seemed to have the blunt; went everywhere, and was well thought of. Not that he cared about that so long as Joan was happy with him. And she was; not a doubt of it. Be no bad thing for little Ellie to nab herself a marquis. No question about *his* title anyway, for the Claymores were one of the oldest aristocratic families in England.

After dinner Adam and Abel made no motion to remain behind with their port. Adam beckoned Ellie to follow him into his study. This elicited no suspicion from his wife, for Ellie frequently gave Adam a hand with ordering his expensive plants. Or it might be something to do with that history she was writing up. Adam knew more about those things than she knew—or cared.

"I have news for you, Ellie," Adam said, as he seated himself in his comfortable chair in front of the grate, and lit up his cigar (imported).

"What is it, Papa?" she asked, with no undue interest.

"Claymore was here this afternoon." He looked closely at her as he delivered this news noticing that she turned a shade paler. It was the only change that did occur, though. He could tell nothing positive from it.

"Oh, what did he want?" she asked.

"He wanted permission to offer for you."

"What!" She stared. Adam stared, too, at her, and there was no doubt in the world she was amazed. So, there had been nothing between them. At least the fellow had told the truth about that. "You—you must have misunderstood, Papa. It was Wanda he liked, and he knows she is engaged, for he came to offer his congratulations before going to Bath."

"There is no mistake. He spoke of Wanda as well. It is you he wants to marry."

"I don't believe it. It is a joke," she said, and if she considered it a joke, she was not amused.

"No joke. I told him it was all right with me. But it is for you to decide."

"I don't understand. Is it a marriage of convenience he has in mind?"

Her father smiled. "Convenient for *us*." He laughed, remembering the settlement. "No, he says he loves you."

It had been my intention to offer for you ... She looked dazed, but a hint of a smile was beginning to play at the corners of her mouth. "I can't believe it," she said, with great truth and simplicity.

"Still, it's true. He comes back tomorrow morning. Think about it. I didn't tell your mother . . ." He let it hang, but what was unsaid was perfectly clear to his daughter.

"Oh, I—I suppose I ought to accept such an advantageous offer," she said rather diffidently.

"Not if you don't like him, Ellie. You are young. Next year you will be presented, meet all sorts of young gentlemen. . . ."

"Yes, I will think about it, Papa," she replied. From the happy smile on her face, he didn't think she would be long in making up her mind. So, she loved him. That was good then. She was hardly likely to do better, no matter how many Seasons she had in London. A marquis, twenty thousand a year. Odd about his fancying Wanda before, though. Well, nothing in that. Wanda appeared prettier at first; once he got a taste of her uppity ways and flirting, he would see Ellie was worth ten of her, if he had a brain in his head.

Ellie wandered from the room, as though in a trance, and went up to her chamber, unwilling to share her precious secret till she had squeezed every drop of romance and glory from it in private first. *It had been my intention to offer for you. . . .* And now he was going to do it, in spite of the horrid things she had said to him. She had thought she had ruined her chances completely that night in the garden when she had said all manner of rude and insulting things to him. Whatever had induced him to change his mind? Oh, what did it matter? She was to marry him! And he loved her—had told Papa so. Many times she relived her first proposal, received in her nightdress through her bedroom window; then she went mentally through their entire acquaintance, trying to spot the exact moment when he had decided he loved her. They had not been often together, and when they had, it was mostly Wanda he was paying attention to. So when had he fallen in love with herself? It was really only at the dance that they had had any private conversation, and it was hardly of a nature to endear her to him. Yet even before that night, he must have begun to love her. The recurrent phrase that had been spinning through her head for weeks replayed itself. *It had been my intention to offer for you.* . . . Her mind ran back further . . . the first night he had dined they had had a few words in the library, but there had been nothing in that. She decided, in some doubt and confusion, that the magic moment must have occurred while Clay was at Bath, absence, apparently, having made his heart grow fonder.

Later in the evening she went belowstairs a few moments with her mama and Wanda, but she could not sit still, or bear to give up her secret so soon. She went back up to her room, and it was very late before she slept. Still, in spite of her late night, she was up early the next morning. She spent a long time in choosing a dress, wishing that she had in the past taken more concern for her wardrobe. There was nothing here worthy of receiving a proposal in. She chose the same sprigged muslin she had worn to Needford and, not having thought to do her hair up in papers the night before, she pulled it back in its usual fashion. She never wore any makeup, but anticipation lent a sparkle to her eyes, and a blush to her cheeks. She could not eat breakfast. She had two cups of tea, and then returned to her room to wait, and was sick.

It seemed an age she waited, alternately sitting on the edge of her bed, then pacing about the room, then going to the window and looking down the road for a sign of his coming. Would he come in his curricle, or on horseback? He didn't come at all. All the morning long she waited—ten-thirty, eleven, eleven forty-five, and still he did not come. There was ample time to imagine it had all been a cruel hoax, a revenge. He had been drunk again—only Papa had not said so. He had changed his mind, had met someone else he liked better. He was as fickle as fate—had dangled after Wanda first, and only because the Rose had spurned him. He was a known philanderer. And why didn't he *come!*

It was just lacking ten minutes of noon when she was called down to the Green Saloon, and confronted with the nervous Marquis, who was biting his lips and silently reminding himself that after Everleigh, he was the best catch in England. He looked at Ellie as she entered, and the first thought that popped into his head was, "Good God, did I offer twenty-five thousand for *her*?"

She smiled nervously, licked her lips, and said, "Good morning, my lord."

He surveyed the washerwoman hair, the pale cheeks, blanched from the strain of waiting, the dreary gown, and an image of the Golden Rose arose before his eyes, laughing, teasing, delightful. Rex had told him that Everleigh had settled only fifteen thousand on the Rose.

"Good morning, Miss Ellie," he replied woodenly. They stood assessing each other, almost like combatants. It was he who finally said, "Well, shall we sit down and be comfortable?"

She sank gratefully onto the closest chair, but no one could be comfortable hanging off the very edge of it, as she was. "I—I didn't know you planned to return to the Abbey from Bath," she said, to fill the resounding silence that thundered around their ears.

"No, I didn't. That is—it was not my intention."

It had been my intention to offer for you. . . . "That's what I thought," she returned.

"Yes, well I suppose you know why I am come?" He tried to sound hearty, but succeeded only in sounding loud, loud and reverberating in the large saloon.

"Yes, Papa told me." He could hardly hear her reply, so softly she spoke.

From the strained expression on her white face, Claymore suddenly conceived the notion that she was going to refuse him. He had not thought of this as a possible reprieve. Of course, she had already as well as refused him!

"What do I do now?" he asked, rather giddy with relief. "Do I go down on my knee and beg your hand?"

"No, you needn't do that, Lord Claymore."

"My name, you know, is Giles. Giles Darrow," he said, as her words began to take on a wonderful significance. "You needn't do that . . ." It was to be a refusal!

"Is it?" she asked blankly. "Fancy that."

"Well, what is your answer?" he asked genially.

"You haven't asked a question yet, my lord," she reproved gently. Her first—her only—proposal. She had to have more than this.

"Will you do me the honor to be my wife?"

"Yes, I will marry you, Giles."

He looked, blinked, and said, "What?"

"I said yes, I will marry you," she repeated in a loud firm voice, fearing that he had not heard her the first time.

"That's what I thought you said," he replied stupidly, his heart sinking. He stared hard at her, comparing her unfavorably with the Rose, and wondering what folly he had committed now. He forgot for the moment that he had already leaked word of his engagement, and a refusal would have resulted in great shame. He remembered only that she had as well as *promised* she would not have him, and here she was, snatching at the title and fortune the minute he offered them. "Well, that's good then," he heard some liar say (the words seemed to come from his own mouth). "That's fine, Ellie." Some unknown force was pulling him to his feet.

"Shall we tell Mama?" she asked.

"Yes, certainly. Let us go and tell your parents." He felt the noose tighten about his neck and gulped.

He looked so strange, so stricken, that she felt sorry for him. "Would you like *me* to tell her? Perhaps you will want a breath of air."

"Yes, air. That's the thing," he rattled inanely, suddenly overcome by a pressing need for air, freedom, for getting away.

"You will return for dinner this evening?" she pressed on.

"Yes. Return for dinner." He turned on his heel and fled as though the hordes of Boney were after him. Ellie sat alone, thinking. It was an excessively odd proposal. She had preferred the first one, even if he had been drunk. "Drunk with love for you, my pretty," he had said. She smiled wistfully at the memory. Well, she supposed it had been a great strain for him. For herself, she had twice that morning been sick while awaiting his arrival. No doubt he had, too, for he acted so very strange. Hardly happy at all that she had accepted him. Almost disappointed, in fact.

She went in search of her mama, and found her in the morning room with Wanda, pouring over fashion magazines from London.

"I have something to tell you, Mama," she said.

"Yes, love. What is it?" her mother asked over her shoulder.

"I have had an offer from Claymore."

"What? Is he back? And what does he wish of you, Ellie?" The books dropped, and her full attention turned on her elder daughter.

"Lord Claymore has made me an offer of *marriage*, and I have accepted."

"Ellie! He never! Surely not an offer ... Wanda, did you hear that?"

Wanda heard, and her pretty little face became rigid. "You're lying," she spat angrily.

"No, he did. Just now. He is coming for dinner."

"Ellie! Wanda!" Mrs. Wanderley was on her feet, turning this way and that, looking at her daughters, while she digested the wonderful news. "Are you *sure*? But how wonderful! How delightful. A marquis, with goodness knows how much money ... we must ask Joan, she will know."

"I know, Mama. It is twenty thousand a year," Ellie said.

"Twenty thousand! Did you hear that, Wanda? Rich as a nabob. And a title. And Ellie never even brought out."

"It's not true," Wanda said, noticing the strange expression on Ellie's face. She would be happier than that if she had really had an offer from Claymore.

"Don't be so absurd," her mother snapped. "Of course, it is true. I must tell Adam. So strange that he didn't speak to your papa first. He ought to have ..."

"He did. Yesterday."

"And he never said a word to me! Such a man, really. But you have had the sense to accept, so it is no mind.

And he comes to dinner, you say. We must have something special. What does he like, Ellie?"

"I don't know." Ellie suddenly realized that she knew virtually nothing about him, except that he had very nice brown eyes, and she felt jumpy when he was near her, worse when he was not. She thought it was love; she hoped she wasn't mistaken.

"Ho, you don't know a thing about him," Wanda threw in. "I don't believe he offered for you either. You are only jealous because I am to be married before you."

"Now, really Wanda," her mother expostulated angrily. "When is the wedding to be, Ellie?"

"We have not decided yet, Mama."

"It can't be till after Wanda's, for we will want a large do—a marquis, after all."

"Did he really offer for you?" Wanda asked.

"Yes, of course he did," Ellie replied, not even offended. The shock to her was not that Wanda did not believe it, but that her mother did.

"He only did it because of *my* accepting George, so you needn't think he loves you. Yes, and he didn't love me either. It is only that he was jilted by Rose, and he would take *anyone* rather than go back to London single. He is excessively proud and rude and *fast*, for he kissed me at the assembly at Needford."

"Wanda!" her mother turned on her in wrath. "Really, that is too bad of you. What would George say if he heard of this?"

"He already knows. He saw us; *I* made sure of that."

Ellie looked at her sister with a black hatred rising in her bosom. "It is nothing to brag about, Wanda. He would not have kissed you if you had not encouraged him."

"Pooh! He likes me better than he likes you. I could have him today if I wanted him. Lucky for you I don't."

"This is the greatest nonsense, Wanda, and I wish you would stop making a goose of yourself. You are engaged to George, and there will be no more of this talk of kissing. I am excessively displeased with you. Even Caroline was not so fast as that."

"He would not have offered for me if he liked you," Ellie said, concealing her uncertainty under a thin veneer of sarcasm. Of course he had always preferred Wanda, and it was only after her engagement that he had offered for herself.

"Yes, and I don't think you care for him either," Wanda shot back. "You are only marrying a title. *I* would never be so crass."

"Well, and what if she is?" Mrs. Wanderley took up the cudgels. "You might have done better than plain *Mr.* Hibbard yourself, my dear. The other girls both got a title."

"Pooh, a phony Polish count," Wanda replied.

"There is nothing in the least phony about Siderow. He is accepted everywhere. And so will Ellie be. The Marchioness of Claymore—just think of it."

"That is not why I am marrying him," Ellie said sternly.

"No, I suppose you are *madly* in love with him," Wanda jeered. "You never spared him a glance or even fixed yourself to look decent to nab him, so don't try to con us it is a love match. He is not nearly so handsome as George, and he is insincere, mouthing all sorts of compliments that he doesn't mean in the least. A desperate flirt—that's all he is, only trying to nab *someone,* some poor credulous creature, so that he may flaunt her in front of the Rose. *I* wasn't so taken in. Little credit *you* will do him in London, in any case. I am surprised he was so desperate as this."

"You are just jealous," Ellie said, and she left the room, storing up every word spoken to be considered in privacy in her room. She was forced to admit there was likely a good deal of truth in them. She had never supposed he had actually *kissed* Wanda. That showed an unsteadiness of character—of affection—that surprised her. Well, maybe he didn't love her yet, but if he was determined to marry someone, it might as well be her, for she loved him. Yes, and he would come to love her in time. She would do her hair in papers to please him, wear lovely gowns and learn to flirt, if that was what he

wanted. Joan would tell her how to go on. She would not
so much mind making her bows in London with Claymore
by her side, to bolster her up. Even if he *did* love the
Rose—and how she longed to catch a glimpse of this
beauty who had set London on its ear—he could never
marry her. She was engaged to a duke, so he might as
well be married to herself as anyone else. He would not
have proposed if he did not at least *like* her. He could
have had his choice of anyone (except the Rose and
Wanda). Funny though, he hardly looked as if he even
liked her when he had proposed.

While Ellie brangled with her sister and worried in her
room, Claymore drove back to the Abbey and demanded
a bottle of wine, and none of that damned home-brewed
ale.

"Ellie turned you down, too, did she?" Rex asked astutely.

"No, she snatched at the chance to get me."

"Why are you in such a pelter then? Said you loved
her."

"She looked like the very devil, Rex. White as a ghost,
and a plain outfit on her."

"Lord, don't let that bother you. The mama will deck
her out to the nines before she hits the Metropolis. Don't
worry she'll look a dowd. As to being a shade pale, well,
you didn't look any too chipper when you lit out for the
Wanderley place yourself. Terrible strain it must be.
Don't know how you all go through it, just as though it
were nothing. Ellie's a fine girl, Clay. Make you a very
good wife. Got countenance, and she ain't the sort will be
cutting capers behind your back either, like *some* I could
mention, but won't. Take that Wanda now," he said immediately, apparently abandoning his noble plan of re-
fraining from mentioning names.

"Yes, she's head and shoulders over Wanda, except for
the looks, of course," Clay agreed. The wine was going
down very well, and easing the strain and disappointment
of his morning's work.

"Yes, and think, too, if she'd said no, after you being
so stupid as to tell Hansom, of all people, that you was

engaged to her. Well, you'd have been ashamed to show your face for a year. You're forgetting, Clay, how well she looked at that assembly in Needford. Daresay she had the hair yanked back today, and one of them drab old gowns she wears around the garden, but they'll rig her up right before you have to be seen with her in London. She'll do."

"She'll have to," Clay said, taking another swig of wine. He was half reconciled to the idea, and wholly unprepared to face London a single man, so he remembered her in Lady Tameson's green gown, and accepted her.

"Shall we take a couple of rods down to the trout stream?" Rex suggested.

"Rather hunt," Clay said, and the subject of brides was closed.

Chapter Nine

Ellie had her hair done up in papers, and sent Wanda to the rafters by soliciting her mama's aid in purloining one of Wanda's London gowns for the dinner that evening. It was a beautiful pale violet silk with overskirt of gauze. There was a narrow band of violet velvet that went with it, to be wound through her hair. The hair turned out very well, with soft curls around her ears. She was so pale from nervousness before going down that she dipped into her mother's rouge pot, and blended a little cream into her cheeks to get rid of that deathly pallor.

Mrs. Wanderley had had the presence of mind to send a note over to the Abbey including Rex in the invitation, as she knew his parents were gone to Bath. George Hibbard was to be present as well. Too many men, with Abel along too, but no matter. It was an intimate family dinner. She glowed to think of a marquis now included in the family. If she had another daughter, she made no doubt she could get a duke for her. And to crown it all, Claymore was settling twenty-five thousand pounds on Ellie. A fortune. She would be independently wealthy if anything should happen to him, God forbid. She crossed her heart, a habit she had picked up in the nursery from her Irish nurse.

Wanda, divining Ellie's plan to shine in her violet gown, donned her white crepe and, with Abel's contrivance, got an orchid from papa's conservatory, which she wore in her hair. She looked, she thought modestly, very like a dark-haired angel. She practiced blushing smiles in the mirror, and noticed that she looked better—there was not much difference—from the left side. She must make sure Claymore got a view of her left profile. She transferred the orchid to the left side, and was bewitched herself at the enchanting picture she made. Claymore would be sorry he had not tried harder to fix her affections. Perhaps she would flirt with him a little, to lead him to believe he *might* have had her, had he only been a little patient.

The two sisters, apparently reconciled, awaited their gentlemen in the Green Saloon. George arrived first, and had to be informed of the shocking news of Ellie's betrothal.

"Only think, George, it was *Ellie* he liked all the time," Wanda smiled, turning her left profile to Hibbard. "And here you thought he was dangling after me. Of course, anyone might have made that mistake, when it was *me* he drove to Needford in his curricle, and he did appear partial. I daresay he was only shy, for Ellie is so intimidating."

George looked at Ellie and frowned in embarrassment. "I daresay that's it," he said.

Later Claymore and Rex arrived.

"Why, Lord Claymore—or should I say *brother*," Wanda trotted up to them, utterly ignoring Homberly. "What a surprise you have given us. And here we thought it was *blondes* you preferred."

"Evening, Miss Wanda," Claymore said stiffly, looking over her head to Ellie, who had turned quite pale, with the two spots of rouge thus highlighted on her cheeks.

He walked past Wanda to his bride-to-be. "Hello, Ellie," he said.

"Hello, Giles. Rex, I am happy you came, too."

The embarrassment of this, their first meeting as a betrothed couple, was alleviated by the presence of Rex. "That chicken I smell, Ellie?" he asked, without even a word of felicitation or any mention of her betrothal. "Nobody makes chicken like your cook. Haven't had a chicken in an age." He sat down, feeling he had done very well by Clay's command that he lend a hand if the conversation flagged.

"We had it last night," Ellie said, seating herself beside him. "The chickens did very well this year."

As Clay made no reply, Rex plunged in again. "Don't they always? Mean to say, may hear of corn or grain having a bad year, but I never heard of it being a bad year for *chickens*." Still no help from Clay, who was—now what the deuce was he up to? He had taken out a snuffbox. "Clay, you ain't never going to take snuff!" Rex shouted in a carrying voice, so that every eye in the room was turned toward the Marquis in this, his first public execution of the tricky business of "taking a sniff."

"Yes, certainly," Claymore replied with a chilly smile. "Will you try my sort, Rex?" He offered the box, to put off the moment when he must do it himself.

"No, no, wouldn't have a notion how to go about it. Silly, dirty habit. If I want to go into a fit of sneezing I'll wear a damp shirt, for it wouldn't be so uncomfortable as that awful stuff."

His effort at sophistication shattered in this miserable fashion, Clay decided to slip the box into his pocket unopened. But he was not to be let off so easily. "Well, you've gone this far, might as well go whole hog and have a sniff," Rex rattled on, revealing to one and all that this was in the nature of an initiation. Hesitating only a moment, Clay flicked it open, attempting to do the whole with his left hand, as he had seen the Corinthians do in the city. Alas, his practice session had been short, and the flick of the lid was given with more force than was required. The little enameled box popped out of his hand, spilling its contents on the sofa, the carpet, and his own trousers.

A trill of laughter from across the room confirmed that

Wanda had been watching the whole performance. "You will require a few more lessons before you manage it with one hand," she called across to him.

Clay began brushing violently at his trousers, and Ellie said, "Pray, wait till I call a servant to do that with a brush, or you will stain your clothing." She arose to pull a bell cord, and in the interval while awaiting the servant she said, "How do you two bachelors go on with no lady in the house?"

"Fine," Clay said. His nerves were too ragged to say more.

"Pretty well," Rex augmented. "Mrs. Ruxted is looking after us. We went coursing hares this afternoon. Got a nice one—*I* did, that is to say. Clay didn't catch anything. Well, he ran a badger to ground, but that's nothing. Daresay we'll have a rabbit stew tomorrow. You like rabbit stew, Clay?"

"Yes, very much," he said, and thought what a fiasco he was making of this important encounter. It was a wonder Ellie was not howling at him, like that viper of a Wanda. The servant arrived, and Ellie requested a feather duster and a whisk and dustpan to clean up "a little accident."

"Had some very nice trout lately, too," Rex continued with their menu. "I caught a beauty of a fellow. Mrs. Ruxted did it up with melted butter and lemon juice. Clay caught an old plaice. I told him to throw it back in, but he lugged it home. The Ruxteds ate it up. Can't abide plaice."

"I like sole," Ellie said.

"Yes, but it wasn't a sole; it was plaice," Rex pointed out.

She demanded a description of this fish while awaiting the return of the servant. Claymore sat like a block, as his friend later informed him. He had never heard such a mundane conversation in such circumstances. Yet he was thankful for Rex's presence, or he feared he and Ellie wouldn't have a word to say to each other. The knowledge that it was his own fault, totally, quite cast him into an eclipse. It was in no way Ellie's fault. She was behaving with perfect propriety and tact, and looking as pretty as she ever had, in a very nice getup.

Eventually the servant arrived, and looked helplessly at her mistress, with no idea what to do. Surely *she*, a menial, was not expected to go brushing at the lord's clothing, yet he made no motion to take the duster from her.

Ellie reached out for it. "Perhaps if you stand up, Clay, most of it will fall off," Ellie suggested. Claymore complied with this request, and Ellie took a few swipes at his legs with the feather duster, then handed it to the servant and directed her to use the brush on the sofa and carpet.

"Sorry to be such a nuisance," Clay mumbled.

"It is no matter," Ellie assured him. "That will be good enough, Mary."

At this point Rex recalled the importance of this occasion, and felt some chivalry was called for. "You look nice, Ellie. New dress? Don't recall seeing that one on Lady Tameson. Your own, is it?"

"Yes," she said, then owned up scrupulously. "That is, it was Wanda's, but it did not quite suit her."

"How's that, then? Same size and coloring as you. Ought to have suited her, for it looks well on you."

"I am a little bigger than Wanda," Ellie said. Actually, the gown was a trifle snug on her, and not very comfortable. She could not breathe as deeply as she would have liked. She looked shyly at her fiancé, and he smiled dutifully, wishing he were elsewhere, or at least alone with Ellie. He felt he could redeem his farouche behavior, if only they were alone, without Wanda staring at him from across the room, and Rex forever saying something to make him look stupid.

Just then, Wanda beckoned to him from across the room, where she sat on a sofa beside the grate. He was happy enough to have something to do, and he excused himself to the others and joined her.

"George has taken the absurd notion into his head that you don't like him, because of that little affair in the garden at the assembly in Needford. I have told him you two must shake hands and be friends, for you are to be connected now by our marriages."

"No hard feelings, Hibbard," Clay said readily, offering his hand.

"Called me a raving lunatic," Hibbard reminded his new friend, but he accepted the hand and nearly wrenched it from the wrist.

Wanda laughed gaily. "That would be because you are so foolish as to offer for *me,*" she taunted.

"Hadn't offered for you then," George reminded her.

Wanda ignored this point. "Lord Claymore has no very good opinion, you must know, of gentlemen who prefer brunettes. Oh dear, how could I forget? He has changed his mind on that score—so suddenly! You *do* prefer Ellie to blondes, do you not, brother?"

"Ain't your brother yet," George said, and was again ignored.

"Yes, I do," Clay replied.

"Do sit down, Claymore," Wanda said, jiggling closer to Hibbard and making room for him at her other side. Then she had things exactly as liked, with all the eligible gentlemen she cared for at her side. Clay sat, looking across the room at Ellie as he did so, and knowing instinctively that he ought to be there with her.

"Now, Claymore," Wanda began, "you must tell us all about how you came to find yourself so suddenly in love with Ellie."

"That is a subject best left to you girls to discuss together," Clay replied briefly.

"Oh, Ellie tells nothing. A regular oyster on the subject. And you, it seems, are another shy one," she quizzed, an arch smile on her face. She had to crane her neck so she was nearly facing the back of the sofa to allow him a view of her left profile with orchid, for she had forgotten and put him on her right side. "You were not so shy . . . on other occasions," she reminded him.

"Not the thing, Wanda," George warned in a low voice, nudging her ribs with his elbow. But Ellie was watching from across the room, in *her* good violet gown and she carried on.

"I collect it must have been love at first sight. You really concealed it very well, sly rascal."

"Yes, I am better at concealing things than some people," he said dampingly, as he arose in disgust and went back to Ellie. What a spiteful, ill-bred girl. Thank God he had not made the mistake of offering for *her*. It was with a sense of relief that he rejoined the other party.

"What's Wanda up to?" Rex demanded.

"Nothing. Merely wishing me happy."

"That so? Thought you looked a bit put out. Was just telling Ellie she was likely needling you about how suddenly you popped the question to her—Ellie, I mean. Never did get around to asking Wanda."

"Mama cannot know you are here. I'll call her," Ellie said, arising from her seat as though she had been ejected, and quite pink under her rouge.

She returned shortly with both parents, and Wanda was forced to behave herself till dinner was served. Mrs. Wanderley had the good sense to seat Wanda well away from Claymore, so dinner passed tolerably well. Clay could hardly fail to remark that across the table Wanda was bestowing languid and loving looks on George in a most common fashion. He assumed that she kept her head averted completely from himself out of pique, not realizing that he was being given another chance to admire the left profile. He was relieved that Ellie behaved herself in a much more becoming manner.

They conversed on trivial topics with sufficient liveliness that the meal did not drag. Rex was surprised to hear that Bath had been much to Lord Claymore's liking, and indicated his surprise by a loud snort, and a swallowed chuckle. Mutterings of Hansom and Bath quizzes and scandalmongering, Clay trusted, went unheard by Miss Ellie. They were all drawn into Adam's plan to grow tobacco plants in his greenhouse. Even Mrs. Wanderley was prevailed upon to give her consent when she learned they were much cheaper than orchids and cattleya.

After dinner the gentlemen hastened through their port, and were soon dancing attendance on the ladies in the Green Saloon. Wanda wended her way to the pianoforte, with Hibbard at her side to turn the pages when she nodded, as he couldn't read a note. Ellie said aside to Claymore, "I have that book I was speaking to you about—an ancestor's diary, you may recall. It is in the library, if you would like to see it now."

"Very much," he said. They arose and slipped out together.

They had not reached the library door before Rex was after them. "You two beating it? Very wise. It'll be the 'Fleuve du Tages' again, I don't doubt."

Claymore regarded his friend and sighed deeply. "I'll tell you what, Rex, why don't you go out and blow a cloud?"

"Eh? Don't have a cigar. Wonder if I could slip one of Adam's."

"On the table in the dining room, if you hurry," Clay told him.

"I'll wait till later," Rex announced, and took up possession of the one comfortable chair in the room.

"No, Rex, you will do it *now*," Clay said menacingly.

"No, no. I can wait. Ain't all that anxious to blow a cloud, actually."

"You wouldn't have a rocket about the house, I suppose, Ellie?" Clay asked, and she giggled at their predicament, though she was not entirely unhappy to have Rex present.

"A rocket? Now what the deuce do you want a rocket for?" Rex asked obtusely.

"To blast you out of that chair," Clay said.

"*Oh. Oh!* You want to be *alone*! Well, why didn't you say so? I can take a hint. Ain't that slow. I'll go." He heaved himself out of the chair and slowly sauntered out the door.

Clay looked at his bride-to-be, and smiled. He found her quite enchanting with that shy, inquisitive smile on her face, her dark curls tumbling about her cheeks, and Wanda's gown lending her an air of distinction. How had he thought he did not love her? "Slow top," he commented to Rex's departing back.

"But very nice. I am fond of Rex," she said, and went

to the table for the book she meant to show him. Opening it, she said, "Here is the passage—"

He lifted it from her hands, closed it, and set it back on the table. "Another time," he said. "We have more important things to discuss."

"What do you wish to discuss?" A little tremble started at the pit of her stomach, of fear and anticipation.

"Our marriage." He reached out and took her two hands in his, and pulled her a little closer to him.

Between the tightness of Wanda's dress and the excitement of being so close to Claymore, Ellie had a terrible premonition that she was going to faint, to expire in his arms from pure elation. "It will not be for some time yet, I think," she said in a stifled breath, looking intently at the buttons on his coat.

"Ellie." His voice was a soft caress. He waited a long thirty seconds till she finally found the fortitude to look at him before continuing. "I don't want to wait. I would like to get married right away."

"Right—right away?" she asked blankly.

"Yes, as soon as possible. Oh, I don't mean in a scrambling way with no notices or anything, but as soon as decently possible. Say a month."

"But what is the hurry?" she asked desperately.

"What is the point in delaying?" he parried.

"But Wanda's wedding is coming up, you know—"

"Devil take Wanda! We need not wait on her. *You* are the elder."

"By ten minutes only," she reminded him. She looked cornered, like a trapped rabbit. Her nose was even quivering, like that hare Rex had cornered that afternoon. A horrible thought assailed him.

"Ellie, you are not being *forced* to accept me, are you? Because of my title."

"No! Oh no, you must not think that. Papa would never . . . it is only that I am not yet quite accustomed to thinking of myself as a married lady."

"Do you think you could become accustomed to the idea in a month?"

She smiled tremulously, some wise intuition urging her on. "Yes, I think I could."

"Good, then we shall tell your parents."

"All right."

He pulled her into his arms and held her gently for a moment. He could feel the stiffness, the resistance in her body, but she made no effort to withdraw. He sensed it would be unwise to go any further, but over her head he smiled to himself, feeling very masterful. He was glad she was shy, not used to men. He remembered with something like disgust the readiness of the Rose, and Wanda, to succumb to a man. He was not so conceited as to think he had been the only one so honored by them. He touched his lips to her hair, and said lightly, in a teasing tone, "Shy?"

Her head nodded, then settled snugly against his shoulder. There was a fragrance of violets in her curls (from Wanda's cut-glass perfume bottle, purloined along with the dress), and they felt soft on his cheek. He felt a passion of possession, of protectiveness well up in him, and he squeezed her harder against his breast. "I love you, Ellie," he said softly, but so ardently that she was sure he must mean it. He could feel the tenseness leave her body. She put her two arms around his waist. She had felt very ill at ease with them hanging down at her side, and as she could say nothing, she wished to contribute in some way to this stirring scene. They held together for a moment, the happiest moment of her whole life, and then he released her.

"We have dozens of things to settle," he said briskly. "Let us sit down and discuss them." She nodded, and had no idea her glowing eyes spoke all she couldn't say. Taking her by one hand, he went to the one upholstered chair in the room, that previously occupied by Homberly, and sat down, pulling her down into his lap.

"Giles! I can't sit here," she said in a voice of pleasant shock, and she tried to arise, which led him to tighten his hold around her waist. A short tussle ensued, and as he had both arms firmly encircling her, and their faces were not an inch apart, he forgot his good intentions and tried to kiss her. Their lips barely met, and he was just preparing with joyful anticipation to do the job properly when she shot from his lap as though sent off by a cannon.

She straightened her dress, and her hair, and said primly, but with a delightful blush, "We shan't get anything settled in this fashion."

"No? In my opinion it is the very best way to settle things." He was strongly inclined to go on settling them in this manner, but Ellie marched straightway to a hardbacked chair pulled up to the table, and he had to join her or shout across the room. They got right down to business and quickly arranged between them that the wedding would best be held in London, at St. George's in Hanover Square, where Joan and Caroline had been married, otherwise the sisters would not be able to attend, as a long trip in their condition was not advisable. Ellie would have to go to London immediately to get her bride's clothes assembled, and no doubt her mama would go with her, as she delighted in any excuse to go to London, whatever the season. Claymore had to go to Claymore Hall in Somerset to break the news to his mother and settle his business affairs. He would bring his mama to London a little later to meet Ellie and her family, and of course she would remain for the wedding.

When all this had been hammered out, Claymore decided to take his leave. The senior Wanderleys had long since been driven from the Green Saloon by Wanda's strumming. In fact, Wanda herself had left, since George had a mare foaling that he wanted to return to, so Rex Homberly sat playing solitaire at a Buhl table. Not even Abel was with him.

"Rex, what shappy treatment!" Ellie laughed. "Why did you not let us know you were all alone?"

"Oh, as to that, already been hinted away once, you know. Didn't want to go making a plague of myself when Clay was trying to make up to you. Wanda was here, but with no audience but me, she soon took off. Cards is better than 'Fleuve du Tages.' You all set to go, Clay?"

"Yes, you go on. I'll tell Mama what we have decided," Ellie assured Clay.

"Eh? Ain't begging off, are you, Ellie?" Rex asked point blankly. "Mean to say, already *been* decided."

"No, certainly not," Ellie told him.

Claymore raised her fingers to his lips and kissed them. "I'll leave for home first thing tomorrow morning, and be in touch with you. I'll write to you at Lady Siderow's, in London."

"Yes," Ellie said, smiling happily.

"Seems a dashed odd time to be dashing off," Rex observed to himself.

"Don't forget what I said," Claymore reminded her.

"What's that?" Ellie asked, for he had told her quite a number of things.

His back to Rex, he silently mouthed the words, "I love you." She blushed, and said in a very low voice, barely audible, "Me, too."

"Eh?" Rex asked. " 'Me, too' what?"

"Come *along*, Rex," Clay said, ushering him briskly through the door.

Ellie, alone now in the Green Saloon, looked at her fingers, so recently bedizened with a kiss, and thought she would burst with happiness. It was all a hum, Wanda's comments about his being in love with the Rose. He loved *her*. He had said so. Twice. And he wanted to get married right away, too, so he must love her very much. She went in search of her mama to tell her the good news.

She ran her to ground in her bedroom, where she was already in bed in her nightgown, with Wanda beside her, looking through the omnipresent fashion magazines. Mrs. Wanderley looked with complacence on her elder daughter, noting how bright-eyed and happy she looked.

"The violet becomes you very well, Ellie. We shall get one made up just like that to fit you."

"Mama, Giles wants us to be married right away."

"*Giles*? Oh, you mean Claymore. But what can you mean, love? You cannot be married right away. You haven't a stitch to wear. And the notices . . ."

"As soon as possible. We thought perhaps a month. . . ."

"A month! Impossible! We shall have to wait till after Wanda is married."

"No, we don't want to wait, and I *am* the elder. There is no need to wait."

"What's the hurry?" Wanda asked suspiciously.

"What is the point in waiting?" Ellie countered with Clay's argument.

"You are a fool, Ellie," Wanda informed her with satisfaction. "He just wants to have you to parade in front of the Rose and Everleigh when he goes back to London. That is what all this rush is about."

"No, it isn't," Ellie replied, so unfazed that Wanda was greatly perplexed.

"I suppose he is so *smitten* with passion that he can't wait to get you to himself."

"Hush, love," Mrs. Wanderley said mildly. "If Claymore wants to do it up right away, I suppose it can be done. We could go to London on Monday, and Joan is not so big yet that she can't come out with us, and perhaps hold a tea for you. There must be something, you know. The notice must be sent in to the *Gazette* immediately. What *is* the rush, Ellie? We could have a better do if you waited a bit."

"I don't want to wait, Mama. And I don't care if it is a small do."

"You're afraid he'll change his mind!" Wanda crowed.

"*Do* stop it, Wanda." Mrs. Wanderley turned on her favorite in vexation and then continued. "All right, then, we'll do it. I shall dash a note off to Joan tomorrow morning first thing, and tell Adam we must have a great deal of money for your clothes. I know he has some put by, else he wouldn't be talking up those old tobacco plants, and him telling me I couldn't have new drapes. Not that it will seem a great sum to *you*, Ellie, with twenty-five thousand settled on you."

"Twenty-five thousand? What are you talking about, Mama?" Ellie asked. "My dowry is only three thousand, like Wanda's and Caroline's."

"Dowry? Lord, love, I am not talking about that shameful pittance. And there is no reason it could not be five each if it weren't for that curst old greenhouse. I am talking of the settlement Claymore is making on you."

"It cannot be so much as that!" Ellie gasped, eyes goggling.

"Of course it is, silly girl. Did he not tell you? Well, I daresay it is nothing to him. Odd, though, that he didn't tell you."

"Oh, it is *too much*," Ellie said. "Why did he make it so much?"

"You have your papa to thank for it, my dear. Claymore only thought to make it ten, but after all, George is settling ten on Wanda, so I think it quite proper your papa held out for twenty-five. With twenty thousand a year, he will never miss it."

"Oh, Mama, I hope Papa didn't *haggle* over it. It is so embarrassing, so mercenary."

"No, he didn't have to haggle in the least. He says Claymore just swallowed once or twice and agreed to it. He must be excessively rich, and I am so happy for you. He said it was much harder to screw Hibbard up to *ten*."

"I don't doubt he would have forked out fifty thousand if he could have had Miss Golden, whom he *really* wanted," Wanda said, angry at her mama's disclosing that George had resisted such a paltry sum as ten thousand.

"Hush up, you silly girl." Mrs. Wanderley turned on Wanda in anger. "It could have been *you* marrying him if you weren't such a widgeon. Well, you have made your bed with a country squire, and now you must lie on it, so stop pinching at Ellie, only because she is sharper than you."

"No, Mama, I prefer to marry a man who truly loves me. I would not be so crass as to marry for a title and a little pile of money, nor so stupid as to marry a man who only wants to *use* me to make his lover jealous."

"Neither would I," Ellie replied agreeably, and she left.

"Don't rub it in too hard, my fine lady, or you'll find yourself unwelcome at Claymore House, and you know perfectly well George won't be hiring you a house for the Season. Play your cards right and you might get Ellie to put you and George up for a few weeks."

"I should be more comfortable with Joan or Caroline."

"Caroline *never* asks any of us, as you very well know, though her place is nearly as big as Joan's. But she was always a nip-farthing. As to staying with Joan again, she had you *this* year. Besides, I doubt Siderow would take to Hibbard. So very different."

Wanda gathered up a handful of magazines and stalked from the room. It galled her that she must bend like a reed before Ellie, whom she was used to lording it over, but she was as needle-witted as her mother when it came to self-advancement, and she determined that she would *try* to be nice to her sister. It was some mitigation that she could at least feel sorry for Ellie in making a marriage of convenience, for that's what it was, of course, while *she* had George, the handsomest man in the whole county, and he doted on her.

Chapter Ten

Lord Claymore was to leave early in the morning as he had a trip of some eighty-odd miles before him. He pointed out to Rex that he would be extremely busy and not free for much sport, but Rex decided that Bath would be equally flat with his mama and Missie to squire about, so he elected to accompany his friend to Somerset. He punctiliously forwarded a note to his mama, pointing out that he had been pressed to go with Claymore to his home, and would present himself in Bath as soon as it should be possible. He never for a moment thought his mama so dull as to actually expect him to show up, nor did she. His letter was of some interest to his parent all the same, as it confirmed the silly story Missie was mouthing that Claymore meant to offer for Ellie. *Had* offered, in fact, and been snatched up as quick as a cat could lick her whisker. The tale lent her a popularity in Bath that she was unaccustomed to enjoying, as she was the only person with any actual hard news on the subject. Its subsequent publication in the *Gazette* next day confirmed her as a bona fide source of news and she was much sought after for a week, till people from London with fresher news arrived to enlarge upon the story. It was quickly circulated

that Miss Ellie Wanderley had got to the Metropolis, and
proved to be just such a ravishing beauty as all the other
Wanderley beauties.

Claymore had no notion of the wonderful surge his
reputation had taken. He was deep into business negotia-
tions at home, trying to raise what part of the settlement
he could. It was no easy matter, and to add to his con-
sternation his mama was acting up, as usual. She was first
put out at hearing rumors of her son's betrothal from
Bath, provoked by Aubrey Hansom's tale, before ever
Giles said a word to her himself. But she was not of a disposition to require any reason for her pique. She was un-
decided whether to take the tack that he had been taken
in by a penniless little nobody, and probably a loose bag-
gage to boot if she was anything like her sister, Lady Tameson, or to treat him as a villain who had coerced some
innocent, witless little country girl into having him, only
to cover his shame at being shown the door by the Rose.
It would all depend on his own attitude. What she never
for one moment counted on was that he actually *loved* the
girl, as he *said* he did. His statement was borne out to
some extent by the fatuous smile she occasionally spotted
on his face, and the number of times he mentioned "Ellie"
in a certain voice. This threw her off her stride, and she
had to reconsider her tactics and see how best to amuse
herself at his expense. Life was a bore in the country, and
one must make the best of it with these little entertain-
ments. Of course, to anyone outside the family she would
tout the whole thing as a wonderful match. No one who
knew her would be so reckless as to say a word against the
match, for in public Claymore was held to be a paragon.

It was from Rex Homberly that she tried to elicit some
news of the girl. Naturally that obstinate creature of a
Giles would say only that she was very pretty, and very
pretty behaved, and such things as gave her no notion of
what she was really like.

The Dowager turned her steely eye on Homberly,
thought him a common-looking fellow, and wondered
what in the world Giles saw in him. "As you are a neighbor of the Wanderleys, you are just the one to tell me

something about my son's fiancée," she began, pleasantly enough. "She has a good reputation, I suppose?"

"Oh no, Ellie has no reputation," Rex replied blandly. "Wanda, now ... you might say *she* has a reputation, I suppose."

"I am not interested in Wanda."

"Twins," Rex enlightened her.

"I know that much. How did it come Miss Elinor was not presented? Sickly is she?"

"No, no. Never sick in the least. Quite a robust girl."

"Well, why then?"

"Too young. Not up to snuff."

"A twin, you say, of the one *who* was presented."

"Yes, but ... well, Wanda *was* up to snuff, you see. That's the thing."

"A gauche, shy creature, you mean?"

"No," Rex answered severely. "Not a gauche bone in her body. Slips around as light as a dancer, and much better behaved than Wanda, if you want *my* opinion."

"Then I don't see why she wasn't presented."

"She was going to be, next spring. A late bloomer, like Lady Siderow. That's Joan Wanderley, or was."

"I am acquainted with Lady Siderow. Would you say Miss Elinor takes after Lady Siderow?"

"She's more like her than she is like Lady Tameson, if you know what I mean."

"I hope I do. Not fast, you mean?"

"Not fast in the least. A very nice girl is Ellie. Like her tremendously. Better than Wanda."

"So you have implied, Mr. Homberly. Twice, and still I have no notion what the girl is like."

"She's a very nice girl, and quite pretty, too, when she's dressed up decently."

"A bad dresser, is she?" The Dowager leapt on this crumb.

"Shouldn't worry about it. Mrs. Wanderley will get her decked out properly, now."

Lady Claymore was forming an impression of a shy, countrified girl without a word to say for herself, and not even fashionable. It did not seem possible Giles would have

offered for such a person. Especially if she were not even
pretty. "She cannot be such a slow top as you are painting
her, if she nabbed Giles within a week."

"As to that, *he* was the one did the nabbing. Took to
her right away. Well, as soon as Wanda got engaged, anyway."

"It was Miss Wanda he actually preferred, you mean?"
she asked astutely.

"He did at first, but he wasn't long in tumbling to what
kind of a girl *she* is."

"I trust her reputation is not so black as to ruin the
whole family?"

"Oh no, she's a cagey one. And now that she's engaged,
it will all come to a halt. Hibbard will ride herd on her
harder than she thinks. It may be all smiles and kisses
now. . . ."

Lady Claymore absorbed this. "This Wanda—would
you say she is the prettier of the two?"

"Everyone thinks so, but I prefer Ellie."

"Yes, you have mentioned it." Was he actually a mental case, she wondered, or just plain dumb? So, Giles had
gone off to Surrey to offer for Wanda, the beauty of the
family, but was too late, so he had taken second best to
save his face in London. She smiled her approval. There
seemed plenty of ammunition here to give him a hard
time. She was in quite good charity with the girl who gave
her such an advantage, and wrote her off a pretty little
note saying she was looking forward to meeting her. If
she had any of the Wanderley looks at all, she would
make a decent showing and Giles might succeed in passing it off as a love match, as he no doubt intended doing,
even to her. She would show the public a satisfied face,
but how she would chide him in private—little slurs and
insinuations. Yes, the immediate future looked rosy.

She nabbed Giles alone in the study before dinner on
the pretext of wanting him to frank her note to Miss
Elinor. "I have written off a note, telling her how happy I
am for the connection," she said amiably.

"I should like to have read it, Mama. I feared you
might not like it . . ."

"Oh pooh, I am not so old-fashioned that I expect my only son to bother telling *me*, only his mother, when he means to marry." She could not refrain from this taunt, though she had meant to be conciliating.

"The decision was reached very suddenly."

"It certainly was! She must be an extravagant beauty. But then, if they have nothing else to offer, the Wanderleys are all beautiful. She *is* a beauty, I suppose? As beautiful as her sister Wanda, who was brought out this spring?"

Clay frowned, not caring for the question. "She is very pretty," he replied vaguely.

"As pretty as Wanda?" his mother repeated the question.

"They are different types. I prefer Ellie's style," Giles stated.

"One can trust your opinion in such matters," his mother said, smiling inwardly at his discomfiture. "No one would disagree with your assertion in a letter to me not a month ago that Miss Golden was the beauty of the Season, for instance. That would be, of course, because Miss Elinor had not made her bows."

"Yes," he said curtly, and turned to the accounts he was working on.

"Troubles?" his mother asked. "An expensive business, marriage, but *her* parents will have to worry about that. I suppose, being a Wanderley, she would not bring much of a dowry. Not above ten thousand."

"No, not above ten," he replied evasively, and buried his nose deeper in his books.

"How much?" the question was rapped out.

"Slightly under ten, Mama," he said, without ever looking up.

"Not a sous above seventy-five hundred you mean." She nodded sagely, and her deceitful son did nothing to enlighten her. "That will mean she has under four hundred a year pin money, Giles. You will have to give her some small settlement."

"Yes, I mean to," he said over his shoulder.

"How much?"

"I am trying to figure out how much I can afford, Mama, if you will leave me alone," he said angrily.

"Hmph. Give her twenty-five hundred. That will give her ten thousand clear, and five hundred pounds a year pin money. It will be plenty, for Homberly tells me she doesn't take much interest in her wardrobe." She looked closely to see how this dart was received. Claymore pretended not to have heard. "I say, Giles . . ."

"I heard you, Mama."

"Well, what do you think?"

"Twenty-five was the sum I had in mind," he said, wondering how long it would be before she discovered it was in thousands he was speaking, not hundreds. "Oh, Mama"—He looked up innocently, the sly wretch—"I must give her a ring for the engagement. She will not want to be going about London without a ring, you know."

"Yes, you must buy her some little thing."

"Well, Mama, the Claymore diamond is our family engagement ring, you recall."

"She won't care for that. Homberly tells me she is not fashionable at all. That little pearl your papa gave me for my birthday will do well enough for her."

"It will not do for *me*. I wish her to have the diamond, as has always been the custom in our family."

"I'm not dead yet, Giles, so pray do not begin stripping the pennies from my eyes."

"I have no notion of stripping you of anything that belongs to you. The diamonds are part of the entailment. Anyway, you never wear that ring."

"I have seldom taken it off this past year," she lied unblushingly, and determined to put it on that very night for dinner.

"Where do you wear it, for you have been telling me you never see a soul but the vicar and the squire's wife. You need not impress them with the jewelry."

"I'll tell you what, Giles," she said cheerfully. "There is no need to settle that twenty-five hundred on her. Wanderley is doing pretty well to get a title for her, without you giving her all that money, too. Buy her a diamond of her own—not entailed you know, but for her own—a sort of investment. Then I may keep my ring, that your father *gave* me."

"Papa didn't *give* you the ring, Mama. However, if you are so particularly attached to it, I can as well give Ellie that emerald with the diamond chips around it. I daresay she won't care."

"Buy her one."

"I can't do that."

"Why not? You were telling me last time you were home how you'd managed to save up ten thousand. You can buy her the ring, and still give her the twenty-five, if you wish to throw your blunt away. We must take into account your unbounded passion for the girl, I suppose," she said in an arch tone.

"No, I have . . . the money is invested."

"Consols? I think you ought to sell out then, for they have gone up remarkably well lately, and I have had my man sell out, just last week. They reached an unnatural high after Waterloo, and he says they are bound to settle down at a lower level soon. I made a packet." She laughed gleefully at her good fortune.

As shrewd as she could hold together, his mama. He wished he had taken her advice and put the money into Consols, but there had been a shipping company that promised greater returns in a shorter time, and not delivered. "No, the money is not in Consols," he said. "You have been more fortunate than I. About the emerald ring, Mama . . ."

"No!"

"Wear it on the other hand?" he asked sardonically.

"She will not like that gothic old emerald. Buy her a diamond."

"Mama, I am not about to *buy* an expensive ring when I have half a dozen sitting in the vault. And you don't wear any of them, so don't try to gull me you do."

"So that is how it is to be! Taking every bit of stone or jewel your dear papa gave me, to shower on that Wanderley chit who hasn't even a decent dress to her name!"

"Mama, where do you get these stories? I must give

her a ring. You know I must. Look, keep the emerald and
the diamond for the time being: I'll give Ellie the star
sapphire."

"No, it is my very favorite of them all! I could not bear
to part with it."

"Dammit, Mama, you're not a magpie! You can't wear
all those rings. *You* decide which one I am to give her."

"Give her the pearl I was speaking about."

"I can't give her a *pearl*, it would be too shabby.
Wanda has a diamond, and she is only marrying a squire's
son."

"Oh ho, *Wanda*, is it? You just want your Ellie to have
a bigger stone than Wanda, that you may let her see what
a bad bargain she struck in turning you down."

"I never made Wanda an offer!"

"No, because some squire's son beat you to it!"

"No, I dislike her excessively."

"Yes, and you dislike your mother, too, that you will
take all my poor bits of jewelry and heap them on that
girl."

"I must give her a ring, Mama. Don't be so unreason-
able."

"Give her the pearl. I won't say a word against it,
even though it is my own, given as a birthday present,
and in no way coming to you. I had meant to give it to
your sister. . . ."

"Do so, by all means, for *I* don't want it, but I *will* require one of my other rings for an engagement present."
He turned his back on her and ignored her, till he heard
the angry whisking of her gown as she turned to the door,
followed shortly by the door rattling on its hinges as she
slammed it behind her.

That night the Dowager wore the star sapphire on her
right hand, and the diamond on the left, and hid the rest
of them under her mattress, along with other necklaces
and broaches that rightfully belonged to her son. Giles repeated his request on two other occasions, but both times
she ranted and raved and refused to give them up, calling
him an *unnatural* son to want to take away her few re-
minders of his papa, so in the end he put it off till some

time when she was in a good mood. Perhaps he could buy some sort of a smallish diamond for Ellie, though where he was to get the money he had no idea, and he had wanted to send the ring to London immediately so that Ellie might wear it. He found the damned pearl ring on his dresser one night, and threw it into the drawer in disgust. It would be an insult to offer it to Ellie as an engagement ring.

He worked hard all day with his bailiff, figuring what repairs and renovations on his tenant farms could be delayed so that he might get his hands on as much cash as possible for the settlement. In the evening he usually had a set-to of some sort with his mama. To add to his ill humor, she, who was practically a hermit, invited a motley crew of neighbors into the house for dinner on the pretext of entertaining Rex, who paid not the least heed to any of them. Night after night they came, and his mother donned her various purloined jewels to show her son how impossible it would be for her to rub along without them. In private, she continued with her barbed comments about Ellie's being unfashionable, about his former preference for the Rose and Wanda, and anything else she could lay her tongue to to annoy him. It was not till he was in bed with the candles extinguished that he had any peace to consider his bride-to-be. He found the image of her face popping into his head a hundred times a day, but he could only have privacy to cherish it at night. He was coming to believe she really was prettier than Wanda, for she had such a sweet, shy smile, while Wanda's was bold and cunning. She was young, bashful, not only of him but of all men, he supposed, and he found suddenly that that was the only sort of girl he could really love. The others were fine for flirts, but when a man was getting married, he wanted a modest girl. He remembered her in the garden at the assembly, telling him how she disliked him (all a result of her shyness, of course), then he smiled softly, for that picture was soon followed by the remembrance of the night he left, in the study, when he had held her, rigid with fear, in his arms, and later when he had grabbed her onto his knee and tried to kiss her. A dozen times he imagined that kiss reaching its conclusion, when she would forget her fright and respond to his ardor.

In fact, it was not till he'd been away from her for two weeks that he realized how much he loved her, and how he longed to be with her again. He had thought to be in London at the end of two weeks, but there was so much to do that he feared it would be three before he could be there, with his wedding only one week away by then. He wrote her a few letters—stiff little things that were completely unsatisfactory to both sender and receiver, but then he was no Byron, and there were so many practical items to be discussed that he deferred his lovemaking till he could see her in person. The short missives he received from Ellie were similarly lacking in emotion.

At the end of the second week Clay's sister, Alice, had a miscarriage at her home in Dorset, and his mama had to go to her, so that she would be unable to attend the wedding. She sent Ellie a note explaining, and Ellie sent back a letter to Dorset expressing her commiseration at the sad event. Claymore made a thorough search of his mother's room after she had left, and discovered to his chagrin that she had taken every iota of his jewelry with her. He was left with the cheap pearl ring, and not enough money to buy a decent diamond. He didn't think Ellie would mind so much, but it angered him. He had been looking forward to seeing her face when he gave her the ring—the large family diamond engagement ring he had decided to have, come hell or high water. It rankled that Wanda would be lording it over Ellie, as he made no doubt she was.

Chapter Eleven

Claymore was out in his fear. It was not easy for a young lady engaged to a squire's son to lord it over one betrothed to a peer of the Realm. What remained in town of Metropolitan society was all agog to see the latest Wanderley beauty. Several departures from town were delayed that a call might be made on Lady Siderow, in hopes of seeing Claymore's new bride. Ellie's splendid catch, made so quickly and quietly in the country, lent her an aura of romance, and the fact that she was virtually unknown only added to her cachet. Her mama, with the help and advice of Joan and Caroline, had taken her to the most expensive modistes for her gowns, had the reigning coiffeuriste called in to style her hair, and Joan had taken upon herself to train her in what was expected of a society hostess. When ladies of fashion called, they bestowed only a fleeting glance on Wanda—oh yes, the one that had made her come-out this Season just past. But at Miss Elinor they looked, ready to be impressed by whatever had impressed Lord Claymore.

It was soon decided that she had great countenance, a nice modest style that so exactly suited a young lady, and, of course, she possessed the Wanderley beauty in full measure. Did not put herself forward in the least, but when spoken to, she responded in a sensible, well-bred manner, with no missish giggling or awkwardness. It was easy enough to see what had attracted Claymore. Not a brash, forthcoming beauty like the Rose to be sure, and what a relief it was for feminine society to have at last someone to take the shine out of Miss Golden, now Duchess of Everleigh, and more insupportable than ever. The Rose had had her Season of glory, had enacted the full fairy story of rise from obscurity to marrying the Duke, and idle minds were now ready for a new divertissement.

Wanda chafed under the attention showered on her sister, and did in private what she dared not do in front of company. The two sisters were never alone that Wanda was not at Ellie, needling her. "Dear me, only two weeks till your wedding, and *still* no engagement ring. I declare, Ellie, I think he has forgotten all about you." Her own diamond would be waved under whatever illumination was present, to catch the light and sparkle blue and orange for the owner's satisfaction.

"I had a letter this morning."

"Ah, that was that flat little envelope from Clay. I made sure it was a bill, for it was the tiniest thing. Only see the *volumes* I have had from George. Three crossed pages, full of the most romantical nonsense. Does Clay write such stuff to you? Only hear what my George has to say: 'Life is empty without you. If you don't come back to me I shall go into a decline and die. My death will be in your hands, as my heart is too.' Whoever would have thought George would wax so lyrical? What had Clay to say to you?"

"He is very busy. It is merely a note."

"A *love* note?" the soft voice taunted.

"A *private* note," Ellie replied dampingly, but her heart sank. Clay never wrote such things to her. Only a brief recital of his activities, signed "Your faithful servant"! Surely he could at least sign it "Love." She could not feel it becoming for her to express such sentiments herself when her lover was so reticent.

"Oh, what a tease you are! I bet he says all sorts of romantic things. Only it is the oddest thing that he never sent the ring. Does he mention it?"

"No, I expect he will bring it with him. It would not be wise to be sending a valuable diamond through the post."

"And naturally the Marquis of Claymore could not afford to send it by a private messenger!"

"It is a valuable family heirloom. Joan says it is an emerald-cut diamond, *bigger than yours.* Very likely he is having it cleaned or reset."

"I wonder he didn't take care of that when he offered it to Miss Golden. Wouldn't it be the *drollest* thing if he has given it to her? Don't look so worried, Ellie. The Duke will make her give it back if that is the case. Oh, how I shall tease Claymore when he comes. *If* he comes, ha ha. Really, one begins to wonder. He was to be here by now, was he not?"

These harrowing interludes left Ellie shaken. Her courtship had been so brief as to be practically nonexistent. It was only too easy to fall into thinking Claymore had changed his mind. His occasional letters did nothing to restore one's self-confidence either. And why didn't he come?

Wanda never tackled Ellie in front of her mother or sisters, so she received no strictures on her behavior. She did, though, recall her mother's admonition that if she were wise she would "keep in" with Ellie, so she interlarded her sarcastic conversations with others of an uplifting sort, which were even more depressing. It was lowering indeed to be told that in a marriage of convenience one must not expect slavish devotion and *billets doux,* and no doubt Claymore would manage his love life very discreetly, so she need not worry about *that.*

Throughout this trying time Ellie had one other thought in her mind besides her husband-to-be. It had become a burning ambition of hers to see the Duchess of Everleigh, before she should be carried off by her husband to whichever of his country seats he decided to visit for the summer. When riding in the park or shopping on Bond Street, she always kept an eye out for a beautiful

blonde, and would make a casual reference to every one
that passed, in the hope that the young lady's identity
would be mentioned. Her vigilance was finally rewarded,
though she didn't have to be told. She knew, sensed somehow, that she was in the presence of her predecessor before
anyone told her. A young lady of exquisite beauty was
seen once being driven past in a dashing high-perch phaeton. She wore a blue suit and a very charming hat with a
golden rose adorning its side. Ellie stopped dead in her
tracks and stared.

"What is it, my dear?" Joan had said. Ellie was with
Lady Siderow at the time, strolling down Bond Street.
Joan followed the line of her sister's glance and said, "Oh,
it's the Golden Rose. This is your first glimpse of her, I
collect? Grand, isn't she?"

The phaeton shot past, and Ellie gathered her wits to
reply. "Yes, she is lovely." It was a foolishly inadequate
answer, for the lady's beauty far surpassed any words that
occurred to Elinor. Her heart sank in her bosom. Anyone
who had loved that vision of loveliness, as Claymore had,
could not posssibly find *herself* the least bit attractive.

"It is nothing to fret about now. She is safely married,
and there is no point worrying she will be dangling after
Clay, for Everleigh won't allow any such a thing, you
know. He is strict as may be with her. They say he is a
demon of jealousy. I bet Miss Golden—the Duchess, I
should say—rues the day she ever accepted him. Though
in honesty, I must say she gives every appearance of liking him. Well, she was a child, and needed a firm hand."

"I bet Clay rues the day she accepted him, too," Elinor
was shocked into admitting.

"No, Ellie, what are you thinking of to say such a
thing? That is all done and past. Everyone was dangling
after the Rose last Season, and you must not take it amiss
that Clay did what every other eligible gentleman was doing."

"But they didn't all offer for her."

"True, but I'll wager she received upwards of a dozen
offers. A diamond of the first water, of course."

It was, however, only one of those offers that concerned

the worried bride-elect. "Now that I have seen her, I am more curious than ever why Clay offered for *me*."

"He would not have done so had he not wished to marry you, and he would not have wished to marry you if he hadn't been mightily pleased with you, goose, so do set your mind at rest."

"She is very beautiful, isn't she? Even more beautiful than Wanda."

"Yes, and rather like our beloved sister in that she is acutely aware of her manifold charms. Has Wanda been putting these ideas into your head? You must know, Ellie, she is green with envy at your match, and you should not be discomposed by what she may choose to say. It is all spite."

"No, that's not what bothers me. It is only that what Wanda says is so very true. He *did* offer for Miss Golden, and he *did* dangle after Wanda when first he came to see us, and I cannot but wonder if he regrets his offer to me. He—he doesn't write much to me, you know, and not at all the sort of thing George writes to Wanda."

"Would you think better of him if he wrote such slop? As to Wanda's regaling us all with his private correspondence . . ."

"Well, I would never do that, Joan. Only I must confess, I do find his notes rather cold, and he didn't send me the engagement ring either, which looks as though he has forgotten all about it."

"Or hawked it, poor soul. You know the *shocking* settlement Papa extracted from him. I should think that would set your mind at rest if nothing else did."

"No, that bothers me more than anything. I cannot think why Papa did it."

"Why, to make *very sure* that your Marquis loved you. Now that we have ascertained that, let us step into this shop and see if we find some rose velvet ribbons to match that sprigged muslin gown you are getting made up."

In this manner Joan tried to calm her young sister's agitated nerves. However, it was not the first time Ellie had spoken to her in this vein, and she was becoming upset herself. Neither the Marquis' title nor his fortune was suf-

ficient to counterbalance a lack of affection. If he did not
sincerely love Ellie, then she could not approve the
match. Having married for love herself and been totally
happy, she did not wish to see her young sister make ever
so grand a match without warm affection. That Ellie
loved her young man was not in doubt; she mooned
around and her only worry was that he did not return her
feelings. Well, time would tell. Even if Claymore put off
his appearance till the very morning of the wedding, Joan
meant to have a good go at him and determine his
feelings before the wedding went forward.

She had not to wait quite that long. At the end of the
third week, one week before the nuptials were to be
celebrated, he appeared in town, and immediately
presented himself in Lady Siderow's saloon to see his
bride. His eager countenance and nervous fidgeting went a
long way toward winning Lady Siderow's approval; his
first words nearly secured it. "Is she here?" he asked.
"She"—very good! There was only one "she" in his mind.
Even his lack of polish in not first saying "How do you
do?" to the hostess was a welcome sign. One did not like
to see a bridegroom too composed.

"She will be here presently," he was informed. "She
has been gone upwards of an hour for a drive in the park,
and is not usually gone much longer. I am happy you
have finally come."

"I should have liked to be here sooner, but there were
many affairs to attend to, you know."

She correctly read into this a reference to the settlement. "Yes, indeed." Condolences were offered on the sister's miscarriage and a mutual agreement voiced that it
was no reason to delay the marriage when it was all set.
The Dowager's absence at the wedding was confirmed—
she could not leave Alice yet. Joan privately thought this
no bad thing as the woman was a bit of a Turk. She had
given Ellie some little idea of Clay's mother, and she assumed others had done likewise, as Ellie appeared to have
developed a positive dread of meeting her. Wine was offered, and within minutes of its presentation, footsteps

were heard at the door, and Elinor came bursting into the room.

"Is that not Claymore's carriage outside?" she shouted. Spotting him, she ran right into his arms, which were out-stretched to receive her, as he had arisen upon her tumul-tuous entry. Before the shocked but approving eyes of her mother and sister, she was folded within his arms, and his dark head went down to hers. Mother and elder daughter exchanged meaningful glances and tactfully retired.

Lady Siderow felt her fears had been allayed, and de-cided against tackling Claymore on the state of his affec-tions. She was not blind, after all.

"Upon my word, Joan, I think he *likes* her," Mrs. Wanderley said, wide-eyed.

"*Do* you indeed, Mama?" She laughed. "And *I* think he gives every appearance of a young man in love."

"Yes, but it is the oddest thing, for I can't imagine when it happened. He did not love her in the least at home. When can it have come about?"

"You have allowed Wanda to mislead you."

"Oh dear, *she* won't like it."

"*Tant pis!*" Joan replied airily, which won a frown from her mama, who had not gone beyond *merci* and *bonjour,* in her studies of the French language.

When they discovered themselves to be alone, the young lovers fell suddenly ill at ease, and pulled apart with a nervous laugh. "I don't know what you must think of me, acting so," Ellie said.

"Well, I think you are not so shy as I have been led to believe," he replied in a bantering tone. He took her hand and led her to the sofa he had just vacated. "I have been wanting to come sooner, Ellie."

"I know you have been busy," she rushed in, ready to exculpate him.

"There were a devil of a lot of things to see to."

"It was that horrid settlement, wasn't it?"

"That among other things."

"I have been busy, too, with all my clothes to get made up, and such a lot of people calling."

"Getting your hair done, too, I see," he said, flicking a

curl with one finger. "You are looking very elegant. Going to take the shine out of Wanda. Is she here?" It was a thoughtless comment, uttered to bridge the tension of their first moments together, but Ellie mistrusted it.

"Yes, but she is out with Lady Tameson today."

"That's good," he said calmly, restoring his bride to high spirits.

"We have had *dozens* of callers," she said, and thrilled him with the recitation of such names as she could remember. Midway through her list he interrupted.

"I daresay you are wondering why I haven't sent your engagement ring."

"No, not in the least. That is, Wanda said, very likely . . . but I was sure you would not like to entrust it to a messenger, and would bring it yourself."

He pulled a dark green box from his pocket, while Ellie prepared to feast her eyes on the radiance of twenty carats, for so rumor had it was the size of the Claymore diamond. Her face fell visibly when her eyes were called on for the viewing of no more than a rather ordinary pearl, set in a flower fashioned of gold lumps. "It—it's very nice," she said, frowning. He had given it to Miss Golden!

"This is not your engagement ring, of course," he rushed in to explain the seeming jest. "The stupidest thing, Ellie. I let Mama get away to Dorset without discovering exactly where she is keeping the heirlooms. I ransacked the house, but couldn't discover them anywhere."

"Do you not keep them in a vault?"

"Yes, usually, but they were not there," he admitted sheepishly. "There is a larger diamond ring I am sure you will like, or an emerald if you prefer. . . ."

All very grand, but what he was holding out to her in his hand was a *pearl* and no very large one either. "You forgot," she said. It was not precisely an accusation, more of a reassurance to herself that the diamond was in fact at his home in Somerset, and not residing in the Duchess of Everleigh's bibelot box.

To add to the vexing problem, Claymore could only explain away his own seeming forgetfulness by asserting that his mother would not let him have any of his own rings. "I didn't forget exactly," he said, still holding his mother's birthday ring, which his fiancée was making no motion of accepting. He removed it from the box and shoved it onto Ellie's third finger. "This is just to let everyone know you are taken." He smiled with what he hoped to pass off as ardor, though it was nine-tenths pure embarrassment.

Ellie looked at the little ring with sinking spirits. So Wanda was right. He had forgotten all about her, all that time he was in Somerset. Had never once thought she might like to have an engagement ring to wear during the two weeks when his mother was home. She knew that if it had been the Rose who was to receive the offering, it would be the diamond, and not this little trinket. She cringed to let Wanda and all her relatives see the pearl, when they had been discussing a diamond of twenty carats for three weeks. It was a symbol of his lack of heart, of interest in this marriage. A little sigh escaped her. Claymore had had grave misgivings about producing the absurd thing at all, and soon came to the conclusion it had been a gross error.

"I daresay you are thinking of Wanda's diamond," he began tentatively. "*Yours* will be bigger, you know, when you get it."

She nodded and attempted a smile, which was such a travesty that she had done better not to make the attempt. Was it possible, Clay wondered, that it was the *ring* she had been so eagerly awaiting, and not himself. He willed down a spurt of anger, and began discussing social trifles. Had so-and-so left town? And had she said the FitzHughes had been to call, or was it the FitzWilliams? Their first meeting, begun so auspiciously, sank into a mere chitchat. After half an hour the Marquis arose and took his leave.

Immediately she had left the saloon where Ellie was entertaining Clay, Joan had sent a note to Tamesons that bore no mention of his arrival, but suggested that Wanda remain there for dinner. Wanda was not reluctant, as she always got on better with Caroline than Joan. So when Claymore returned to Grosvenor Square to dine at seven-thirty, it was only the Siderows, Mrs. Wanderley, and

Elinor who sat down with him. Siderow, who was a diplomat by vocation as well as by nature, soon had the table agreeably discussing social nothings, the only topic in which his mother-in-law might take an interest. The lack of vivacity between the lovers was put down to Ellie's well-known shyness, and the meal was considered a success.

After taking their port, the gentlemen rejoined the ladies for tea, and after a discreet interval, the older members of the party discovered they had each a pressing matter to attend elsewhere, thus affording the younger some unwanted privacy.

"I can't stay long," were Claymore's first unpromising words, which were met with a worried frown. Ellie became every moment surer he did not care for her in the least. "I want to get to Claymore House, you know, and get the servants to set it to rights. I am hoping you will come with me tomorrow and inspect it."

"I should like to," she answered stiffly.

That would put her back in high gig. His London residence was considered one of the city's finest. She would see she was not making such a bad bargain after all. "You may care to make some changes, I daresay. Mama has not been in the habit of coming to town the past few years, and it is in the way of becoming a bachelor's home."

"Joan tells me it is very fine. I doubt I will want to change much."

"It will have to be in the afternoon. I'll have to see my man of business in the morning." And try if I can't wring some money out of him for a curst diamond ring, since that is what is putting you in a pucker, he thought, but naturally did not say.

"The afternoon will be fine. Wanda and I planned to go shopping in the morning. She is collecting her things, too, you recall."

He nodded in recognition of this startling intelligence, and then silence descended like a pall over the room. Claymore regarded his thumbs, which had taken to whirling round each other in a most nervous fashion. Gathering his courage, he said, "Ellie, I'm sorry about the blasted ring!"

"It—that's all right," she said.

"If I had realized how much it meant to you, I would have . . ." Rung Mama's neck, he thought, but again kept it to himself.

"Oh, Clay, it's not the *ring*," she said, her voice trembling on the verge of tears at what she wanted to say.

"What is it, then?" he asked, nudging nearer to her on the sofa, and laying one arm along its back, behind her shoulders. "I know something is bothering you, and I wish you would tell me. Has Wanda been ragging at you?"

"No. Well yes, that, too, but that's not what . . . what troubles me."

"What is it, Ellie?" he asked gently, in a coaxing tone, while he let his arm slip from sofa to shoulders.

"You were away such a long time, and I hardly know you. I thought we would have longer to become acquainted."

Claymore relaxed, feeling the tense nerves of his body ease, and a warm urge to reassure his bashful bride arose. "I came as soon as I could. We have a week, Ellie, and a lifetime after that. For myself, I know you are exactly the girl I want."

"Yes, but are you *sure*? I cannot think—"

He silenced her doubts by covering her moving lips with his own.

Lady Siderow, passing by the door and stopping to put her ear to it, was assured by the silence within that things were proceeding exactly as they ought to be. As duenna, she could not leave them too long alone, so she made a great racket with the handle before entering, and gave them sufficient time to compose themselves, but not time enough to remove the stars from their eyes.

Claymore soon took his leave, and when she was alone with Ellie, Joan said, "Well now, are all your little doubts set at rest?"

"Oh yes," her sister sighed happily. "Now I am quite

at ease and can listen to Wanda rant on all day, for he is here, and I *know* he loves me."

"Yes, and so do we all know it. He never looked more moonstruck, even when he used to tag along after the Rose." It was meant as a joke, but Ellie immediately took alarm.

"Did he behave so with her, too?" she asked jealously.

"No, I think the look of idiocy was less pronounced." Joan laughed. "What is that little ring you're wearing? I noticed it during dinner. Did Clay give it to you?"

"Yes," Ellie said, and swiftly covered it with her right hand.

"You would do better to wear your diamond for these last few days," Joan suggested. "I am curious to see it, and so must everyone be. We have been hearing about the Claymore diamond forever, but I can't recall that I ever saw it on the Dowager."

"It . . . he . . . his mother has it, you see," Ellie explained in confusion "She went off to Dorset to her daughter in such a rush that she forgot to give it to Clay."

"Did it on purpose *I* bet." Joan shrugged. "Lady Castlereagh, who is a bosom-bow of hers, tells the most gothic stories."

"I expect she dislikes the match, for Clay might have done much better for himself, and then the huge settlement on top of that. . . ."

"She wrote you a very pretty note, you recall. And as to the ring, you'll have it soon enough. How I should have loved to see Wanda's face, though! Lord, if she has flashed her rock under my nose once, she has done it a hundred times."

"Mine is bigger," Ellie defended her desultory provider.

"Yes indeed, love. I was not trying to steal your thunder. Quite the contrary. I don't doubt he'll have it here before the wedding."

Ellie had not thought to discover this. "I don't care about the ring," she said.

"No, why should you? You have the Marquis!"

Chapter Twelve

It was a regular cavalcade that wended its way to Claymore House the next afternoon for the viewing of the mansion. Mrs. Wanderley was excessively eager to see its elegance, that she might take home a detailed description to regale Mrs. Homberly and her other social cronies. For five years she had been enduring Marie's casual comment that Rex was "putting up" with the Marquis during a visit to London, now he would be "putting up" at *Ellie's* mansion, but that would soon come to a halt. He must hire a room at a hotel like anyone else, for she would not abide his sponging off *them.* Lady Siderow, Ellie's favorite sister, had been invited, and Lady Tameson descended on the family in such a pique at not having been invited to dine with the Marquis the night before that the only way to soothe her ruffled feathers had been to include her in the invitation. Indeed, it was perfectly clear that she meant to tag along whether invited or no, for she said a dozen times, "Well, I'll not be left out *this time,*" and never removed so much as a glove during her entire visit, lest they try to slip off without her being quite ready. This left Wanda at loose ends with all her chaperones occupied, so she went along too. The last thing she wanted to see was more glories being heaped on Ellie, but she owned (to herself) that she was curious to see the fabled mansion. The crusade was met at the door by, not a butler, nor even the host, but Rex Homberly, who had come to town with Clay and was staying with him.

"Ah, I see Claymore is making you earn your keep, Rex," Mrs. Wanderley said with a glittering smile. She must speak to Ellie about this business.

"Lord, what are all of you doing here?" he demanded genially, and stood firmly fixed in the doorway, barring entry, till Clay told him to stop being such a ninnyhammer and move aside.

He enumerated each visitor as they entered. "Mrs. Wanderley, Lady Siderow, Lady Tameson, Wanda, Ellie. Where's Abel? You've left one of the family behind, Ellie."

Ellie, already in confusion at the uninvited entourage that had come along, frowned at her neighbor. "He and Papa don't arrive till tomorrow," she said.

"Bringing them along for the tour tomorrow, are you?" Rex asked. Aside to Clay he added, "Ought to charge a shilling a head, Clay. Make a fortune."

"And a crown a head for *overnight* boarders, Claymore," Mrs. Wanderley added with an arch laugh. "Then you wouldn't have people forever billeting themselves on you."

"You see I make him work off his charge by acting as my butler." Clay smiled, and bowed his guests in. To Ellie he said, "Do bring your papa and Abel tomorrow, if you think they would be interested."

"I daresay Papa would like to see where I shall be living. I ought to have waited till everyone was here."

"Adam won't care a fig," Rex told her. "Ain't a fern or a palm tree in the whole place."

The crowd was finally in, pelisses and bonnets stashed away, and the ladies huddled in a group admiring the black and white marble floor of the hall, the curved staircases that branched off to left and right, giving on to a walkway on the next story, and the rather ugly statuary residing in niches along the walls. Claymore had little experience in conducting tours, and asked if they would like a glass of wine before commencing.

Lady Siderow observed his uncertainty, and took him in charge. "Let us have a look around first, then refresh ourselves with wine. There is no need for us to see more than the downstairs. May we begin with this saloon here on your right? How lovely and spacious it is. This would be your main drawing room, I collect?"

The throng followed in and gaped around at the large room, the *two* Adams fireplaces, the Persian carpets, were treated to an exposition by Lord Claymore on the efficiency of gaslight—his own sole improvement to the mansion. He was mute on such subjects as Chippendale stands and Queen Anne chairs, paintings by Canaletto and French desks, but their worth did not escape the assessing eyes of the Ladies Siderow and Tameson, who raised their eyebrows at each other in appreciation. Lady Tameson thought, when she spotted a Chinese Chippendale stand that would just suit her small sitting room, that the room was perhaps slightly crowded, and she would offer to relieve Ellie of a few pieces. Mrs. Wanderley, following slightly behind the others, unobtrusively turned a few pieces of ornamental porcelain upside down to determine their value, but the name of Meissen meant nothing to her, and a blue F, surmounted by a crown, indicating the Furstenberg factory, was even more mysterious.

The tour continued, guided by Joan, through the library, with its intimidating array of leather-bound volumes, the ballroom, composed of two large rooms with a sliding wall to permit part or whole to be used, according to need. Mentally comparing it to the Hibbards' tiny dancing parlor, Wanda felt a sharp twinge of envy. The dining room was admired, and here Ellie saw the one feature she intended to change. She could not think she would enjoy eating with various scenes of carnage of the hunt bleeding before her eyes. Mrs. Wanderley observed that the drapes in here were nearly as shabby as her own, and said aside to Ellie that if she would like new draperies for a wedding gift she would not in the least mind returning the silver tea service, for she had already marked *three* quite similar, and Rundell and Bridges were very good about taking things back. Overhearing this remark, Caroline reminded her mama that she and Harold hadn't received a silver tea service for their wedding.

"Oh well, if *you* want to buy it, Caroline . . ."

The matter was allowed to drop, as Caroline very seldom wanted to *buy* anything except new gowns. "Harold is not really that fond of tea," she said.

Wanda, irate with the praise her sister's home was eliciting, asked, "What, is there no picture gallery in the house? At the Manor they have a great long gallery."

"Our family portraits are in the gallery at Claymore Hall, in Somerset," Clay told her, "though there is a small gallery here." He opened a paneled door into a "small" gallery fifty feet long, which was also used as a music room and occasionally for small impromptu dancing parties. The walls were hung with landscape paintings and some lesser portraits not deemed worthy of inclusion in the Somerset gallery. A pianoforte stood in one corner, with a harp standing beside it.

"Ah, a music room," Wanda laughed. "What a pity you cannot play better, Ellie. You might try the harp, for you will not want to assault your poor husband's ears with your pounding on the pianoforte." She strolled toward the pianoforte as she spoke, intending to give the Marquis a morsel of the music he would be missing.

"Let's split," Rex said to Clay and Ellie, who stood on either side of him, "before she strikes up the 'Fleuve du Tages.' "

A general exodus, prompted perhaps by the same fear, left Wanda no option but to follow, before she had completed two bars. "Quite out of tune," she whispered loudly to Caroline, whose thoughts were running elsewhere. Ellie had never taken any interest in the harp, whereas *she* had had half a dozen lessons two years ago, and given it up. She would like to resume, if only she had an instrument.

"There's not much more downstairs," Clay said. "A breakfast room in there." He opened a door to allow a peek, but did not bother to enter.

"Forgot the visitor's parlor," Rex reminded Clay.

"Oh, that's nothing."

"My favorite room in the house," Rex opined.

"It's along here," Clay said, leading the band forward to a room he had not intended showing, for it was his favorite too, and as it had had considerable rough use over the past five years, and no redecoration, it was not in the best repair. There always exists in every home one spot where the inhabitants relax and do whatever they dislike to do elsewhere because of the resultant mess. It was here that Clay and Rex shared a bottle, neglectful of circular stains on the table surface, smoked a cigar, occasionally adding a black burned hole to some piece of furniture, entertained at one time a mongrel mutt they had picked up, to the detriment of the sofa's upholstery, played cards with their feet on the table, and had even been known to shoot darts at the painting of an unknown relative with giant mustachios. A hit between the two curls of the mustache was counted a bull's eye. This being the owner's favorite room, and vacated not two minutes before the guests' arrival, there were several pieces of personal debris strewn about it. Unanswered invitations, a discarded cravat, and a pair of worn slippers were noticed at a glance. As soon as his visitors were within its doors, he recalled that there were as well some amorous memorabilia in the desk under the window. Stuff that must be burned before he brought his bride to the house.

To his chagrin, Rex came in, plopped down on the tatty sofa, and said, "Time for that wine you promised us, Clay."

"We will not want to take it here," Claymore said, striding firmly to the door.

Alas, it was a large house, and Mrs. Wanderley a large woman, unused to prolonged exertion. She, too, sat with a sigh of relief that boded she would remain exactly where she was.

"We will be more comfortable in the Green Saloon," Clay urged, at which juncture Wanda sat on the chair by the desk and said, "I'm thirsty. Let us have our wine."

Lady Siderow took her host's reluctance to be due to a

most natural desire to entertain his guests in a better room. "This is very comfortable," she told him. "Very like Papa's study, is it not, Ellie?"

"Yes, even the smell," Wanda replied for her.

"That is stale cigar smoke you're smelling." Clay leapt at the excuse. "You ladies will not be comfortable here." It had been borne in on him that not six inches from Wanda's chair there lay a drawerful of incriminating evidence. A telltale lock of golden hair and a dried yellow rose were by no means the worst of it, though they were bad enough to cause a tremble There were notes from Miss Golden, and the discarded beginnings of replies, even—how had he come to forget it?—an oval miniature of her, given to him on the occasion of his last birthday, also their last kiss.

"We are used to the smell," Mrs. Wanderley replied. "My whole house reeks of it."

"Ellie!" her fiancé said in a desperate voice. "Pray, let us remove to the Green Saloon. I have had Mulkin lay a fire. We will be quite comfortable there."

"Don't need a fire," Rex said. "Dash it, Clay, it's *July*."

A servant bearing a silver tray with wine, glasses, and biscuits passed the door en route to the Green Saloon, and Rex hailed him. "In here, Mulkin." The servant entered, deposited the tray on the battered table top, and the thing was settled.

Claymore had no choice but to acquiesce, doing his best to conceal his annoyance. Conversation resumed with the passing of wine, led, unfortunately, by Homberly, who never knew when to hold his tongue.

"Remember the last time we was in this room together, Clay?" he said. Clay remembered, and frowned at him. "The morning I brought the announcement of—" A resounding kick at his ankles brought him to an abrupt halt.

"Of what?" Wanda asked, a mischievous smile on her pretty face.

"Of . . . of," Rex muttered.

"Princess Charlotte's engagement, was it not?" Clay inserted.

"Oh fire." Wanda laughed. "You must do better than that. That was announced last winter; she has been *married* since May second. I think it must have been a *different* engagement."

"No such a thing," Rex said. "It wasn't her."

"What a whisker," Wanda teased with a knowing glance at Claymore. "And *you* pretended you didn't know about it when first you came to Surrey. *I* was not so taken in as some," she told him, with a nod of her head at Ellie, who was discussing with Joan a redecoration of the room they sat in.

Claymore glared at her, but Rex chuckled good-naturedly. "Got you dead to rights this time, old boy. Right in this very room. Don't you mind, Clay, I was here tossing cards into my hat and you came in looking blue as megrim."

"Yes, I recall the incident, Rex. There is no need to bring that up." He rose abruptly. "Will you not try this madeira, Mrs. Wanderley? I cannot vouch for that ratafia you are drinking. I fear it has been in the house forever, since the year Alice made her come-out."

"Just a wee bit then," she said, passing her glass. Her only thought on the discussion was that Rex had been entrenched for a long time, and he would be a hard one to uproot.

Claymore felt a profound relief when his servant came and summoned him to deal with a person at the door, who sought his contribution for a charity.

Wanda was becoming bored with no one to pester, and began fiddling with the drawer of the desk before her. She slid it out a little and peeped inside. She was rewarded with no more than a general clutter of papers. She pulled one out at random. "Your Marquis has paid three guineas for a curled beaver hat," she said to Ellie. "That is a very expensive chapeau, is it not, Rex?"

"Don't snoop, Wanda," Mrs. Wanderley said, reaching out her hand for the bill. "I wonder if he has paid it. It is not receipted. Perhaps you had better give it to him, Ellie."

"Mama!" Ellie said in disbelief. "Pray put it back. How

horrid and nosey we should look if he saw us prying into his private papers. Close the drawer, Wanda. Close it at once."

"You're not the mistress here yet," Wanda retaliated, and pulled the drawer out further. Her eye fell at once on the lock of golden hair, nicely tied up with a silver ribbon, and she snatched it up. "Only look what I have found!" she chirped.

Lady Tameson arose and took it from her. "This looks mighty familiar," she said to the company at large.

"Yes, it might be anyone's," Joan replied. "Clay's sister has hair just that color." She glanced at Ellie as she spoke, and knew her ruse had not succeeded. Ellie was looking at the hair as though it were poison.

"Alice's hair is *mouse*-colored," Caroline said.

"It is Gloria Golden's!" Wanda announced triumphantly, shuffling through the jumble of treasures. She extracted the oval miniature, which was quickly snatched from her fingers, like the lock of hair, by Lady Tameson. "I am surprised she would part with a lock of it, even for Clay."

"Deuce take it, Wanda," Rex said in anger, "if you ain't a gudgeon. There is nothing in that. Every gentleman has a batch of such things. St. Ives keeps his locks of hair on a special board, all labeled."

"But *most* gentlemen dispose of them when they are on the eve of their nuptials, do they not?"

"You may be sure he plans to."

"He seems to have gotten rid of the others. He only kept Gloria's," Wanda said, sticking her hands back to the back of the drawer in an effort to find more hair.

An ominous silence fell, and into it came the sounds of footsteps approaching the door. The relics were hastily passed to Wanda, who stuffed them back into the drawer, just as Lord Claymore entered the room. To fill the resounding silence, Rex asked, "Who was that to see you?" and Clay explained the nature of the visit.

Joan thought it no great thing that he should have a few keepsakes he had not thought to dispose of. He had scarcely been in his townhouse since Gloria's marriage, and no doubt intended to discard all such things before bringing Ellie home. The only pity was that that fiend of a Wanda should have discovered them and made a to-do of them.

The visit broke up shortly after his return, and with such a surfeit of carriages at their disposal—for Joan and Caroline had each brought her own—it was not necessary for Claymore to accompany Ellie to the Siderows'. She went with Joan and her mother, while Wanda accompanied Lady Tameson. Joan gave her view of Wanda's discovery, making little of it, and even going so far as to invent an amusing story, similar in nature, involving herself and Siderow. Ellie was inclined to agree with her sister, though she was naturally sorry to have been so mortified before her family.

"You are very wise to make little of it, my love," her mother said. "We never thought he was a saint, and so long as the connection is broken now, there is nothing to become excited about. Both Joanie and I agree that he seems to be becoming quite *fond* of you. And in any case, everyone says Everleigh is a very jealous husband, so Claymore will not be able to get near the Rose."

"There is no reason to think he will *try*, Mama," Joan said, stressing the more important aspect of the case. She then entered immediately into a discussion of wedding arrangements, professing great concern for Ellie's bouquet, which had not yet been decided upon.

As soon as the Wanderley crew had departed, Rex felt it his duty to inform Clay what had transpired during his absence, and did so, in his usual roundabout fashion. "You'll have to watch that Wanda," he said, thinking to soften the blow.

"Yes, particularly when she has so willing an accomplice as yourself. What the devil got into you to go bringing up that business about Gloria's engagement?"

"Nothing in that," Rex defended. "Everyone knows she got engaged. Had to learn of it sometime and somewhere. No place more likely than this room right here, which anyone could see you *live* in."

"The only difficulty being that I let on at Wanderleys

that I didn't know of it when I went there. However, we brushed through it fairly well, I think. Ellie wasn't paying much note, do you think?"

"Not *then*," Rex allowed leadingly.

"No doubt her sister will unfold the tale when they are home."

"That, too."

Rex was wearing his wise face, a sure sign that he had news to impart. "Out with it. What's happened?"

"Thing is, Clay, that Wanda, no trusting her."

"So you said. What has she done?"

"Been routing around in that drawer," Rex replied, lifting a stubby leg encased in biscuit-colored trousers, and indicating the drawer with the toe of his hessian.

Clay turned a shade paler. "You didn't let her get into that drawer!" he shouted.

"No stopping her. *I* tried. Ellie tried. Think her mother said something, too, or ought to have. Wonder Lady Siderow didn't give her a heavy setdown. Anyway, she was into that drawer."

Clay strode to the drawer and pulled it out an inch, hesitantly, to see what this malevolent Pandora's box had unleashed on him. The first object that hit his eye was the lock of golden hair, of which a piece of silver ribbon actually protruded still from its hasty return. He swiftly shoved the drawer shut, closing his eyes as though to block out the sight. "The hair," he said in a flat voice. "Did she see it?"

Rex nodded, then, noticing his friend's closed eyes, said, "Yup."

Clay opened his eyes, pulled the drawer out a little and said, "And the miniature?" Rex nodded in the affirmative.

"I'm sunk," Clay said, and slammed the drawer closed so hard that the whole desk rattled. For a moment he stood silent, his chin cupped in his hand. "I suppose it's too much to hope that she didn't show these curst things to Ellie?"

"Afraid so."

"She *did* show them?"

"She did, yes."

"Well, I wonder I didn't get my eyes scratched out when I came walking innocently into this room."

"Ellie ain't the kind to cut up stiff. Didn't say a word when Wanda pulled 'em out. Just sat there, looking sort of *paralyzed*, if you know what I mean."

Strangely, this bracing statement did nothing to reassure the worried Marquis. "Is that the whole of it, or did that viper of a Wanda get into the letters too?" he asked, in the voice of one inquiring whether his death was to be by gun or sword.

"Didn't get around to the letters. You came back too soon. Just a bill for a hat. Three guineas. Took exception to that."

"Damn that woman!"

"What's in the letters then?" Rex asked, and tugged the drawer open to see for himself. A moment's rifling was rewarded by discovering one of Gloria's notes, and he opened it to peruse it. His eyebrows raised, he pursed his lips and whistled. "That Gloria Golden's a dashed loose girl," he said.

Clay snatched the letter from him, read it, and blushed. "This isn't what it sounds like," he said angrily.

"By Jove, should hope not! 'My heart flutters when I am in yr arms,' he quoted. Tell you what, Clay, you want to burn this lot. Ought to have done it before. If Everleigh ever gets his hands on this mush, he'll call you out."

"I know, I know. But that was written after our first waltz at Almack's. That's the only time she was in my arms. Except for . . . well, never mind that."

Rex fumbled through the drawer till he found another of the infamous missives. "What's this, then? 'You are hansomer than anyone.' That girl can't spell, Clay. Can't spell worth a peg. And she don't put a period where she ought either. 'I will be in the Park this afternoon I hope you can come, if not I will see you at Almack's tomorrow and you better be there!' Bold, too. Bold as brass." He read on and his blue eyes popped. "Well, if this don't beat the Dutch," he said. "Listen to this bit. 'You are so hansome'—spelt wrong again—'I tingle at your touch.' Where the devil did you touch her, Clay? You've got to

get rid of this. We'll burn 'em before they fall into Everleigh's hands." He walked to the grate as he spoke, still
reading and clucking.

"Let's get them together," Clay said. He pulled the
drawer open and yanked out all the papers. Then he and
his friend began sorting out letters from bills, invitations,
and other useless pieces of paper that had found their way
into the drawer.

"What's this?" Rex asked, lifting out a lock of Titian
hair. "*This* ain't the Rose's hair. Now how did Wanda
come to miss this? Whose is it? Don't recognize the tint at
all."

Clay regarded it dispassionately. "I think her name was
Morin," he said. "Or possibly Morgan."

"Morton," Rex corrected. "Recognize it now. Jane
Morton. You'll find one of these pieces in most gentlemen's possession I fancy. I wonder that girl has a curl left
on her head. And she's *plain*, too. Don't know why you
all went getting a hank of *her* hair."

"Well, she and Sara Grant were the only redheads, and
Sara wouldn't part with a single hair. I needed it to complete my collection."

"*She* must have needed it to complete her coiffure;
must be two feet of the stuff here." He flung it into the
wastebasket, to be consumed with the rest of the evidence.

During the afternoon Mrs. Homberly and Missie arrived in town, having been invited for the wedding, and
coming early to spruce up their country gowns with city
feathers and bonnets. They were staying in Rex's apart-
ment, since he was at Claymore House (with no apparent
intention of *ever* leaving, as the mother of the bride occasionally mentioned). They called at the Siderows', and in
order to have a good private cose with Missie, Ellie bor-
rowed her sister's carriage for a drive in the park. They
exchanged confidences, with Missie having great affairs to
relate, for she had attracted the attention of a gentleman
of the first stare in the Pump Room in Bath, and had to
describe in detail how ingeniously the gentleman had

made their acquaintance by discovering she was Rex's sister, and he had been to Oxford with Rex. This, her first affair of the heart, loomed larger in her mind than her friend's marriage to a marquis, and made up the major part of the conversation. Ellie was content to let her ramble on and fed her just enough questions that she didn't have to do much talking herself. With such interesting new developments in their lives, neither of them even mentioned their previous plan of taking to the boards at Drury Lane.

Chapter Thirteen

Forewarned that his bride-elect had been witness to the objects in his drawer, Claymore knew he must bring up the subject on their next meeting and try to explain them away. The opportunity occurred that same evening. Claymore, the Wanderley family, and the Homberlys were invited to dine at Lady Tameson's. Even if Lady Siderow had not seen fit to invite *her* to dine with the Marquis, she was not so mean-spirited, she said half a dozen times, as to refuse to include Joan in her invitation. Joan need not think *she* was to have the running of the Marchioness' social life, as she clearly did, and besides there were the Chinese Chippendale stand and the harp to consider.

The evening passed pleasantly. Caroline did not frequently bestir herself to entertain her family, but she was by no means backward in the social graces, and knew how to put on a show to impress a marquis as well as anyone. She limited herself to two courses and two removes, but served such a quantity of side dishes that the most gluttonly of her guests, her husband, had no cause to complain. Her orange and lemon soufflé was a particular success, and she looked forward with pleasure to having it at the Siderows', for she had told Joan the recipe, cutting the sugar in half.

It was not till Claymore and Elinor were alone in his carriage on their way back to the Siderows' that he raised the subject that had been bothering them both all evening. He took the precaution of getting his arm around her before he began. He remarked that she had been in the sullens during the dinner, and lay it at the door of Wanda's having exposed him.

"I know you are angry with me," he began apologetically. She had on her paralyzed look, and he found it difficult to explain the matter as glibly as he would have liked. "And I know why. It was those stupid things Wanda found in my desk."

"Oh, Rex told you," Ellie exclaimed, nearly as mortified as he was himself, to see a member of her family so disgraced.

"Yes, he told me, and now I am going to tell you how it came about. You know I fancied myself in love with Miss Golden last Season."

"Everyone knows it."

"Yes. Well, we exchanged a few notes and things, but I have gotten rid of them. I'm sorry as may be that this happened, but let's not have it ruin our relationship."

"Do you *truly* no longer care for her?" she asked.

"Ellie, I never did! Not as I care for you. It was just— oh, an infatuation. She was the belle of the Season, and everyone was dangling after her. I wanted to prove, I suppose, that I could outdo them all. I never felt for her as I do for you."

He felt sure this ardent speech must make all right between them, and wondered at her reluctance to throw herself on his chest in tears and recriminations for her mistrust. But she was shy, of course.

"And you don't see Miss Golden—the Duchess, I ought to say—anymore?"

"No, there is the best of good reasons *not* to. Everleigh is so jealous it would be more than my life is worth to try to see her. I have not the least desire to do so in any case—ever again."

"But she is so beautiful, Clay. I don't know how you can *not* love her."

He grabbed her to him convulsively and tried to shower kisses on her face. She turned her head aside to hide the tears on her cheeks, and he could only reach her ear. "She is not half so beautiful as you," he said into the ear, and resigned himself to doing no more than holding her in his arms. Till they were married, he must control his impulses.

At her door he said, "I love you very much, Ellie. Don't let this business come between us." He kissed her lightly on the cheek, and she ran up the stairs to her room to be alone in peace.

How could she doubt his words? His voice shook with emotion when he told her he loved her. Anyone might have fallen in love with Gloria's beautiful face, and if Clay found herself twice as beautiful, he must love her very much indeed. One thing she was sure of: she loved him, as she would never love anyone else. Gloria was married, her husband fiendishly jealous. Whatever had been between Clay and the Rose would die a natural death when they were both married to jealous demons, for she acknowledged to herself that she was every bit as jealous as the Duke of Everleigh. She would have Clay, and if Gloria ever tried to get him away, she would scratch her beautiful blue eyes out of her head, and tell the Duke, too. On this outrageous thought she slept.

The week between Claymore's arrival in town and the marriage was to have been a period for them to become better acquainted. It turned into a gay social round with no time for anything but parties and fittings and shopping. They were frequently together, but they were seldom alone together. Mr. Wanderley and Abel came to town; various of Claymore's relatives paid calls on the bride and held parties for the couple. When they hoped to slip away by themselves for half an hour, Rex and Missie would suddenly decide that they, too, would love a turn in the park. George Hibbard had come for the wedding, and he and Wanda were frequent and unwelcome companions.

When Ellie read in the *Morning Observer* that the Everleighs had left for Brighton, she shoved Rose to the back of her mind. She heard on all sides what a fortunate creature she was, making such a fine match, and her fiancé so devoted to her. Even Wanda let up on her haranguing, determined to make herself beloved to the couple who had such a handsome London residence, with plenty of room for George and herself. With George at last present to compare favorably with the Marquis, she had no more to say than it was odd Ellie didn't receive her engagement ring. Claymore did not find it possible, after a prolonged discussion with his man of business, to divert a thousand pounds to this purchase. Ellie appeared to have forgotten it, for she didn't mention it to him again. There were presents to open, plans to make for a honeymoon, arrangements for a dresser for Ellie, for she presently shared one with Wanda, and a battle was pitched over this important point.

Miss Pritchard had "done" for both girls since they had begun putting their hair up, and they both laid claim to her continued services. Ellie carried the day by telling her mama Wanda was to remain practically at home among all their old friends, while she was to be launched among strangers, and must have one old friend with her.

"Yes indeed, and besides you are the *elder*," her mother replied. Had she been the *younger* by ten minutes, that would have been the excuse. The *reason* was certainly not mentioned: that a daughter with the great fortune to nab a marquis might have whatever she wanted.

Miss Pritchard smiled happily, relieved that she must not state publicly that she wouldn't do for Miss Wanda if she had to starve in a gutter first.

Miss Wanda's beautiful nose was further disjointed by the discovery that a young lady making a grand match required a more valuable gift than one marrying a mere squire's son. Silver wrought into every conceivable shape and form was hauled in for Ellie, and rather than expressing surprise that the relatives were so generous, it was stated that "you can't go giving just anything to a *marquis*."

She was similarly told that Ellie, who would soon be coming into a settlement of twenty-five thousand pounds, must be outfitted in the first style *before* this time, for after all, she was marrying a *marquis*.

"Next you will tell me she must have a bigger dowry than I, because she is marrying a *marquis*," Wanda raged, and regretted her words when she saw the light of interest go on in her mother's eyes. Mr. Wanderley scotched this idea, however, having already ordered a hundred tobacco plants, which required the enlargement of his greenhouse. Even Caroline, with an eye to her Chinese Chippendale stand and her harp, turned traitor and supported Ellie's cause. In fact, it was only the recipient of all this largesse who stated in an unheeded voice that many of the wonders bestowed on her were neither necessary nor wanted, and that if *she* got six bonnets, Wanda ought to as well.

"You are forgetting we had all the expense of outfitting Wanda for her come-out this spring," her mother said. "And she has still half a dozen gowns she hasn't even worn. Who will see her, stuck out in the country anyway?"

"I don't intend to remain stuck in the country!" Wanda fired back.

"You will if you don't mind your manners," her mother reminded her eliptically, and Wanda smiled grimly at her sister, who had snatched the Marquis right out from under her own nose, in the slyest manner imaginable.

The day for the wedding finally arrived. The gowns were prepared, the flowers on hand, their price and quality strongly derided by Adam, the church suitably trimmed with white lilies and white bows on the seats, the wedding feast prepared at Siderow House, the carriages washed and polished, Claymore House stood in readiness for the nuptial night, with Rex Homberly finally (to the bride's mother's relief) dispatched to Fenton Hotel, and far away in Somerset Claymore Hall was being turned out to receive its new mistress. This was to be the destination of their honeymoon. Everything but the engagement ring was taken care of. The wedding ring was purchased on credit, a circle of diamond chips set in a golden band. The party wended its way to St. George's in Hanover Square, and the ceremony was performed with all due pomp and circumstance, crammed in between the weddings of Sir Geoffrey Haskin, Bart., and Captain Lawrence McMaster, for it was a very busy edifice at this time of the year.

It was agreed that the bride looked stunning, and the groom excessively handsome, and St. George's had not seen so ideal a couple before, not since Sir Geoffrey and Miss Milne had entered its door an hour previously, and would never see such a sight again till the entry of Captain Lawrence McMaster and Miss Lanctot an hour later.

When the fateful words of the occasion were being enunciated in a low tone by the bride, Wanda reached out her hand and took ahold of George's fingers. They exchanged a meaningful smile, and Wanda even squeezed out a tear. She hoped they would be very happy, and thought it a gross mistake for Ellie to have chosen the Spanish lace mantilla for a veil, for it stood up so very high, and made her look like a giant at a raree show. *She* would wear Mama's, or perhaps the lovely one Caroline had worn. That would be her something old, and Caroline need not think she could palm it off as her wedding gift either, for she had given Ellie two sterling silver goblets, duplicates of which would look very handsome on the Hibbards' fireplace shelf. Joan worried whether she had reminded the housekeeper to clean the extra batch of silver that would be required, and was almost certain she had forgotten. She admired Ellie's Spanish lace mantilla, such an original idea, though it made her look nearly as tall as Clay. Caroline, glancing across the aisle to the groom's side of the church, wondered whether Lady Jane Blackmore wasn't pregnant *again*, for her gown was hanging at a peculiar angle. Surely the baby wasn't above four months, and she was already showing! If her own bambino proved to be a male, she would try not to have another for years and years. Lord, she hoped she wasn't going to be sick! She overcame her nausea by the delightful notion of asking Ellie whether she would mind leaving the harp with her while she and Clay were in the country, for it would pass the time during the next few months when she couldn't get about much. This settled, she set her inventive brain searching after an excuse to get the Chinese stand, temporarily. Mrs. Wanderley dabbed at a tear and considered how long she ought to wait before going to visit Ellie in Somerset, and whether her husband would go with her, or must she make do with Abel. Lord, and not mention a word of it to the Homberlys, or Rex would tag along. Adam mentally toted up the price he would have to fork up for the wilting lilies, and regretted that he had not thought to provide flowers himself.

In less than an hour the ceremony was over, and the party repaired to Grosvener Square for an afternoon of overeating, drinking, dancing and general revelry. Everyone complimented the young couple and insinuated with ingenuity that each was fortunate beyond just expectations in having snared the other. By way of complimenting them mutually, Rex, slightly bosky with wine, said, "Well, Clay, you said you was going to buy the prettiest girl in England to spite the Rose, and by Jove, you've done it."

"That is not precisely what I said," Clay replied, frowning heavily.

"The gist of it anyway. The morning you proposed to . . . well, well, never mind that. Wasn't supposed to mention it. Very nice wedding, Ellie. Your mother did you proud." He shot a guilty glance at the groom, hunched his round shoulders in apology or desperation, and thought of a way to retrieve his slip into veracity. "Clay tell you about our little bonfire?" he asked genially, having found no opportunity to perform this office for his friend. "Burnt up all the Rose's love letters. Whole slew of 'em."

"Yes, he told me," she replied, torn between amusement and chagrin.

Rex said aside in a perfectly audible voice, "Glad to oblige you, Clay. Any time," before stumbling off to tell Wanda she'd have to go some to beat this do.

Clay was naturally eager to avoid any further obligations Rex might wish to perform, and tried to keep out of his way, but alas, he was soon back. "Where's Miss Simpson?" he demanded, in a voice becoming surly.

"Who is Miss Simpson?" Ellie asked.

"Who's Miss Simpson? Well, if you ain't a flat, Ellie. Miss Simpson's the prettiest girl in London."

"How does it come you didn't marry *her*, Clay?" Ellie asked archly.

" 'Cause *I'm* going to marry her, that's why," Rex said. "She's too tall for Clay. About as tall as you are today, with that lace scaffold you've got on your head. What in the deuce made you wear it? Wanda put you up to it to make a sight of you? Going to marry Miss Simpson. She'll have to stoop a little. Daresay she won't like it. Wanda didn't." He roamed off again, without waiting for any answers, in search of Miss Simpson, who was in Bath with her parents, receiving the attentions of a very *tall* Officer of the Guards.

"Poor Rex is all about in his head," Claymore was happy to inform his bride. "There is no making any sense of him when he's in his cups."

"He made pretty good sense to me," Ellie said, then she turned abruptly away to receive yet more compliments from the Hibbards. She contrived to stay away from her husband for the next hour, till she should get her feelings under control. It was no easy matter, for he pursued her relentlessly, but at least they were not private, and he could hardly go into complicated explanations about having *bought* a bride at his wedding feast. Instead he consumed a great deal of wine to fortify his courage for the ordeal ahead of him. He was determined to get the subject of Gloria cleared away once and for all.

By the time the couple was waved from the door in a shower of rice and ensconced in Claymore's carriage on their way home, he was as well foxed as Rex, and even Ellie had consumed more than she was accustomed to. Besides their reeling heads, they had their separate problems to consider, so that conversation was slight, and lovemaking nonexistent. Clay struggled inadequately in his mind with words to explain how he had gone to Surrey seeking just any beautiful woman to marry him, and found there the girl of his dreams. Ellie, even more distracted, considered her nuptial night. She knew some unprecedented thing was going to happen to her, but had very little idea what. Her mama had told her ominously that "what was expected of her" on that night, and subsequent nights at her lord's pleasure, was little enough price to pay for the privilege of being the Marchioness of Claymore. Joan might have been more explicit but for Mama's comprehensive statement that she "had gone into all of that" and there was no point in throwing the poor girl into hysterics by harping on it. It was, strangely, Lady Tameson who had given her some hope by exclaiming with a titter that she feared she must be an *abandoned* creature, for she had come to enjoy it. Wanda, who was present on that interesting occasion, appeared to know more than her twin, for she, too, confided that she was looking forward to it. Ellie could not bring herself to proclaim her ignorance before these two women of the world and was wallowing still in a sea of doubt and misconceptions. She had heard her Aunt Elaine once tell Joan that she had locked herself in the closet on her wedding night, and though she had laughed at the time, she was coming to think it a very good idea now. She pulled into her own corner of the coach and bit her lips in apprehension.

When Miss Pritchard, a spinster, of course, had arrayed her in her finest chiffon nightgown, brushed out her curls and said in a bracing accent, "Buck up, it won't kill you," Ellie was as prepared as she would ever be to receive her husband—or perhaps lock herself in the closet. A cursory examination revealed there was no lock on the closet, and besides she thought she would feel very foolish to be found crouching in amongst her suits and gowns. Before she had time to discover whether the spot under the bed was deep enough to conceal her, there was a tap on the door, and Claymore came in, fully clad she was happy to see, and carrying a tray with champagne and two glasses.

"Well, here we are, alone at last," he said in a voice that was trying hard to sound jolly, and failing miserably.

"Yes, indeed," Ellie replied in a similar tone, casting

one last longing eye on the closet, and backing away from him.

Claymore set the tray down on the table and took up the bottle of wine. "I thought we might drink a toast to ourselves," he suggested, and made a prolonged ceremony of removing the cork.

"Oh, yes indeed," Ellie replied. Her retreat had led her to the bed, and she fell backward on its edge with a plop.

Clay poured the wine and advanced toward her with a glass in either hand. Seeing that her eyes were wildly dilated and her fingers clutching at the counterpane, he said, "Not nervous, are you?" as he handed her a glass. His own hand was shaking so violently that half a glass of champagne sloshed over onto her new gown. "You can see *I'm* not nervous," he laughed inanely.

They drank for two minutes in silence, the only sound that of the wine going down their throats. "It's good champagne," he said at last, desperate to introduce some talk to the occasion. For one wild moment he even wished Rex were there.

"Yes indeed," she said again. They seemed to be the only words she knew. With an effort she added, "Very good wine," and she emptied her glass.

This opened a whole new sphere of activity. Claymore could now pour her another glass, and suggest playfully that he hadn't realized his wife was a tippler, and he had better get cracking, or she would finish the bottle on him. "And don't say 'yes indeed,' Ellie," he added, in quite a natural tone. Her patent terror had served to put him relatively at ease. What he must *not* do was rush at her again, as he had in the carriage, and scare the daylights out of her.

The lovemaking advanced by such slow stages that it could hardly be said to advance at all. Lord Claymore's passion, however, proceeded apace. He could no longer restrain himself, and sit mouthing platitudes on his honeymoon, when his bride sat not six inches away, looking very fetching in her diaphanous gown. Before he quite knew what he was about, he left his chair and was on the edge of the bed beside her, and within two seconds she was in his arms, struggling violently to get out. Just as she was about to give up the struggle, for she was human after all, and felt suddenly a certain intuition as to what he was going to do, and no terrific reluctance for him to do it, he pulled back.

He looked at her a moment, his face rigid and flushed. "I can't," he said, and he arose from the bed.

"Can't what?" Ellie asked in a shaken voice.

"Poor girl," he said with a soft smile. "You've had enough horrors for one day. Stop worrying; I'm not going to ravage you. Go to bed."

"I am in bed," she pointed out.

"So you are. Go to sleep then. We'll talk about it tomorrow."

"Clay! You are not leaving me!"

"Ah yes, my pretty," he stroked her cheek with a warm finger, feeling very debonair. "Do you think I can trust myself with you?" He laughed softly, blew out the last burning taper, and walked from the room, bumping tables as he went, and sending a glass to the floor. His gallant exit was marred by the sound of shattering crystal, but in his new guise as master of all situations, he did not utter a single expletive.

He walked to his own chamber, feeling unfulfilled, and very noble. He marveled at her shyness, her inexperience. He even managed a twinge of remorse at his scarlet past. He would woo her slowly—wait another whole night if necessary—so that her initiation would not be of a harrowing sort that would give her a disgust of him. He recalled the unwisdom of a friend, Raleigh, who had bragged of his exploits on his wedding night, and within a year his wife had left him. Didn't see how a fellow could be such a gudgeon. He doubted if Ellie appreciated the sacrifice he was making, though.

In the next room Ellie beat her pillow in frustration, and told herself she had known all along he didn't love her, and this proved it. He was *disgusted* with her; couldn't bring himself to touch her; had only married her to spite the Rose, as she well knew, and was very likely sneaking off to see her at every opportunity.

In the yawning darkness (naturally, she had nothing to rekindle the taper the brute had blown out on her), she considered a just punishment for him. Her first ideas of throwing herself into the Thames, or perhaps consuming deadly nightshade, were seen upon further consideration to inflict some small damage on the innocent, as well as depriving her of witnessing his guilt. She turned her wrath to lesser revenges. She took some consolation from envisaging herself a scarlet woman, infamous throughout all of Europe for her wanton ways, but that, she felt, would not be quite comfortable. Well, she had lost comfort forever in any case; how could she be comfortable under the roof of this unfeeling wretch? This belligerent thought gave birth to another and more hopeful one. Why must she reside under his roof? She was not his wife in anything but name. He was *using* her to spite the Rose, whom he simultaneously loved on the side, and had probably promised *her* that he would never love another. It was this awful darkness that muddled her thoughts so. Or perhaps it was the wine. Why had she drunk so much? It was only the embarrassment of being alone with Clay, on their wedding night.

Her thoughts took a lachrymose turn to *her* part in the debacle. Certainly she had behaved rashly. Very likely he had taken the notion she didn't *want* him to touch her, only because she had backed off a little at first, out of shyness. If *that* was what he thought . . . she threw off the blankets and hopped out of bed, determined to go to him at once, for of course he loved her dearly. She would explain this whole nonsensical misunderstanding away. In the darkness she stepped on the broken crystal, and felt a large chunk sink into her heel. She hobbled to the door, whimpering, and in the hall a lamp was burning. By its dim light she pulled the sliver of glass from her foot, before limping along to Clay's room, feeling very like a true heroine, braving all dangers and losing half an ounce of blood, to go to her beloved.

What a sad comedown that he was laid out on his bed, fully dressed still, and *snoring*. But a candle was tilting at a precarious angle, rammed into the top of a wine bottle, and obviously endangering his life. How very like him! He thought to blow out *hers*, but not his own. The gaslight, of which he was so proud, appeared to stop at the ground floor. Her heart melted with tenderness to see him in such peril.

"Clay." She laid a hand on his brow. "Clay, wake up," she said, softly in his ear. He snored on, and the fumes of wine were breathed in her face. "Clay, it's me," she crooned softly. "I love you. You know I love you. I don't care if you used to love Gloria. I still love you," she insisted to his inert form.

Perhaps some words penetrated his sleep. Perhaps the word "Gloria," as he then turned his head and grabbed her hand and said, "Rose. Golden Rose."

She pulled her hand away as though it had been scorched. For a moment she stood motionless, only her chest moving in agitation, before she turned and ran from the room. Then she returned and took up his candle, not that she cared a hoot if he burned his stupid old house down, but only because she didn't want to go back to a dark room. She was breathing hard, in quick, shallow breaths. This was the final degradation! He was dreaming of the Rose, and on his wedding night! She was humiliated, hurt, angry, and determined to leave his roof at once. Only her heel was bleeding like the very devil, and paining her too. Very likely she hadn't got all the glass out. She sat on the side of her bed and made plans in earnest. Real plans this time, not maudlin stuff about killing herself. Kill *him* was more like it! She would leave and never see him again. See how Miss Golden Rose liked that, and the Marquis of Claymore, with his twenty thousand pounds a year. *Buying* the prettiest wife in England, to spite the Rose!

She got dressed in a new scarlet suit, put on a hat, and headed for the door without packing a single stitch of her trousseau. Then she remembered that it was packed, in a trunk somewhere, ready for the honeymoon trip, but she had no notion where it might be. It was while she stood at the door considering this that it first occurred to her she must have somewhere to go. Not to the Siderows. That would be the first place he'd look. And not Caroline's either, for *she* would only say she must return to him, and very likely begin nagging at her again for Alice's harp, which was in the music room. No, what she must do was to go home, to Papa. *He* would understand, though her mother would kill her. Well then, she must get home without Mama's knowing anything about it, which meant not *with* Papa, for they would both be going home with Abel in the family carriage. Her next thought was the Homberlys'. She would not like to tell her story to Mrs. Homberly, but Rex would stand her friend. And he was, fortunately, not with his mother, but at the hotel—the Fenton Hotel was the name she had heard mentioned by her mama.

A rational consideration led her to the conclusion it would be foolhardy to go before daybreak. Rex had been foxed a few hours ago (only a few hours ago; it seemed eons), and would be of no use before morning. Very well then, she would wait. She sat in the chair by the table, and within ten minutes of sitting down was fast asleep, her head resting on the hard wood. The candle, still leaning dangerously in the bottle, contrived to burn itself out without setting the house afire, and when she awoke several hours later, the room was half bright, with a red rising sun visible through the window.

She picked up her reticule, limped to the door of her room, checked the hall for lingering servants, and, observing the path to be clear, made a hasty flight along the corridor, down the broad staircase, across the vast marble hall, and out the door to Curzon Street.

Chapter Fourteen

She had, fortunately, only to walk around the corner to Tiburn Lane and down the two blocks to Picadilly before she managed to hire a hansom cab to take her to the Fenton Hotel. Mr. Homberly was not at all pleased to be dragged from sleep not two hours after his dizzy head had hit the pillow, and long before the inebriating fumes had dissipated. Still he was sober enough to realize that a thing of unparalleled interest was in the process of enactment when he glanced at the hasty note Lady Claymore had sent up. He was soon into his blue coat of Bath cloth with the buttons of brass, big as saucers, and his yellow trousers. The exigency of the occasion decided him against arranging a time-consuming Waterfall, and he contented himself with a natty dotted Belcher kerchief round his neck.

He was happy to see Ellie had had the sense to take a private parlor to await him, unaware of its being the proprietor's idea, when he recognized the early caller to be a swell of the first stare. "What the devil's happened, Ellie?" he asked in a surly tone. "Where's Clay?"

"He is at Claymore House. I've left him," she asserted bravely, her chin up.

"Left him? Good God, you can't do that! Haven't been

buckled twenty-four hours yet. Never heard of such a thing in my life. Why did you go and do that for?"

"For—for private reasons that I can't reveal, even to you, Rex, but you must believe they are *very good reasons*." She limped toward him as she spoke, her glass-infested heel hurting madly.

"Good lord, you never mean he *beat* you!" Rex exclaimed, approaching sobriety with the shock this circumstance dealt his reeling mind. Why, the poor soul could hardly drag herself along at all.

"Certainly not! Why should he do that?" she asked, feeling a bothersome desire to defend her awful spouse.

"How should I know? Why are you dragging your limb then?"

"That is not of the smallest importance. An accident merely. The thing is, Rex, you *must* take me home."

"*I* must take you home? Well, if you ain't a Johnnie Raw, Ellie. All you've got to do is hire a cab. Any number of them around. No need to have gone hauling me out of my bed. What I want to know is what you're doing *away* from home at this ungodly hour."

"I don't mean back to *him*," she explained. "I mean home to Papa."

"Back to Sussex? You've lost your marbles, my girl. You can't go back home. You're married."

"I have left him I said. Oh Rex, you are foxed still."

"No such a thing," he replied, wounded to the quick. "Might be a trifle tipsy, not foxed. Come, let us have a chair, and a cup of coffee to clear our heads." He summoned a servant to bring coffee, and then demanded an explanation of his caller's errand.

A young lady reared in accordance with the strictest principles of propriety could no more tell what was bothering her than she could fly. She had to content herself with tales of her husband not loving her, and having been in love with Gloria all along, and even talking about her in his sleep.

When the waiter returned with coffee, Rex stepped to the door under the pretext of conversation of a harmless sort with him, and said in a fierce undertone that he was to get a message to the Marquis of Claymore in Curzon Street to get over here *at once* on a most urgent matter dealing with "he knew who." The servant blinked, said "Eh?" in a mystified voice, listened again to the same message, then left with a knowing wink. Rex returned to his caller and began reassuring her in what he took to be a kind, avuncular manner.

"Well, Ellie, and to think I thought you was a knowing 'un," he began. "Why, there's nothing in what you've been telling me. Nothing at all. Of course he was in love with the Rose—you always knew that—but as to still being in love with her, why it's no such a thing. Wouldn't dare go chasing after her now she's riveted to Everleigh. He'd have his skin. Anyway, the attraction was mostly on the Rose's side. Clay's letters to her weren't half as silly as hers to him. Outside of telling her he'd be in hell till she came back from somewhere or other she was going, there was nothing in them at all."

These encouraging words had the inexplicable result of hardening Clay's wife against him even further. "In hell," she said in a suppressed squeak, "and he only told me he would see me soon, and wrote the stiffest notes you ever saw. He didn't even sign them 'Love' or anything. 'Your faithful servant' he signed them," she charged, daring her comforter to explain away this monstrous behavior.

"You must remember, Ellie, you're his *wife*. A man don't go writing that sort of tommyrot to his *wife*."

"I was not his wife when he wrote that," she countered.

"You was about to be; same thing. You don't have to be making up lies when you mean to win a girl fair and square, and marry her."

He was saved from elaborating on this excellent theme by the arrival of coffee. The serving was accompanied by a sage nod and a wink behind the lady's head. All was well. Rex relaxed and tried to institute a complimentary conversation on the wedding party, but met with opposition.

"And besides," she cut into a neat declaration that *he* hadn't thought her wedding veil looked so bad, whatever

everyone else said, "he didn't even remember to give me
my engagement ring."

The battle for the jewels had been fought in private between the Marquis and the Dowager, so Rex was at a loss
to explain this solecism. He had to try new tactics. His
poor brain had not been so challenged in years. "I begin
to think Clay was right, and you only married him for his
money after all. I'm surprised at you, Ellie."

"Did he say so?" she snapped. "Pray, what can a man
expect when he sets out to *buy* a wife?"

"Deuce take it, the price he paid for you he can at least
expect her to behave herself."

An acrimonious discussion of this sort continued, interrupted by the servant with more coffee and a plate of
buns, as they had neither of them eaten breakfast. Rex
was becoming fidgety, wondering if his message had gone
astray. He was relieved to hear the angry banging of heels
on the floor outside, and arose just as the door was flung
open.

"Hallo, Clay," he said. "Glad you finally got here."

Ellie looked, turned an angry pink, and gasped, "Traitor!" to Rex. "How *could* you serve me such a turn?"

"No, really," he said, backing away from her, toward
the open door and safety.

"Thank you, Rex," Clay said, his face glowering. "Perhaps you will be kind enough to leave me private with my
wife now."

"Too happy," Rex agreed, sidling past. Out of the corner of his mouth he said in a stage whisper, "Sore as a
boil about not getting a ring, Clay. Get the girl a diamond
or you'll have no peace."

Rex pulled the door softly to behind him, and, unlike
the hovering waiter, felt not the least desire to know what
went on behind that wooden facade. His duty done, he
had earned a glass of something wet, and went to claim
his reward.

Clay, like Rex half an hour before him, had been un-
ready to face the world so soon. His hung-over head had
been further jarred to receive news that something of interest awaited him at Fenton's Hotel. He knew Rex was

putting up there, and his first impulse had been to send the nervy fellow who brought the message away with a flea in his ear. It was the man's knowing smile that there were a *lady* in the case, a *young* lady, dark and pretty-like, that had aroused his interest. His mind immediately flashed to Ellie, only to abandon so preposterous an idea. Still, it bothered him enough that he took a quick peep into her room, and discovered her gone. He had not waited to disturb the servants. The fewer who knew of the affair the better. He shrugged himself into a fresh shirt and jacket without help from his valet, and he, too, opted for a Belcher kerchief to save time. He was first worried that something dreadful had happened to Ellie, but no concatenation of events he arrived at could account for her having gone to Rex, at an hotel, rather than to himself, her own husband, right next door to her. He reviewed his quixotic chivalry of the preceding evening. At least he was blameless on that score, as he had sacrificed his own desires heroically rather than discommode her in the least. Worry led to anger, and by the time he arrived, he had worked himself into a fine lather.

"Well, Madam Wife," he said stiffly, "I trust you have a good explanation for this flight."

"You know well enough why I left," she countered.

"You are mistaken. I have not the least notion. I wish you would tell me. I cannot believe the hunger for diamonds has led to such wanton misbehavior as this."

"Wanton misbehavior! You, *you* of all lecherous creatures dare to accuse me of that!"

He was stymied. His behavior had been so far from lecherous that he could only stare, his mouth open. He tried to recall with accuracy what had passed between them before he went to his room last night. Perhaps he had been a little rash but the woman was his wife after all. She must have some idea what was expected of her. "If you find *my* behavior lecherous, I can only say it is well you didn't marry anyone else."

"I wish I *had* married anyone else but you," she flung at him.

He went from incredulity to cold anger. "A wish in

which you are not alone, ma'am. However, the damage is done. We *are* married, and I did not pay twenty-five thousand pounds for a wife, only to have her make a laughing stock of me."

"No, you did it to spite the Rose!"

"No indeed; I have not the least desire to spite such a charming lady."

"Oh, how dare you."

"My mistake was all in my lack of daring. I have been too considerate of you, for I see you are not so sensitive as I had thought."

"I can't imagine what a miserable creature like you would want with a sensitive wife. You never loved me; you *know* you did not. You had better married Wanda."

"You are not so unlike her as I had thought. Merely you are more subtle. She doesn't bother to hide her mercenary streak. Yes, and she is a deal prettier, too," he threw in, to wound as deeply as possible this woman who was driving him distracted with her freakish starts.

"I am leaving you," she said in arctic accents, her head high. "I am not going back to your horrid house, so don't think it."

"You are going back immediately, before the whole of London hears of your flight. It is well we leave for the Hall today. Before we return, I shall have taught you how to comport yourself as the Marchioness of Claymore."

"And I am not going to Somerset with you either," she went on, turning a deaf ear on his statement.

"The bargain is struck, my lady, however much we may *both* regret it. When you have considered the matter further, I think you will be satisfied with your rewards. The diamond will be forthcoming, along with a few other baubles you are unaware of. Then, too, there will be your allowance—five percent of twenty-five thousand pounds is not an insignificant sum. Come, we will leave before the streets are full."

"I am not coming with you," she maintained firmly, but already doubts were assailing her as to what she would do, since Rex had failed her in a most ignominious and chicken-hearted manner.

"You would do well to obey me, Ellie," he said, so menacingly that she arose, with a pathetic effort at dignity, and hobbled toward him.

"What is the matter?" he asked in alarm, noticing her slow progress. "Have you hurt yourself?"

"Certainly not," she replied, and put her full weight on her sore heel with a concealed grimace. It was only his anger that let her keep her composure. If he became sympathetic, she would be undone entirely.

Having gained his point, Claymore was much of a mind to mend the breach with his wife. He realized with every difficulty that arose that he loved Ellie more, and tried valiantly to talk her around. "It was all that waltzing at our wedding yesterday has raised a blister," he suggested playfully when he remarked that she was walking hesitantly. She glared.

"It was *you* who was doing all the waltzing," she reminded him. "You know I cannot waltz in public yet."

"You can now. You are a married woman. You see, there is another advantage you have forgotten."

"*Another* advantage?" she asked, the implication being that it, such as it was, was the sole one.

"I have brought the closed carriage," he pointed out, "so that we won't be recognized."

"Your crest is quite unknown, is it?" she asked, viewing his coat of arms emblazoned on the panel.

He could think of no reply, so he handed her in in silence. Once they were headed back to Claymore House, he regaled her with a description of the delightful summer that lay before them. "We will leave early this afternoon," he began enticingly. "The traveling carriage is all loaded and as soon as I have attended to a little business, we can begin our trip." He had decided he *must* buy a diamond, whatever his man of business said. "We'll cover about fifty miles today—spend the night at Basingstoke, and set out early next morning. We'll make it into Somerset before dark and have only forty miles to complete our journey home. We should arrive around noon next day. Mama will be back from Dorset by then, and be waiting for us."

"You said your mother would be moving into the Dower House," she reminded him, having a very natural desire not to share her domicile with this termagant.

"Yes, but she won't have moved yet, because she has been with Alice, you recall. She hasn't been home to get her things packed. Besides, she usually goes to Bath for six weeks in the summer, and will likely wait till she returns to make the move."

"Must we go to Bath, too?"

"Certainly not, if you don't want to. We'll stay at the Hall. We can take the *Stella Maris* out in the Channel. That's my yacht. Do you like boating?"

"I've never tried it."

"You're bound to like it."

"I expect I'll get seasick."

Ellie proved such a recalcitrant conversationalist that before they were halfway home Clay sank into silence. Try as he might, he could find no cause for this Turkish treatment he was receiving. Rex's urging that he get her a diamond seemed his only hope of bringing her around to humor before they left. Go downtown that very morning, before they leave, and buy one on credit. Serve his mother well if he sent her the bill—all *her* fault for not letting him have his own. Only natural a bride should be piqued at not getting an engagement ring, especially when her sister, marrying a squire's son, had such a whopper.

At home he accompanied Ellie into the Green Saloon. "I have to go out, but I'll be back within the hour. Why don't you speak to the housekeeper and tell her what you want done while we're away? I expect you'll want those sheets on the sofa and what not."

"She will *know* that," his wife informed him in a tone of withering contempt. "Have you ordered the shutters locked and the knocker removed?"

"They will know that, too," he replied, gritting his teeth and wondering what had happened to that shy little girl he had married.

"Are there any valuables to be taken with us?"

"No, the jewels and valuable things are kept at the Hall, and there will be Meecham and his wife here to keep an eye on what remains—the silver and so on, till we return."

"Where are you going?" Ellie asked.

"Out."

"I *know* that. I am not a complete simpleton. Where are you going out to?"

"I hope you're not going to be one of those pesky women who try to keep a fellow leg-shackled twenty-four hours a day," Clay said irritably. The ring was to be a surprise.

"You took it hard enough when *I* went out."

"That was different. And you're to stay *in* till I get back."

She narrowed her eyes at him, then sat down suddenly to take the weight off her foot. The poor unsuspecting housekeeper came wandering into this scene of marital conflict, and very nearly got her nose snipped off.

"How does it come you haven't got the furniture in Holland covers?" the young Marchioness asked in a haughty manner, to let her husband see she was not the least bit scared of his servants, as he probably thought.

"Why, we were waiting till you'd left, milady," the good woman said with trepidation. So much for their hope the new mistress would be a biddable one. A dead ringer for the old lady. She dashed off to inform her spouse of this piece of intelligence.

"You didn't have to snap at her," her husband chided when they were again alone. "The Meechams have been with us for years."

"Yes, and a soft touch they have had of it. This place is a mess." She peered about for dust and dirt and was soon rewarded, for with the master away for a month, the place was not in prime shape.

He regarded her closely, a frown on his youthful countenance. "Who was it told me you were the shy one?" he asked.

"Some poor misguided soul. Homberly perhaps."

"He was certainly misguided." She scowled at him, and he suddenly smiled at the ludicrousness of their plight. Here were they, not yet married twenty-four hours, and already into their first fight. He had been convinced that what he wanted was a shy little wife, like the old Ellie. He came suddenly to see he liked her, perhaps even better, in this new guise of jealous woman. How adorable she looked, with her little face formed into a pout. The thing was, he loved Ellie whoever or whatever she was. He came up to her and on impulse kissed the tip of her nose. "I will be back soon, wife, and I want you to have a breakfast waiting for me. Steak and potatoes, and no fobbing me off with bread and tea. We might as well get started for Somerset before noon, since we are up so early."

She sniffed in an injured fashion, but felt herself weakening against his smile. Claymore, sensing her sinking resolve, put his two arms around her. "I have been the greatest fool in captivity," he said. "But I'll tame you yet, woman." He regarded her in an anticipatory manner, laughed softly, and left.

Alone, Ellie took off her shoe, rubbed her heel, and cried. It was in this deplorable state that she was discovered by the housekeeper, coming with Holland covers to prepare the house for their remove.

"What is the matter, milady?" she asked.

Ellie lowered her head to hide her tears and replied, "I have hurt my foot. Perhaps you will be kind enough to have some warm water and a plaster taken to my room."

"Indeed I will, ma'am. Shall I call a doctor?"

"No, that is not necessary."

"I did wonder, milady, when Betty told me about the blood all over the floor—" She stopped suddenly at this revelation of servant gossip, and dashed off to do as she was bid.

Ellie climbed up the stairs and tended to her foot. With a rather cumbersome wad of cotton under her stocking, she went again downstairs to order steak and potatoes for her husband.

Her emotions were in a turmoil. She was embarrassed at having been brought home like a fractious schoolgirl, heartsore at Clay's cruel words at the hotel, yet not completely despondent. She didn't think his eyes would have sparkled so if he had not cared for her. She supposed he was trying, in his own way, to comfort her by discussing plans for the summer. If only it weren't for Gloria Golden. This naturally called to mind the hated room where the discovery of the lock of hair had taken place. She roamed around through halls and drawing rooms till she found it, and went like a homing pigeon to the desk.

The hair and the miniature were gone—she already knew that. A thorough probing of the remaining contents revealed a few remnants of the Rose's reign. There were discovered, besides a dried yellow rose, hiding under a Psalter, bills for eight dozen yellow roses, bearing various dates, bills for a fan and an ormolu hand mirror, and another scrap of poetry, having to do with violins singing sweeter than his love, and orchids having a perfume more rare. That was so unflattering she wondered whether it had not been composed for herself. Ah no, here was the proof in the last couplet:

> *My heart is ever Rose's, for no one else to share*
> *I send these dozen roses, to my own Rose so fair.*

She squeezed it into a ball in her angry passion and flung it to the floor. Then she walked into the hall, and upon encountering Mrs. Meecham, said stubbornly the master would like bread and tea for breakfast, in perhaps half an hour. She went to the breakfast room immediately herself and sat down. Over tea, she tapped the tables with her fingertips and considered how to wreak her revenge on him. A brief reconsideration of last night's plans proved unhelpful. Rex was now struck irrecoverably from her list of supporters. She had only her own wits to rely on. The half-hour came and went, making up the hour he had said he would be gone. Another half-hour dragged by, and still he did not come. He had left at eight; it was finally ten, and still she waited.

It was patently obvious he was doing this to annoy her. Showing her a lesson. He would "tame" her, would he, as though she were some wild animal! Teach her to comport herself like the Marchioness of Claymore. Well, she would

teach him a thing or two as well. She was interrupted
from these edifying thoughts by the arrival of a letter
from Lady Siderow, wishing her a bon voyage. She read
it, tapped her toe on the carpet, and came to a decision.
The bell was rung to summon Mrs. Meecham, who came
hopping.

"I have had a note from his lordship," Ellie lied affa-
bly. "He is detained and I shall go on without him."

Mrs. Meecham's bleary eyes bulged at such goings on.
"You'll never go alone to Somerset, ma'am," she had the
temerity to say.

"Certainly not. My Miss Pritchard will accompany
me." It seemed insufficient somehow, and she added a bit
of substantiating material. "The Dowager is fallen ill, you
see, and wishes me to come to her at once. His lordship
will follow at his leisure."

"But why would she want *you*? She doesn't even know
you!"

"That will soon be remedied. Will you have the carriage called, please? It is packed and ready to go. I daresay Claymore will be following on horseback, and catch
me up before noon."

"Oh. Oh, I see. Yes, very likely," Mrs. Meecham said,
yet it seemed odd to her. "Taken a bad spell, has she?"

"Yes, very bad," Ellie confirmed, and whipped past the
servant to tell the same lie to Miss Pritchard, whom she
feared would not accompany her if she knew the truth.
There seemed no great advantage to being a marchioness
after all, if one still had to make excuses to servants to get
them to do one's bidding.

Miss Pritchard had no reason to suspect all was not
well between the newlyweds. An early peep into Ellie's
room had shown her bed to be vacated. She could not
bring herself to look into the Marquis' room, but made
no doubt that was where they were. She later discovered
both bedrooms to have been deserted at an early hour,
but again had no reason to suppose they had not arisen
together. Gone for a ride in the park perhaps. Miss Ellie
liked a ride above anything. The broken glass on the floor
explained the few drops of blood on the carpet, and a

single question confirmed that it was Ellie who had stepped on it, with no fatal results. The only uncertainty to be cleared away was why they must go on ahead of Claymore. An ingenious thought having to do with the desired presence of the Dowager's solicitor from London for some last-minute changes to the will accounted for Claymore's delay, as well as buttressing the story of the Dowager's sad state of health. They were into their bonnets and pelisses and out to the carriage in a flash. Blackie, the groom, certainly thought it unusual to be setting out without the master, but then a mistress in the house was bound to be upsetting things, and he went, along with a footman, without a suspicion of involving himself in a plot. His new mistress found immediate favor by advising him to "spring them" as soon as he he hit the open road. He was more than happy to oblige and whip the team up to a spanking pace. If they *had* to have a woman around their necks, he was happy it wasn't the China doll, whom he well knew could stand nothing above a strict trot. This dame now was more like!

Ellie fretted during the trip. They had left around tenthirty. Till luncheon she was hopeful, but when still Claymore had not overtaken them by nightfall, she was beginning to panic. To have to go *alone* to meet the Dowager, bad as it was, was not the worst of it. Why had not her husband come?

Chapter Fifteen

Due to the early hour of Elinor's flight to Fenton's Hotel on the morning following her wedding, and the rapidity with which her husband had brought her home, he ended up downtown trying to buy her a diamond an hour before the shops were open. This naturally played havoc with his given schedule, so that while his wife awaited his return for breakfast, he was still cooling his heels outside Van Ark's Jewelry Shop. Even when he was finally admitted by an apologetic clerk, the purchase of the stone proved difficult. The matter of credit was no great thing—set up as soon as the proprietor arrived half an hour later, by which time the Marquis had examined every diamond in the shop and found them all too small, which is to say, smaller than Wanda's. A small tray of larger stones was brought forth from some hidden vault with great ceremony. They were examined, admired, and finally one, larger than all the others, was chosen. The proprietor had to explain in minute detail how this was a brilliant cut, with seventy-two rather than thirty-two facets because of its huge size. It was hefted, held to the light, admired once again, and then the jeweler inquired what setting was desired.

"Setting?" Claymore said. "Oh yes, I see what you mean: I want it put into a ring. Right away."

The jeweler rubbed his dry hands in glee and settled in for what he supposed would be a pleasant hour's discussion of claw settings and diamond clips and so on.

"Whatever you think best," Claymore said airily. "I want it right away."

"Certainly, my lord. It can be ready in a day or two."

"A day or two! No, no. I need it immediately."

"Oh, my lord! Do but consider. A stone of this beauty and value must have a setting worthy of it. It is unique. We will not want to destroy its appearance by an overly-hasty job of mounting. Leave it to me, and by tomorrow I shall have it set in a way that must please you."

"Waiting twenty-four hours does not please me," Claymore replied haughtily. "I'm late already. Haven't you got some setting you could stick it into?"

A hasty consideration that the mounting made for Lady Teasdale's sapphire was about the right size and could be duplicated before her return to London settled the matter. "As you wish, Lord Claymore. I will have it done immediately."

"Immediately," however, turned out to be a good half-hour, and when the ring was finally presented to the fuming Marquis, it was found to slide over his own finger with ease, thus ensuring that Ellie could wear it for a bracelet. Having already made himself two hours late, he could not return home with a ring that didn't fit. He paced up and down the shop, his watch in his hand, receiving frequent and impatient glances. Finally the thing was done, to no one's entire satisfaction.

Van Ark wiped his brow and said to his assistant, "What a fellow. Still, it pays to cater to these lords. He might buy any amount of stuff, now he sees how eager we are to help."

Claymore jammed the box into his pocket, and as he slammed the door of the shop he promised to himself, That's the last time I come to this old fool. Lord, he would keep me here all day while he talks of facets and brilliants, as though I were buying a dozen tiaras. He was pleased with the ring's appearance, though. Plenty bigger than Wanda's. He could hardly wait to slip it on Ellie's finger, and see her eyes light up.

When he came into his home, he went first into the Green Saloon, thinking she would have finished her breakfast long since. She was not there, so he went along to the breakfast room. All traces of food and dishes had vanished; the room was empty. Becoming slightly annoyed at the delay in finding her, he took the stairs to her room two at a time. Drawing the box from his pocket, he held it behind his back and tapped at her door. It was opened immediately, but it was Betty, the upstairs maid, who stood looking at him, and who very nearly received a little black box, for it was already being brought around.

"Is your mistress not in here?" he asked.

"Oh no, sir; her's gone long ago. I've got the bed made up and the clothes put away, the glass swept up and the dusting done and all. Should I be taking the bed curtains for a good airing while you're away?"

"Where is she?"

"Her's gone, milord."

"Gone where?" he asked, reining in his temper.

"As to that I couldn't say. Mrs. Meecham could be telling you, for she were talking to the mistress."

"Thank you." He turned on his heel and flung himself downstairs, trying hard to suppress that rising panic. "Gone" didn't mean anything. Gone from the room was all Betty meant. Besides, the girl was obviously a cretin. Mrs. Meecham would have the explanation.

She was in the hall waiting for him, having been apprised by her husband, the butler, that his lordship was home and would likely be wanting a bite before he set out for Somerset. "Where's my wife?" he asked, rather sharply.

She looked her surprise. "Why, she's left already, my lord. Set out an hour ago, as you requested."

The panic could no longer be damped down. "Set out for where?" he shouted.

"For Somerset, to go to your mother. How is she, my lord? Not too severe an attack, I trust?"

"What, was there word from Mama? Is she ill?"

The two exchanged blank stares. "I thought you knew . . . that is, she said . . . and there was a letter. . . ."

"From Mama?"

"I don't really know," Mrs. Meecham replied. "I thought she said it was from *you*. Her ladyship received a letter, then she told me that your mother had taken ill, and she was going on ahead, and you would ride after her and overtake her along the way. I assumed the letter was from yourself, giving her instructions. . . . But then, I have remarked she is very decisive. The letter may have been from the Hall, and she made the decision on her own, expecting me to tell you."

Claymore, somehow, did not think any such thing. "Do you think you might find the letter?" he asked, trying not to rip up at her.

"She was in the breakfast room at the time, and left the letter on the table as it happens, which I naturally did not open and read, but put it up on the side table. I'll get it for you."

His lordship had no such scruples about reading his wife's private correspondence. A glance was sufficient to inform him the whole thing was a hoax. "You're positive this is the same letter she received this morning?" he asked.

"Yes, and I do recall for *sure* now that she said it was from you, for she called you 'his lordship' and I was wondering before that how she'd refer to you, as 'his lordship' or 'my husband.' I thought it'd be 'his lordship' she'd say," she added in a knowing tone. "Not from you, eh?"

For a fraction of a second Claymore considered prevaricating to hide his wife's lie, but with Mrs. Meecham as his sole source of information, he decided she must be taken into his confidence. "No, not from me. She left half an hour ago you say. How did she go? What carriage I mean."

"Why, the traveling carriage, that was all packed and

ready to go. Took her Miss Pritchard with her, which
made it seem all right to me, for if she were sheering off
on you, I shouldn't think she'd take the loaded traveling
carriage, with your luggage on it, as well as her own."

"Blackie driving?"

"Yes, and Pottrell went along too, so she's safe at
least."

"It's not her physical safety I'm worried about," he
said.

"After her accident last night I thought maybe . . ."
She let it hang mutely. She was too experienced a retainer
to let the least degree of encroaching curiosity show, but
inside she was bursting to know what was afoot. So odd,
Claymore getting hitched all of a sudden to a young girl
none of them had ever heard of, though her connections
seemed decent enough. Odder still that *two* beds should
have been tossed the morning after their wedding night,
and them up and streaking out of the house at the crack
of dawn, not together either, whatever that blind Miss
Pritchard might think, or let on to think. As to the
shambles of milady's chamber with broken glass and
blood all over—well! And now this; bolted on him, plain
as the nose on your face. It looked black indeed. Anyone
who hadn't known the Marquis forever would be forgiven
for thinking he'd misused the poor girl, but that she did
not believe. Oh, he had the devil's own temper and would
say mean things when he got riled up, but as to laying a
hand on a lady, it was no such a thing. No, and a body
couldn't credit that the brass-faced young lady he'd married would put up with any bullying from him or anyone
else either. Still, he must have done something to set her
off in such a pelter.

Claymore was only half listening; the greater part of his
mind was occupied with figuring where the devil she'd
gone off to this time. "Accident?" he asked, as the word
finally penetrated. "What accident?"

"The broken glass in her room. And the blood all
over. . . ."

At this recital, all other preoccupations left him, and he

came to rigid attention. "What blood? How does it come I wasn't informed of this?"

"I thought you knew," Mrs. Meecham replied. "Betty said there was blood all over the carpet and the sheets. She got it cleaned up before I saw it. You must have noticed milady was limping."

"No! That is, I did notice—but it was only a very little, surely."

"She was crying with the pain, but wouldn't let me call the doctor."

"You should have called him," Claymore said, visions of his wife dragging around London, her foot all but severed from her leg, coming into his head.

"I wanted to, but she wouldn't have it. Well, I fancy you know she's not one to be told what to do."

"My wife is shy," he said. "Her abrupt manner is a result of shyness merely. You ought certainly to have called a doctor, Mrs. Meecham."

She did not take well to being charged with negligence, and bristled. "Too late now." She clamped her lips shut upon the deliverance of this platitude. She awaited instructions, but as Claymore fell into a daze of concentration, she spoke again. "What are we to do?"

"Bring me some wine," he said. "I'll be in the little parlor."

She could only stare. His wife cut to shreds and bleeding all over the place, lying herself blue and peeling off on him the very day after the wedding, and he orders himself up a bottle of wine. Loony. The man had taken leave of his senses. She'd better get the wine, or he might become violent.

This taking of wine was not quite so cavalier a gesture as she supposed. Claymore's mind was working furiously. It had many things to sort out, and he wished peace and quiet to do so. The little parlor was his thinking room. Chair tilted back, feet on the desk was his thinking posture, so that is how she found him a moment later when she brought the wine.

"Quite comfortable, my lord?" she asked in a voice of

deep sarcasm. Having known him since he was breeched, she dared say what other menials would not.

"Shut the door when you go," was her only reply.

Claymore poured a glass, retilted his chair to a dangerous angle, closed his eyes, and sipped the madeira. He had wanted port or claret. This dashed stuff was sickeningly sweet. So, she had gone again. Where to this time? Rex? Hardly, after her last encounter with him. Taking the traveling carriage indicated a longish trip. Not, he was certain, to Somerset. She'd said she wouldn't go, and he was fool enough to think she hadn't meant it. Making up that Banbury story about his mama being ill, and having got a note from himself was all fudge, to deceive the servants. Wanted them to tell him where she was gone, so clearly she had gone off in another direction entirely. He realized how little he knew his bride when he tried to think where she could possibly have gone. Doubtless she had many friends to whom she might run in this case, but he knew none of them. Only her family. If she hadn't gone to one of her own sisters or to her home in Sussex, he was sunk. He hadn't the faintest notion where to start looking. There were the Homberlys, too. She and Missie were chums. Might plan to join Mrs. Homberly and Missie at Bath; they were going to return there after the wedding. She knew his mama planned to go there though, and she went rigid at any mention of his mother. Probably not Bath. His possibilities quickly reduced themselves to three locations: the Siderows', Tamesons', or directly to her father's house in Sussex.

He cringed in his boots to show up at the Siderows' and ask if Ellie were there. God, what would they think? What could she possibly have told them to account for so unlikely a circumstance as leaving him the very day after their wedding? The embarrassment, the shame of it, made him writhe, and he felt a pronounced desire to have his wife's white throat between his hands. He was mad enough to kill her. This tender thought called to mind the accident of which Mrs. Meecham had spoken. But he brushed it aside—stepped on a bit of glass very likely. It wouldn't kill her. He took the ring box out of his pocket and admired the many-faceted stone, sitting majestically in Lady Teasdale's setting. She wouldn't have gone scooting off if she'd known this was waiting for her at home. Maybe he should have told her; he always seemed to do the wrong thing. No, dash it! Why should he have to bribe her with diamonds and riches? She was his wife. He opened the drawer and put the box inside the desk. He wouldn't even give it to her for a while, that'd show her.

No matter how long he kept putting it off in this fashion, there still remained before him the humiliating job of going to Ellie's family and confessing that she had left him. He heard some commotion in the hall, a deep voice, and he jumped up. Siderow must have brought her back! Thank God. He opened the door.

"Hallo, Clay," Rex said, and ambled in. "Thought I'd drop by and see how you and Ellie's making out. Got her back all right, did you?"

"Oh, it's only you," Clay said, disappointment visible on his drawn face.

"Who was you expecting?" Rex walked past Claymore and deposited his chubby frame in a chair. "I feel like the very devil today," he continued, rubbing his eyes. "Too much wine at your wedding, that's the trouble. That, and Ellie having me dragged out of bed in the middle of the night. Where is she? Off catching up on her rest, I expect. Don't call her on my account. Fancy she won't want to receive me for a while."

Clay slumped on to a sofa. "She's not here," he said.

"Good. Gone trotting over to Siderows' to say goodbye to the family, I suppose? I came at a good time. How come you didn't go with her? Ought to have, you know, Clay. Really ought to have gone the first time. No need to go every time, but today it seems to me you should have gone along for the looks of it."

"I don't know where she is. She's run off on me again," Clay admitted shamefacedly.

"Eh?" Rex jerked to attention, his little blue eyes fairly starting from their sockets. "You don't mean it! You haven't let her get away again. Deuce take it, Clay, you'll have to mount a guard on that girl. Gone again." He shook his head in amazement. "How come you ain't out bringing her back?"

"I don't know where she is."

"Well, dash it, man, you can't sit here slugging wine when your bride's out careering all over town for all you know, making a show of the pair of you. Don't know what you're thinking about, sitting here moping."

"I don't think she's careering around town. She took the traveling carriage, all loaded for a trip."

"Hmph, that's odd. Would she have gone on to Somerset, do you think?"

"No, I do not, though she would like me to think so."

"Must have gone home then. To Sussex, I mean. Nowhere else she could have gone, is there?"

"I guess not," Clay sighed. Just as the sigh was expiring, he was visited with a very face-saving idea. His eyes brightened, and he settled back, smiling fondly on his visitor. "Have a glass of wine, Rex," he said, and poured as he spoke.

"Huh, don't mind if I do. Madeira, eh? Sweet, sticky stuff. Never could stand it," he stated, just before tossing off the glass at a gulp.

"Yes, poor stuff," Clay agreed, refilling his glass. "Do you know, Rex, I am glad you came by. You're the very chap to help me out a little."

"Any time. Always glad to oblige a friend," he said, sipping on the much-maligned madeira with apparent relish. "What can I do for you?"

"I want to make sure my wife is not with her family before I set out in pursuit. Perhaps you would be so kind as to call at the Siderows'—her parents and Wanda are staying there, too—and see if she is there. If she's not, drop by the Tamesons' and see if she is by any chance with them."

"All right. I'll do that. Come back here and let you know."

"Thank you, Rex. Oh, and by the way, there is no point in giving them a fright. Don't say you've been here first, or mention anything about her disappearance."

"Oh, so that's why you don't want to go yourself?

Can't say I blame you. Must be a lowering thing to be so repulsive your wife can't stand one night with you. I won't say a word. Trust me. Can't undertake to bring Ellie back, though. She wouldn't come with me after this morning."

"I'm not asking that. Just let me know if she's there. You'd better get right along."

"Ain't finished this rotten wine yet."

"Leave it."

"Huh? What's the rush? Didn't see *you* bestirring yourself to find her. You know what, Clay, I think Ellie might have a point. You *do* use people." On this defiant note he arose, finished the wine, and stomped from the room, feeling he had put Claymore in his place, for once.

Neither chastened nor repentant, Claymore went to the door with him, dictating orders all the way. "Don't sit around chatting for half an hour, Rex, or stop for wine. Just nip in smartly and find out if she's there, without letting on she's gone. Can you remember all that?"

"Ain't a complete dunce," Rex replied. "Course I can. First Siderows', then Tamesons'. Far as that goes, Tamesons' is a waste of time. She won't be there. Don't care for Caroline above half. It'll be Siderows', or she's dashed straight off to Sussex."

"Go, anyway, just to be sure."

"All right, all right. Your own fault. Don't see why you couldn't have got the poor soul a diamond ring."

"Hurry!"

"I'm going!"

He went, finally. Claymore returned to his little parlor, but found himself unable to sit still, or to think coherently. Either she was there, with Joan or Caroline, or she was not. He forced himself to concentrate. All right, so if she was there, he'd have to go, tail between his legs, and get her. They'd set out for Somerset immediately, without even waiting to hire a guard. If she wasn't there— Siderows' or Tamesons'—he'd assume she'd gone directly to Sussex, and have to go after her. He'd take his curricle. They might enjoy driving in the open carriage if the good weather held up. Why were these irrelevant thoughts intruding at a time like this? Images of himself and Ellie, cutting along in the curricle with the sun in their faces and the wind in their hair. He recalled his curricle ride with Wanda, that fiasco that had turned him against her entirely, though he hadn't realized it at the time. He had never ridden with Ellie—never done anything with her. And Rex said she was a bruising rider, too. Their curricle was replaced, in his mind, by a pair of bays, and they were dashing through fields, side by side, over hedges and ditches. Oh damnit, why couldn't he concentrate? He had to get her back.

All right—one way or the other, he'd be traveling. Get ready then. His valet would have a light traveling case packed. Lord, he hadn't even shaved, in his mad morning's excitement. He dashed up to his room, made his preparations, got some money from the safe in the study, and was just coming into the hall when Homberly was admitted again.

"In here," Clay said, and hustled Rex into privacy before he opened his budget.

"She ain't there," Rex said, coming right to the point for once. "Went to Siderows' and Tamesons', and she ain't with either one. Hasn't been there. Had my groom take a look around the stables, too, in case they was lying for her, and there was no sign of your carriage, so she ain't there."

"Sussex then. I'd better get going."

"I wonder. . . ." Homberly assumed his wise face, lips pursed, eyes narrowed.

"What, have you thought of something?"

"Thing is, Clay, I don't see Ellie going back home. Besides her mama cutting up stiff—which she *would*, you know—there'd be Wanda's taunting to put up with. All I can say is, she must have been awful desperate to go pitching herself into that cauldron."

"But where else could she be?"

"Your place. Somerset."

"No, I'm convinced she's not gone there. She always pokered up at any mention of my mother. Besides, she's *left* me; she wouldn't go to *my* house, would she?"

"No, but I can't see her going to hers either. She was always wonderful close with my sister. Used to talk of going on the stage together. Was going to pretend they was sisters. Just foolish child's talk, of course, but . . ."

"You are not seriously saying you think my wife plans to go on the stage!"

"No, but she might have gone to Bath with Mama and Missie. They left about an hour ago, before I came here. I was there to see 'em off."

"Well, was my wife with them?"

"No. No, I'd have told you if she was, but she might have been planning to meet 'em along the way."

"I don't think so. Mama will be going there. I told you, my wife is afraid of her."

Rex was frowning at Claymore, an intent spark in his blue eyes. "That's three times you've said it inside of a minute."

"Said what?"

"*My wife.*"

"Well, what of it? We are discussing my wife; why should I not use her name?"

"You never do, though, use her name. You always say 'my wife.' Slides off your tongue as easy as if you'd been married a decade. I should think it'd take you a while to get used to it."

"No, I am used to it already." He stood a moment considering this speech. He was not at all used to it, of course; how could he be when to all intents and purposes he was not married, did not have a wife? It was only the frequent and repeated uttering of the mystical words "my wife" that brought any feeling of reality to that charade that had been performed at St. George's.

"It gives the impression you think of Ellie as a *thing*," Rex charged. He marveled that this wonderful insight had somehow occurred to him, and added, "Just a thing, like a horse or a carriage. Something to *use.*"

"That is the second time today you have accused me of using people," Clay fired up. "I can assure you I have not used *my wife* as a *thing.*"

"You've used her bad anyway, or she wouldn't have

left you. I begin to regret I ever called you to come and get her this morning. Tell me truthfully, now, Clay, why did she go? I won't tell a soul, but I feel it's my fault she married you, for it was me put the notion into your head."

"I don't know," Clay said, and clamped his jaws shut.

"Seems hard you didn't even get her a diamond ring, Clay, with all the jewels you've got locked up in a box somewhere. Everyone knows it. Shows a lack of respect, of interest in Ellie." He waited for some response, but the locked jaws didn't budge an iota. "*I* think she's hurt. Thinks you don't care for her a jot. If that's the case, you shouldn't have married her." Rex was sure this would bring some response, possibly even physical, but still Clay stood with his mouth shut and his tongue between his teeth.

"Didn't even sign your letters 'Love' or a thing, after all the warm stuff you scribbled off to the Rose."

At last he got his response. "My w—Ellie doesn't know what I wrote to Rose, and how does it come that you know what I wrote to Ellie?"

"She told me, this morning. Bawling her eyes out, too. She's jealous of the Rose, Clay. If you ever hope to get this marriage off the ground, you're going to have to explain to her you're all through with the Rose. Even if you don't love Ellie, you owe it to her—"

"Of course I love her. Why do you think I'm half distracted with worry! Rex, I can see you've made some sort of a botch of this morning."

"*I* made a botch of it! Well, if that don't beat the Dutch! *You're* the one made a botch of it. Seems to me something happened last night! You did something stupid, Clay. Don't know what it was, maybe it's none of my business, but *something* turned her sour between the time she married you and this morning, when she came limping into the hotel. You didn't—you didn't *beat* her, did you? She denied it, but then she would, I suppose, for the disgrace of it. It's been preying on my mind, thinking I led that poor girl on to marry a beater. She was limping something awful when she came in, which is why I mention the beating."

"No, she cut her foot on a broken wine glass. The limp, Rex, surely it was not at all pronounced. I was hardly aware of it."

"Daresay *you* was hardly looking. It was very noticeable. Who smashed the glass?"

"That was an accident." Clay waved it away with a fluttering hand.

"Drunk, was you?"

"Certainly not."

" 'Cause if you *was*, daresay you might have got carried away and pounced on her. Scare the wits out of a shy girl like Ellie."

"No, there was nothing like that."

"You must have been foxed, Clay. What she said—well, there was no other way of reading it, though, of course, she couldn't come right out and say what she meant. Said, though, that—well, I don't remember word for word, but said you proved you didn't love her. Yes, and you was talking about Rose in your sleep, too. Should think *anyone'd* know better than that."

"But we weren't even in the same room," Clay said, and immediately the words were out he realized the chasm at whose brink he hovered.

"Eh?" A sapient blue eye was fixed on him.

"I mean, for *sleeping*—and if you tell a single soul, I'll break your face," he added, plunging with two feet into the abyss.

"Well, if you ain't a slow top. The Marquis of Claymore!" Rex went off into uncontrollable whoops of laughter, till the tears were trickling down his face. Between gasps for breath he exploded, "Separate rooms . . . said you didn't love her . . . no wonder . . . gudgeon . . . and *I* thought you'd *pounced*."

"Stop laughing like a hyena and get out of here."

"Didn't even creep up like a pussycat." Again he was off into chuckles.

"That's a lie! If you breathe one word of this, Homberly, I'll call you out."

"The fellow doth protest too much, methinks."

"Shakespeare! You're quoting Shakespeare at me," Clay said, incredulous. "I don't believe it. At a time like this. My best friend, sitting there quoting Shakespeare at me while I am in the worst toil of my life."

"Sorry." Rex sobered up immediately at the seriousness of the charge. "No offense. Didn't know it was Shakespeare. Heard St. Ives say it t'other night. Thought it had a pretty grand ring to it. Might have known it wasn't his own." Unfortunately, he again fell into titters.

"You'd better go, Rex. I'm setting out for Wanderley's place in Sussex right away."

"I'm off to Bath then. Tell you what, Clay, you won't find Ellie at home. Know that as well as I'm standing here. I'll keep an eye out along the way to Bath. Inquire at the toll gates if your carriage has been through. Won't seem anything odd in that, for anyone who recognizes me will know we're close as peas in a pod. If I discover Ellie's gone that way, I'll let you know. Where should I direct a message?"

Clay listened with some interest to this opinion. Not that Rex had so much as a suspicion of a brain, but he *did* know Ellie pretty well. "You can send word here. If she's not at her home, I'll come back here, I guess."

"All right then. If I hear anything at all I'll write to you here."

"Yes, thanks, Rex."

"Sorry about—you know—all that laughing and Shakespeare and so on. Fair floored me, though, to think of you being so slow." His only absolution was a snort and a sheepish look from his friend. Rallied by these, Rex said, "Say, Clay, why don't you come along to Bath with me? Just like old times. We might race—"

"Rex, be sensible. I can't go racing with you."

"No, no. Forgot. Your wife, of course. Well, I'm off then. Happy hunting and all that." He went to the door, chuckling into his collar stealthily. "Pussycat by Jove, Marquis of Claymore. Clunch."

Mrs. Meecham accosted Claymore as he was gathering

up what he needed for his trip, and inquired whether he wouldn't have a bite before leaving.

"No, I am in a great hurry," he said. It was well past noon, though, and he was suddenly aware of violent pangs of hunger from his long fast.

"You have to eat," she pointed out. "Might save yourself time if you did it here. There's cold meat ready and some soup."

"Well, if it's ready," Clay allowed, and was taken to the breakfast room, while Mrs. Meecham poured consoling words regarding "keeping up his strength" over his head, and hot coffee into his cup. At last, his body fed with food and his mind with worries, he left for Sussex.

Chapter Sixteen

He wasted the rest of that day in a fruitless trip to Sussex, was forced to stay overnight at an inn to rest his horses, and arrived back in London the next day around noon, no further ahead than when he had left. She was with none of her relatives, neither the Siderows, the Tamesons, nor her own mother. She must have gone to Bath after all with the Homberlys, as Rex had suggested. Wait to hear from Rex then. He waited the remainder of that day and the whole interminable night with no word from Rex. By morning he could wait no longer, but had his curricle hitched up to go to Bath himself.

He kept a spare team stabled at Reading, so he was at least sure of good horses for the remainder of the trip. He made it without hindrance to Gay Street, where Mrs. Homberly annually rented lodgings for eight weeks, then found he hadn't the heart to face yet another batch of people and lie again. He headed to the York Inn, but realized he was likely to meet a dozen people he knew there, and drove around instead to the Pelican, a respectable place, but not quite of the first stare. He dispatched his valet, who did not take well to becoming a general factotum, with a note to Gay Street. It was while he was refreshing himself with a bottle in his suite that Rex came in.

"What in the world are you doing *here*?" he asked. "She ain't here, nor hasn't come this way, for I've asked everyone. Slyly, of course. Very slyly."

So great was his shock that Clay didn't even take him up on this ominous addendum. "What do you mean, she's not here?" he asked, turning a shade paler.

"Told you I'd drop you a line if I heard anything. Well, I didn't. Hear anything I mean, or drop a line either, far as that goes. So why are you here?"

"She must be here."

"No, she ain't."

"But she is not at her father's either."

"Told you she wouldn't go there."

"You said she would be here."

"Well, what I said was if she hadn't gone to your mama, she might be here."

"She is most certainly not there."

"Certainly not here either," Rex advised, and flopped into a chair, from where he could reach the bottle and a glass, both of which he put to use without further ado.

Clay began beating a tattoo on his knee with his closed fist. "She is ill," he said. "Got an infection in that cut. That is what must have happened." He closed his lips and frowned.

"No reason to go thinking that," his friend reassured him. "No saying she got one of them terrible infections. Though, of course, there's no place likelier than a foot to get one in, what with having to put on an old sock, and walk on it and all. And it was certainly a terrible cut; the poor soul could hardly stand up when I last saw her. Still, that's not to say she did get an infection like my old Uncle Harry. Ever tell you about him? Let a little scratch go—on his foot, just like Ellie—and before a week was out, it had puffed up like a balloon, right up past the ankle. They thought they'd have to cut it off, the foot, but he was too scared, so he just let it go on swelling. Can't say I blame him."

Claymore, visibly shaken, listened in horror to this recital. "Well, what happened?" he asked sharply.

"Nothing. It went down after a while. He lived for a couple of years, and even got around a little with the help of a stick. Never could stand the pressure of a boot on it again, though. Had a kind of a loose sock thing made up out of a cowhide, so he could go out in the winter, so you needn't worry she's *died*, or anything of that sort."

"No, she can't be dead," Clay agreed. This lugubrious possibility went beyond the worst he had envisioned thus far.

"I'll tell you what," Rex said suddenly, and from the settling on his features of his wise look, Clay came to attention, trying manfully to cast off the mental image of his bride, laid out on a slab with her foot inflated like a balloon.

"What is it?"

"Just remembered, you have *the gift*."

"Yes, I have it right here," Clay replied, patting the pocket where he had stowed the diamond ring for safe keeping.

"What, in your pocket?" Rex asked, startled.

"Yes, I am carrying it on me for safety's sake."

"I thought you'd keep it in your head."

"My head?" Clay asked, dumbfounded. "Where, stuck through my nose, or wound through my hair perhaps?"

"Inside your head, of course."

"I take it the gift we are discussing is not the diamond ring."

"No, did you finally break down and take one out of your box?"

"I bought her a new one." He took it out and showed it to Rex. "It's bigger than Wanda's," he could not resist adding.

"Very nice. Couldn't bear to part with one of the heirlooms, eh? Shouldn't let yourself get so attached to them bits of glass and metal, Clay. They're only things. The gift I meant, though, was a different one. Don't you remember, the first time we went to Wanderleys, you said you had the gift, and could hear your love calling to you, so you knew which room she was in? And you was right, too, only it was Ellie that was calling, and not Wanda, as we thought at the time."

"Have you taken leave of your senses?"

"No, but I think you have. Remember distinctly you heard Ellie calling to you over the miles, or maybe it was feet. Anyway, you said you had the gift. And you have, for it worked. Well, thing to do, use the gift. Have a chat with it and find out where she is."

"I haven't the least idea what you are talking about. I never heard anything so stupid in my life."

"Thought so at the time, but it worked. No denying it was Ellie that was calling you, for she came to the window right away, and started hollering down to us to shut up."

"Did she?" Claymore asked, and rather thought he did recall some such event. The idea of the gift, however, was disdained. Upon repeated urgings from Rex he did at last lie down, close his eyes and concentrate, but his gift refused to give him the least help, now that he needed it.

"You want my advice," Rex said, "go home. Got to be there. No place else she could be."

"Home to the Hall you mean?"

"Yes, got to be there."

"But if she ain't there, Rex—and really, you know, I don't think she would go and tackle Mama all alone— well, where am I? All I have done is give my mother a club to hold over my head. You know how it would please her for me to have made a muddle of the whole thing. I'd never hear the end of it, nor would Ellie."

Rex began to shift uncomfortably in his chair, fearing he would be chosen as the intermediary. This excellent idea did not, in fact, occur to Claymore till Rex began wriggling. The movement was a signal that his guest was uncomfortable, and before many moments went by, Clay knew why, and wondered that it had not occurred to him sooner.

"I suppose you wouldn't . . ." Clay began coaxingly.

"Rather not," Rex replied promptly. "Thing is, don't think your mama has much of an opinion of me."

"No, really, she often—mentioned you."

"Might's well go yourself. Save time. Mean to say, if she *is* there, I have to go, and come back, and then you set out and go. It's forty miles one way. That's what—a hundred and twenty miles—when forty will do it if you just buck up and go yourself."

Clay considered this. "Very true. I can see I must go, too."

"There's no 'too' about it. No point my going if you're going."

"Just to make the actual knock at the door, you know. I could wait half a mile down the road, and you could come back and let me know what's up."

"Dash it if you ain't a chicken-hearted fellow. Afraid to go to your own mother's—in fact, *your own* house—and knock at the door, to see your own wife. I'm surprised at you, Clay. Thought you had more gumption. Though I ought to have known after your wedding. . . ."

"Rex, you know I would be there in a flash if I thought there were any chance that she *is* there. But I fear she's not, and I don't see any point in giving Mama the satisfaction of ragging at me."

"Seems a perfectly bird-witted way to go about it, if you want *my* opinion."

"But I don't, Rex. I only want your help. Will you come?"

"Supposed to be taking Missie and Mama to the Lower Rooms tonight. Cotillion Ball. Daresay Miss Simpson will be there."

"Rex, if you will help me, I'll *buy* Miss Simpson for you."

"No, dash it, keep your damn purse in your pocket. It's your buying Ellie that has got us into this pickle. Besides, Miss Simpson ain't for sale. Ain't a bit like that. Thing is, Clay, she's got this guardsman trailing after her everywhere she goes. Tall as a lamppost, way up past her head. Handsome, too. He'll be at the Cotillion Ball."

"There is nothing like absence to whet the appetite," Clay began persuasively, and added many suggestions having to do with Miss Simpson keeping an eager eye on the door the whole night long, waiting for him to enter. Rex was half convinced, being very gullible, that she would be his for the asking by morning, if only he could drum up the fortitude to stay away for one night. From this state it was easy to coerce him into going to Somerset, for he knew himself too well to think he could stay away from the ball if he were in town.

Then after all this had been gone through, it was decided that they would leave in the morning, it being already dark out, and Rex decided he might as well go to the ball after all. Might hear something about Ellie.

True enough, he heard many rumors, of so strange and varied a nature that he was quite at a loss to explain them to his friend the next morning, when he presented himself at nine o'clock at the Pelican to go with Clay to the Hall. "Did my best to squash 'em," he said, which hit his friend's ear with an ominous note.

"What did you say?"

"Told that Banbury tale about your mama being sick, and said you came from London by way of Bath to pick her up some medicine from her apothecary here. Anyway, there's such a batch of different stories going around, no one knows what to think. If you could just get Ellie back and show up here with her a few times, the world would conclude it was all a tempest in a teapot, and forget all about it."

"Yes, that is what I must do. Let's go."

Chapter Seventeen

The bride's dilatory flight to the Hall was prolonged with as many stops for tea and even sightseeing as she dared to suggest, or could cajole her companion into accepting. While she dallied along, Rex arrived at Claymore Hall, where he was informed in a very civil manner that Claymore and his bride had not yet arrived, but were expected that very day. They were already a day late. He was even invited to attend their arrival, for the Dowager was bored and restless with the waiting, and thought this booby entertaining enough in his way. Having received no orders from his general as to how to proceed under this circumstance, Rex accepted the offer and sat down with the Dowager to a cold luncheon, while Clay walked his horses for over an hour, fuming with frustration and impatience.

The Dowager queried in vain as to how the wedding had gone off, but could discover only that it was "a pretty good do."

"I expected they would be here by now," she said. "Clay thought they would arrive last night, and he is usually a few hours earlier than he says, but perhaps his wife does not like to travel at his speed."

"You're out there. Ellie likes a good hot pace."

"Does she indeed? They are well suited then in that area. I wonder if they did not decide to come by way of Bath. The road is better, and they might have stopped to have the servants get the house ready for my remove."

"No, he didn't."

"Ah, you have been to Laura Place then?" she asked, rather curious.

"No. No, that is, uh, sent a note around, you see."

Now why was he coloring up like a schoolboy caught with his hand in the cookie jar? "And they are not there?"

"No, she—they ain't there. Already told you," he added in a surly tone.

The Dowager's sharp eyes narrowed, and her heart quickened with the thrill of the scent. She considered her strategy carefully, but when she spoke, it was in a nonchalant manner. "I wonder where she can be," she said. With her eye on her plate, she still discerned the rapid movement of his head, jerking to sharp attention. So that was it—*she* wasn't at Bath.

"Eh?" he asked suspiciously. Deuce take it, did the woman know already?

"I said, if she is not at Bath, and she is not here, I wonder where she can be."

"*They* ain't at Bath you mean," he challenged.

She regretted that she had flushed her quarry too soon, but smiled agreeably. "*They,* of course, is what I meant."

He breathed a perfectly audible sigh of relief. "Thought that was what you meant."

"To be sure. What else could I mean?"

"Heh, heh. What else indeed? As though she would have gone into a snit and left him, when they are only married a few days."

"It is surprising, though. Sometimes trouble develops the very first day," she suggested in a leading fashion.

"Or night," he agreed with feeling, and bit his lip in a cunning effort to stop from laughing aloud. His shaking shoulders told the secret, and from then on this uneven match between a bantling and a game cock was over.

"Oh, naughty Mr. Homberly," she chided gaily. So that was it!

"Only funning," he assured her. "No trouble between them two anyway. Nothing of the sort. Daresay if he'd given her a diamond ring as he ought—not that Ellie is a *grasping* sort, but it looked odd, you know, with Wanda sporting a diamond as big as a hen's egg."

"He ought certainly to have given her the Claymore diamond," she agreed, with shameless calm.

"Told him so. Dam—dashed silly to go buying another diamond when he has a boxful of them already. You can grow too attached to *things*."

This home truth glanced off her. "So he *did* buy a ring for her. And was she pleased with it?"

"She hasn't seen it . . . *hadn't* seen it, till—er—till after the wedding." He grabbed his glass and drank deeply. The woman was worse than a dashed Spanish Inquisitor.

"I daresay she will like it. Women always do like diamonds. Is it a good stone?"

"Oh yes. Pretty big, you know. Bigger than Wanda's. Ought to do the trick."

"Yes, that should patch things up," she said offhandedly, and looked out of the corner of her eye as his head slewed around to regard her.

"Do you know, I've just remembered something," he said, rising to his feet halfway through his omelette and cold cuts. "I'm late for a very important appointment. Just remembered it this very minute. Pray, don't interrupt your meal. I can see myself out."

The Dowager said, "Give Claymore my regards."

"Yes, I'll tell him. That is, when I see him, though *you* will likely see him before I do. They ain't at Bath, so you'll see them first."

"Do you think so?" she asked innocently. He glared at her, gave a stiff bow, and wobbled from the room.

The account he gave his waiting friend was garbled at best, but the one fact of real importance was clear enough: "Ellie ain't there."

"I knew she wouldn't be," Clay said, crestfallen.

"Well, it seems dashed odd to me, and why was your

mother making sly remarks about trouble developing the first day after being married, and where could 'she' be, if she don't know something?"

"Someone has been running to her with stories, I suppose. She is not so far from Bath, and the tale is rampant there."

"Anyway, Ellie ain't there, for I took a good look about your stables, and there were none of your London bloods, and nor the traveling carriage. Your loose boxes are in a terrible state, Clay. Boards falling off them and what not. Ought to get 'em attended to. If some stupid groom goes shoving your grays into them they'll tear their sides off."

"I mean to attend to it this summer. Did you see my Barb?"

"Yes, and they've been overfeeding him, and not giving him enough exercise. Didn't like the looks of him at all. Fat as a flawn."

"I paid five hundred pounds for him," Clay said wearily. With these two minor worries added to his load, Clay turned his curricle back to Bath, for lack of any more reasonable plan occurring to him.

Forewarned by Homberly's visit that all was not well with the newlyweds, the Dowager was not so surprised as she would otherwise have been when her daughter-in-law came trailing in alone, except for her servants, late that same afternoon. The terror of this, her first meeting with the dragon, lent a sparkle to her eyes, and a flush to her cheeks, that might have been taken for good health, or perhaps a raging fever. Certainly it added something in the way of beauty. The Dowager traced a learned eye over the nicely-tailored blue traveling suit, the neat bonnet with enough trim for fashion, and not too much for a young lady, and was satisfied that Mrs. Wanderley had got the girl rigged up in style. The face was good, especially the gray eyes, and what could be seen of the raven hair. Always liked those pitch black curls, perhaps because she had had an unsightly ginger colored mop herself, now turned to an equally unsightly buttery yellow. Not nice bluish-white, as some lucky dames acquired in old age. These few advantages of appearance would have been outweighed by malice had the bride come waltzing in, simpering and smiling on the arm of a doting husband, but to have to face the ignominy of coming *alone* on her honeymoon, deserted by that clod of a Clay, was something to endear her to her new mama.

Scared stiff, and on the verge of tears, poor thing. "Welcome home, Daughter," the Dowager said, wearing the merriest smile imaginable. She even came forward and pecked Daughter's cheek. "I have been waiting this *age* for you to come."

"I had to make a slight delay in my journey, ma'am, for I was feeling rather poorly this morning."

"Ah, travel is a curse. I have given it up entirely, but for my yearly jaunt to Bath. Come over and let us be comfortable on the sofa. Why has Rigmore not taken your things? Rigmore! Rigmore, I say. Come here and remove my daughter's hat and, oh, you are not wearing a pelisse. July, of course. How quickly it has come round." She chattered on, making her guest feel at home till tea was brought in.

For quite ten minutes they discussed the roads, the weather, even the wedding, without either of them mentioning the rather prominent fact that the groom was absent from this meeting. At length, it was Ellie who broached the ticklish subject, thinking her hostess believed him to be delayed at the stables.

"Claymore did not come with me," she said, and licked her bottom lip in a nervous gesture, waiting for the boom to fall.

"No, I thought as much," was the perfectly civil reply, as though it were the natural thing. "Had a call from Homberly this morning, seeing what he could find out. Sent by my son, I have not the least doubt. They are cooped up in Bath, I believe."

"Bath! But why should he be there? I told him I was coming straight to you."

"Did you indeed? I rather supposed you had dashed off without letting him know where you'd gone." This threw the Dowager off her stride, though she tried her best not

to show it. She assumed the nervous bride had bolted after her first encounter with her conjugal duties, and not
solely because she had not received a diamond ring. She
noticed Ellie wasn't wearing the pearl, nor the new diamond either—hadn't even *seen* it no doubt, but a cheap
little band of diamonds that you'd need a microscope to
see.

"Oh no, I told him—that is, I left word with the servants where I was headed, and thought he would overtake
me long before this."

"Never thought you'd have to tackle me alone, eh?"
the Dowager said bluntly, and with a delighted cackle.

Ellie opened her mouth to contradict this bald statement, but a nervous laugh escaped her, and as it did not
appear to offend her new mama, she confessed shyly that
she had been a little nervous of the encounter.

"Well, there's no need to be nervous, my dear, for I
won't eat you. I wasn't half sure how I would like you, to
tell the truth, for that fool of a Homberly as well as said
you was not elegant, but I see he got it all wrong, as I
might have expected. You'll do very well for Clay, and
what we must do now is *find* him. I won't be pestering
you with questions as to why you left. Private is private,
though I would just hint that you oughtn't to make a
habit of it, for it would only set tongues wagging, and that
I am not fond of."

"Joan, my sister—Lady Siderow, you know—has already told me so, only I never thought he would not come
after me. I had no thought of making a scandal."

"You haven't taken him in dislike then?"

"Oh no! No indeed. It was merely a lovers' quarrel."

This set the Dowager's mind at rest considerably. Her
earlier suspicions that Claymore did in fact love the girl
had been bolstered at seeing her. He was always soft on
those big-eyed dark-haired girls. If the whole thing were
only a plain lovers' quarrel, it might be settled in two
minutes by throwing them together in private. But why
had Clay not followed her? Here was something odd. Her
suspicions flew to Homberly. If Clay had used *him* for a

confidant—and God help them, mentor!—anything might
have happened.

"I'll have to get a message to him," she decided.

"And you think he is at Bath? I cannot imagine what
led him to go there. He must have known I would not be
at *Bath*."

"Yes, particularly as you told him you were coming
here."

"Even if he didn't think I was coming here, I should
think he would have gone home—to my papa's home, I
mean—or to Lady Siderow's, but not to Bath."

"Do you have some reason to suppose he would think
you *weren't* coming here, when that is the word you left
him?"

"Well," she confessed, "he knew I was a trifle nervous
of meeting you."

"Scared the wits out of you, did he?" she asked with
satisfaction.

"No indeed, it was Joan—oh, not actually *scared* me,
you know. . . ."

"I see." The Dowager nodded. So Lady Siderow had
stuck her oar in, had she? Well, perhaps she had a bit of
a reputation in London. Never one to keep her tongue between her teeth. She understood her son enough to know
he would have warned Ellie to expect a chilly reception.
He underestimated the girl, though. More bottom than
he'd given her credit for. He, obviously, had overesti-
mated the quality of their little quarrel, and supposed Ellie had flown to hide herself. But still, why Bath? Was it
possible Homberly had come from London, and not from
Bath at all? Yet he had stated quite positively that Ellie
was not in Bath. He was such a ninny, he would have let
something slip if he had come from London. She still
placed her hopes on Clay's being at Bath. Lord, known
by every quiz in town, too, and making a cake of himself
by mooning around, very likely.

"Tell me," she went on, "though I promised I wouldn't
pry, and don't intend to, what excuse did you make to the
servants to account for your leaving alone, before your

husband? I should think Meecham would have thrown a rub in your way."

"I'm afraid I dragged your name into it, ma'am," Ellie admitted, with a fearful glance. "I hope you are not dreadfully angry with me, but I said you were fallen suddenly ill, and I was going on ahead to save time, as Claymore had to see your solicitor before he left, and could easily overtake me."

"So that is the story that is around London by now, is it? Princess Esterhazy will have me in my coffin with the lid nailed down, and she dancing on top of it, if I know anything. She was always jealous of me, silly creature. At least it accounts for your being seen leaving the city alone, as I make no doubt you were."

"I don't *think* anyone recognized me."

"Would have recognized the carriage; everyone knows the crest," she was told. "Besides, you were two nights on the road. It is too much to hope you were not seen and recognized. We'd better wait and hear what lies Clay's spinning before we settle on a story to tell the world."

It was a new experience for Ellie to find herself a subject for discussion by the "world," by which, of course, the Dowager meant only polite London society. "I still can't imagine why he went to *Bath*. I fear he cannot be looking for me at all." She looked so woebegone that her hostess feared she would turn into a watering pot in a moment, and sought to reassure her.

"And didn't send that great lummox of a Rex Homberly here to find you either, I suppose? No, my dear, for some reason he took into his empty head that you were at Bath, and that is where he has gone looking for you. I wonder if Meecham got it mixed up, and told him I was taken ill at Bath. I do go there every year, and am usually there before this. No doubt that is what has happened."

"No, for *Claymore* knew you were here. He said you would be here waiting for us."

"Yes, that's true. I'd forgotten that."

"He is not looking for me at all. I shouldn't be surprised to hear he is gone to Brighton."

"No indeed. He never goes there. He is much too young for Prinny's set you must know."

"*That* was not the set I had in mind."

"Was it some particular set you had in mind, then?"

"I was thinking of Everleigh's set," Ellie replied, being unaware that her mama-in-law knew all about Clay's infatuation with the Rose.

"No, he's not pining over *her*," she replied. "I know my son well enough to know he had forgotten her by the time he offered for you. I couldn't get a rise out of him at all with her name."

"Oh!" Ellie gasped involuntarily at this maternal show of mischief.

"Wicked, ain't I? Still, I am not a fool, like my son, and will send for him at once."

Ellie repeated once more that she could not think Clay was at Bath. The Dowager charitably assumed she was tired, and not really witless, and suggested a lie-down before dinner. Her guest was only too happy to comply. To add to her uneasiness, she had to listen to Pritchard's worries about what was keeping his lordship while she disrobed. She offered no idea at all. Some other story would have to be woven to fob her off. Bad enough that the Dowager was showing not the least sign of being ailing, and a near miraculous cure invented for her. "I'm burnt to the socket, Miss Pritchard," she said, and escaped to her bed.

Sleep did not come, nor even much rest. Half of Elinor's perturbations were banished at having survived the ordeal of meeting the Dowager. Not so bad as she feared, yet a sadly unfeeling parent, when compared with her own dear papa. And mama, too, she added dutifully. She almost seemed *happy* at the difficulties her son was confronting, and hadn't asked about him at all as regards health or happiness. A strange, protective feeling swelled in her breast at this poor treatment her husband was receiving. And *where was he?* Surely not at Bath. There was no conceivable reason for him to be there; none having to do with her, at least. She enjoyed a good spurt of tears, but stopped in time to descend to dinner without the disgrace of red eyes.

Ellie was not looking forward to a formal dinner *tête-à-tête* with the old Marchioness, but like their first meeting, it went off better than she had dared to hope. The discussion turned to family lines and genealogy, for of course it had to be determined exactly who Claymore had brought into the family, and there was little chance of discovering it from *him*. Her writing of the family history was a support in this catechism, and when she could mention names going back to the sixteenth century and decorate the names with a dab of history and lore along the way, she was judged to be a better than average sort of girl.

"I hope you will induce my son to take his place in Parliament," the Dowager suggested. "With your interest in politics, you might have some influence with him. He has taken his oath, but has never spoken in the House, and it is high time he did."

Ellie goggled to hear such weighty matters were to make up her new life, and confided diffidently that Papa was not at all political.

"He has a large conservatory, I hear."

This was good for the second remove, and was finally terminated by the suggestion that Ellie might be able to do something with that scraggle of weeds in the yard that was supposed to be a rose garden. She observed that her new life was not to be an easy one, and any talents she possessed were to be put to good use.

It was over the sweet that the first mention of Clay's absence was raised, it being tacitly understood between them that they wouldn't let him ruin their dinner.

"I have sent a note off to Bath while you rested," Ellie was told. "I doubt we will see him before morning."

"I cannot think he is there." If she had not just distinguished herself by knowing more history and horticulture than her mama-in-law, she would have been considered quite a wet goose. As it was, she escaped with a curt "We'll see."

The note had been dispatched by a footman within

minutes of Ellie's first retiring to her room. One copy was taken to the Dowager's quarters at Laura Place, where servants were in residence, and a duplicate to Homberly's place on Gay Street, but, of course, none was delivered to the Pelican. In fact, the Dowager had never heard of it. The York was part of her world, but the Pelican was unknown to her.

It would have done no good had it been sent to this den of outer darkness. Clay and Rex were both there, but in no condition to be reading, or hardly even sitting up.

The two gentlemen, disgruntled by their wasted afternoon, drowned their woes in brandy and a futile discussion of what they ought to do next. It was well past midnight when Rex reeled from the room, and was put to bed in the inn by a servant.

Chapter Eighteen

Claymore was furious with himself when he awoke in such sad disarray in the morning. He had wasted a whole night when he might have been out looking for Ellie. But where was there left to look now? He had been to the obvious places, the less likely ones, and finally to the Hall—the unlikeliest of all. The affair was taking on a new seriousness in his mind; no longer a prolonged game of hide-and-seek, instituted by a piqued bride. Ellie was *gone*, vanished entirely, and he had to find her. He made a hasty toilette and was about to go below stairs for breakfast when a light tap sounded on his door. His hands trembled, and he whispered the word that was uppermost in his mind—"Ellie."

The door opened before he reached it, and a puffy-eyed and extremely disheveled Rex Homberly shuffled in.

"I seem to have spent the night here," he said, yawning.

"We drink too much, Rex, you and I. You are your own man, of course, and I don't mean to dictate to you, but *I* mean to limit my drinking to a reasonable level." He walked to the dresser and handed his friend a clean shirt and cravat. While these raiments were put on, the lender delivered a short sermon on the evils of drink and general dissipation, none the less sincere for being hackneyed.

As Homberly put the finishing touches to his ensemble, he said in a hushed tone, "Clay, you ain't setting up to become a *Methodist*, are you?"

"Certainly not. Order breakfast, then come back."

Rex was so impressed with the austere countenance of his reformed friend that he went without a single complaint. Over breakfast they discussed their next move in the search for Clay's wife—a phrase never uttered between them without restraint at the wording thereof.

"I shall return to London," Clay said, but he sounded by no means confident that he was doing the right thing.

"Can't think she's there."

"No more do I, but if she means to try for a divorce, you know—"

"Or an annulment," Rex threw in slyly, reminding his friend that his marriage was unconsummated.

"Or an annulment, I expect that is where the papers would be prepared."

"Lord yes, her mother'd never let her do it at home. But you don't think it will really come to that?"

"I hardly know what to think. Clearly, she is hiding herself from me. It doesn't seem to me that she has any thought at all of ever living with me. I expect it will be better to legalize the estrangement."

"I can't picture little Ellie being a divorcée. Seems so dashing, you know, and her such a shy little country-bred girl."

"I cannot picture myself in the role either."

"Oh, suits *you* well enough," Rex replied heedlessly. "Ain't so bad for the man, but a *woman* . . . well, gives a girl a bit of a fast reputation, if you see what I mean."

"*I* don't intend to divorce her."

"No, she'd never give you the grounds. Not the crim con sort. Take Wanda now . . ."

"The devil take Wanda! But if Ellie wants to leave me, I expect some sort of hoaxed-up arrangement can be made. I will be happy to stand as the offending party."

"That's big of you, Clay. 'Pon my word, that's very broad-minded."

"It is not what I *want*, of course."

"That makes it all the bigger. Really, I don't know how she can have the heart to divorce such a thoughtful fellow. If she only knew how reformed you've become, I doubt she'd divorce you at all."

This taking of his divorce for granted set up Clay's hackles, and he said stiffly, "It is by no means certain there will be a divorce. I shall try for a reconciliation first."

"I'll be your second."

"I said *reconciliation*, not duel."

"That's so. Very true. Still, I'll act as your go-between if you like."

"Thank you, Rex. You have been a true friend through all this ordeal. I have to find her first, though. I must go to London."

"That's where we started, ain't it? And I still don't think you'll find her there."

"I don't think I will *ever* find her. It is become a nightmare, as though the earth had just opened up and swallowed her."

Rex's eyes were on the verge of spilling tears. They were swimming, but had not yet overflown. He sniffed, and said, "Thing to do is start all over again. She's just a simple little girl, Clay, and there's no point thinking she's gone slipping off to Paris or something, for she wouldn't even think of that. She's with some of her family. Her papa, or Joan, or Caroline. Retrace your steps and you'll find her at one place or the other. Easy enough to have missed her on the road. If her carriage was in an inn yard or what not when you passed by, you know, you'd never know you'd passed her. Take my word, she's sitting right at home now, waiting for you to come and fetch her, or at Joan's or Caroline's."

"I'll start at London then. First the Siderows', then the Tamesons'."

"That'll be *my* job, I fancy," Rex said with resignation.

"No, it is *my* job, and I shall do it."

"Lord, but you'll feel a fool, Clay, telling 'em what happened."

"I'm past all that. I should have told them the truth on the first day, and they might have told me where to find Ellie. It is this damned pride that has hampered my search. Four whole days I have wasted. I can't stand it anymore, Rex. If I don't find her by today, I will put an advertisement in the papers, and let the whole world know she has left me, and see if someone can find her."

"Can't think your mother would like that."

"She would be delighted to see me sunk so low."

"There's the Bow Street Runners. Could call them in to help. Townshend's boys are very good at finding a lost person."

"Them, too. I'll try anything."

"Shall I go with you?"

"It might be better if you stay here, on the off chance that she shows up in this neighborhood. You might ride over to the Hall and tell Mama the truth, and tell her to notify me in London immediately if Ellie goes there."

"Yes, I'll do that."

"Good. I'm off then. You'll keep an eye peeled, and an ear, too. Don't bother sending me every rumor you hear, though. If you discover any *facts*, let me know."

Clay arose and was soon leaving. Rex sat behind to finish the coffee and make his own plans. First, go home and change into some decent duds. Looked like a hooligan in this outfit he'd slept in. As Rex left the inn, Clay's curricle was just setting out. He raised a hand in salute, and Clay tried to smile at him. Poor devil. Looked like death warmed over. Face white as a sheet, and his eyes all circled in smudges. Taking it very hard. Be an old man before he was thirty at this rate. Rex had his own curricle harnessed up and rode over to Gay Street to make a fresh toilette. It was quite as an afterthought, some half-hour later, that Rex asked the butler if there was any mail for him. He was handed the letter for Claymore, and asked where he should direct it, or if milord was expected at Gay Street.

"Well, if you ain't a cloth-head!" Rex said to his butler, and snatched the envelope from his hand. He immediately recognized the writing and seal as belonging to Claymore's mother, and wondered what to do. He first thought of setting out after Clay immediately and seeing if he could overtake him. Then he considered what the envelope might contain. No saying it had anything to do with Ellie. Might be no more than a request to get Laura Place ready for her arrival. Seemed to him she'd mentioned some such thing. Old devil of a woman, and after he'd told her half a dozen times Clay wasn't at Bath. He deemed the circumstances extraordinary enough to permit him to open and read the letter, and quickly did so under the disapproving eye of the butler.

The Dowager's style of communication with her son did not allow of any misunderstanding: it was immediately clear where Ellie was. Told him so half a dozen times, and why must he go dashing off to London to get divorced? He had his curricle hitched up for the chase. Here was a rig very much to his liking. Clay would have an hour's start on him by the time he got off. Wouldn't let his horses full out, for he wasn't half eager to go to London. Moseying along at a canter is what he'd be doing. Thing to do, spring his own team and try to catch Clay up as soon as possible. He set on Marlborough as the closest spot for overtaking Clay. That with good luck. With bad, it would be Reading, where Clay kept a spare team stabled. He'd be sure to stop there and freshen up and change horses. It was not till he was several miles out of Bath that it occurred to him he should have sent a note off to the Hall, to allay their fears. Still, if he'd done that, the old Tartar would know he'd opened and read Clay's letter. What wouldn't she make of that!

At the Hall, Ellie enjoyed all the lively humiliation of knowing that *if* her husband deigned to return to her at all, it would be at his mother's command, a circumstance that did not augur well for their future happiness. When she sought refuge in her room from the Dowager's painful attempts at entertainment, she was met with Miss Pritchard's wounded countenance. Pritchard had patched

together the true story from bits and pieces picked up
from the servants, and from the evidence of her own eyes.
She bustled about the room, muttering animadversions
against "sly and deceitful creatures," and "a viper in my
bosom." Gaining no response to these leading sallies, she
said outright, "Had I know what lay before me, milady, I
would have preferred doing for Miss Wanda."

"Do be quiet, Pritchie!" Ellie exclaimed, and when her
mistress burst into a flood of tears, the servant forgave all,
and cuddled her in her arms as she had not done for ten
years.

The Dowager bore up well, for she enjoyed a good
set-to, and there would be a fine one before this day
was over. Yet she became fidgety as the day progressed,
and still no signs of Claymore. Shouldn't have taken him
more than a couple of hours to come from Bath. In as-
sorted attempts at conversation with her daughter-in-law
it came out that the marriage settlement had been
twenty-five thousand, not hundred, as she had thought.
She choked on the sum, and was more convinced than
ever that Clay *must* love the girl, so why did he not
come? Then she fell to wondering how he had contrived
to purchase a large diamond in the circumstances to which
the settlement must have reduced him. She understood for
the first time his eagerness to get ahold of his jewels. She
could not but feel culpable, and thought it might be politi-
cally wise to turn the heirlooms over to the bride now, before Clay returned.

With an anguished heart she did so, only to have Ellie
look at them blankly, declare them very fine, and shut the
lid of the chest without so much as lifting one of them up
to try on, or admire. Whatever else the girl was, she was
not grasping. The young maw-worm of Clay's had been
right about that at least.

By dinnertime both women were distracted with waiting and worrying. When the meal was finished, they retired to the Blue Saloon and Ellie offered her services to
work one corner of the tambour frame, on which a canvas
firescreen was being embroidered. "This is for my Dower
House," she was told. "I'll be removing there after I return

from Bath. I don't intend to billet myself on you and Clay."

Ellie had already been assured of this by her husband, but was happy to hear it confirmed. "I hope it is not too far away," she replied, by way of appearing friendly.

"Only a mile. Close enough, but not too close."

"Just a pleasant walk."

They worked on till ten, both with one ear to the door, and not even half the other on their conversation. "He won't be coming tonight," the old lady announced as the clock chimed ten dolorous clangs. "Might as well toddle off to bed."

Ellie was happy enough to do so. Even if he *did* come, she would prefer to have the first meeting take place in private. The Dowager sat up alone, long after Ellie retired, thinking about the scrape, how to disentangle them all, and later fell into a reverie of her future life. Much as it pained her to admit it, she was getting old. Couldn't hack the London round anymore, and this great rabbit warren of a place was too much for her. The gardens were a disgrace, and she hadn't been up to the third floor for two years. Her little brawls with Clay were becoming more of a nuisance than anything else as well. She'd be glad when this one was over. Lud, she hoped she didn't become one of those *mellow* old ladies, smiling at her children and grandchildren, and slipping them money and sweets, respectively, on the side. She was forced to admit, though, that she felt a very unaccustomed pity for Clay's young wife. Actually thought she might turn out to *like* her, which she had not counted on. She had rather liked Lady Siderow, whom she knew a little the year she was married to her Polish lord, or whatever he was.

She got up and went to examine the corner of the tambour frame Ellie had been working on. Well, she was a nice little thing, but she was no needle woman. This pleased her rather than otherwise, for she was a bit of a dab in that line herself, and didn't much relish competition. Bad enough to be put to the blush by the girl's knowing so much about history and gardening. One had to maintain one bastion of supremacy. She was not ready to abdicate completely. The girl was no musician either, if that one off-key little song she'd strummed tonight was any example.

She was just putting away her threads and needles when she heard a clatter of hooves on the drive, going round to the stables. She was finished when she heard a footfall in the front hallway, and went out to see who it was. She hardly recognized her son, he looked so pale and worn. She expected some sort of rip-up from him, but he said only, "Hallo, Mama," and pecked her on the cheek. "I got your note. Thank you for sending it. Is Ellie all right?"

"Yes, gone to bed long since. Come in and have a glass of something. You look dead beat."

"I am. I have been riding since morning."

"Lud, Clay, Bath is only twenty-five miles away."

"Yes, but I was at Reading when I received your note." He sank into a chair, and she bustled off for refreshments. Looked as if he needed more than a glass of wine. She had a servant bring cold meat and bread into the Blue Saloon, for she hadn't the heart to ask him to stagger into the dining room.

"Ellie is asleep, you say?" he asked when she returned.

"Yes, gone to bed hours ago."

"I won't disturb her then. I suppose she told you . . ."

"I ain't blind, Clay. She has told me enough."

"Yes, I know I acted the fool, Mama. Pray don't scold me. I will be in fitter trim to spar with you tomorrow."

Again she felt that weakening stab of pity, and for her own son, too. She softened her barb. "Why did you not follow her on, as she seemed to expect you to do?"

He raised his two hands, palms up, and shrugged his weary shoulders. "I didn't think she was coming here. We had had words, you see."

"Pooh! A lovers' quarrel. She expected you to go after her."

"Mama, I have been 'going after her' these four days past. Chasing all over England looking for her. I didn't think she'd have the bottom to face you alone. I made sure she had gone off to her papa."

"She showed more sense than you then, for she came here, just as she ought."

"I hope you like her." The son cast a wary eye on his mother as he uttered this hope.

"Yes, we go on very agreeably. She is not in the least a dowd, as that friend of yours said, but very elegant, and with excellent conversation for a *young* girl. She is nothing special with a needle I find, but then one can't expect all accomplishments to be hers at so young an age."

"She is rather shy, and I suppose I warned her you are—"

"Yes, I make no doubt you gave me a ferocious character, and it seems Lady Siderow backed you up, but we got on in spite of that. I would not say she is *shy* precisely, by the by."

"Well, not *precisely*," he agreed, with a strange smile on his wan face.

"I take it this breach between you two is not irreparable?" the Dowager asked, eyeing his smile.

"Since she is come here, I have some hopes it may be repaired."

"Yes, and if you saw her eyes light up every time your name is mentioned, you would have no doubts of *her* feelings at least. Very fine eyes, incidentally. Rather like Lady Siderow's."

"Better than Lady Siderow's," he pointed out.

"I can see I'll have to step up my comparisons, or eliminate them entirely if she is to be an Incomparable."

"Just so."

"And well she might be, with a settlement of twenty-five *thousand* pounds!"

"Ah, you have discovered that, have you?" he asked, with an arch glance, not completely devoid of horror.

"I have, but it's *your* money, and you may squander it as you please. It is nothing to me. Well, it's all in the family, as far as that goes. And had you told me the *truth* of the matter, I should naturally have given you your ring, and other things. Gave 'em to her, by the way."

"Thank you, Mama," he said, feeling the words

hopelessly inadequate to the occasion. Truth to tell, he was so tired the whole conversation was like a dream.

"Don't thank me. They're yours. Not that they made much of an impression."

"Did she not like them?" he asked, surprised. There were some fine and costly pieces among the Claymore heirlooms.

"Hardly glanced at them, to tell the truth. Your foolish friend mentioned something about your buying her a diamond ring."

"My foolish and *well-meaning* friend, Mama. You underestimate Rex. He has bent over backward to help me all through this awful business."

"Let's see the ring. Do you have it?"

"Yes, I have it here." He pulled it out of his pocket and showed it to her.

She did not quite whistle, but her lips took on the look of it. "Very fine. Must have cost you a bundle. How did you swing it with the settlement to make?"

"I haven't. Paid for it, I mean."

"Maybe you could take it back, since she's got the others now. Your *well-meaning* friend told me you'd already given it to Ellie. Wondered that she wasn't wearing it."

"I'm sure he thought he had a reason for telling you so. No, Mama, in a way this ring is responsible for our—altercation, one way or the other, and I mean her to have it. Now if you would care to *lend* me—"

"I haven't given you any gift yet. If you would care to consider it as your joint wedding gift, I'll make a present of it to Ellie." Good God! Here was she, slipping her children money, as she was determined she would not do. "And you can give me back my pearl," she added, to salve her conscience.

"It would be highly appreciated, Mama. I don't mean to make a habit of outrunning the grocer, if *that* is what has got your brow wrinkled."

"Very well, that's settled. Give me the bill when you get it. I shan't ask the price, for I want to get some sleep this night. Now we must consider what to do about the scandal broth that I make no doubt is brewing, what with you two dashing all over the countryside in separate carriages. Ellie tells me I am ill, and she came on ahead here to tend me, while you followed behind."

"And Rex told someone or other I came here by way of Bath to pick some medications up for you. It is such a tangled skein there is no hope of unraveling it. I doubt any two people think the same thing on this matter. And for myself, I don't care a tinker's curse what anyone thinks, except Ellie."

"But for the looks of it, Clay, I was thinking whether we couldn't all go together to Bath for a few days. I'll lay low to lend credence to my illness, just letting a few crones in to see I am really there. If you and Ellie are seen about together, it will give the lie to the stories. I'll even make an appearance at the Pump Room and have a glass of that awful water, to prove I am not well, though the stuff would be enough to really sicken me."

"I won't ask such a sacrifice of you. No, you go ahead to Bath. Ellie and I will rusticate here a while. Perhaps we'll join you later for a few weeks."

She was about to persist, but upon noticing a certain rigidity settling in along the line of Clay's jaw, she refrained. "I shall do what I can to scotch the rumors in any case."

"How many times tonight have I thanked you, Mama?"

"More times than the rest of your life put together. You are become a pattern-card of civility."

"And *you* are behaving very much like a mother. You weren't used to, you know."

"Ah well, I grow old. I can feel the rust creeping into my hinges; that's what my mother used to say—seems like a million years ago. But she lived twenty years after that. I may be back to my normal unmaternal self by tomorrow and renege." Glancing at his tired face, she changed tack. "Go on up to bed, Clay. You look dog tired."

"Yes, I will. Where is Ellie sleeping?"

"In the master bedroom. I had it prepared for the two of you. You see how you have misjudged me? I moved out, just as I ought."

"I am embarrassed to say thank you again. What shall I say instead?"

"Say good night, before you fall on your face. All this cordiality is tiring me out. I'll go up with you."

They proceeded together up the staircase, each half dragging himself, and half dragging the other. "Quite a pair of relics," the Dowager said. "It'll be good to get into my snug little cottage."

"Bath will rejuvenate you."

"Let's see if marriage rejuvenates you."

At the top of the stairs the Dowager turned left to what was now her suite. A sad come-down from the master bedroom. Still, it suited her age and encroaching infirmity. Smaller, and less draughty. It could be the north wind howling through the windows in her old room that gave her those painful twinges in the knees and shoulders.

Clay turned to the right and went to the door of the master bedroom. His mama had not turned it over to him upon his father's demise, as she should have done. He would have felt an intruder had the room been vacant. Knowing that his wife was within, he felt the veriest interloper. He supposed she was asleep, and wanted only to take a peek; to reassure himself that she was really there, under the same roof as himself, after all these weary days of pelting about England looking for her.

She was there, and she was asleep, her dark curls spread out on the pillow, the shadow of her lashes elongated on her cheek. She looked about six years old. He stepped in and closed the door behind him, but as deep darkness followed this step, he reopened it to light the single taper by her bed before closing the door again. Perhaps the sound of the door awoke her, or perhaps her troubled spirits allowed her only a fitful doze. In any case, she opened her eyes and blinked twice at him, before springing up to a sitting position.

"Clay! Is it really you?" she said, her voice sleepy.

"I didn't mean to awaken you," he apologized, yet he was not sorry to have this glimpse of her with her eyes open. He came closer to have a better look. "I think it's me, but I am so tired I hardly know."

"You look haggard," she agreed. "You had better sit down. *Here!*" she added, patting the bed, as she noticed he looked around the room for a chair. "And tell me what has fagged you so."

"Well, Ellie," he began uncertainly, "it is chasing from here to kingdom come looking for *you* that has fagged me so. What did you think?" He perched, rather tentatively, on the outermost edge of the bed as he spoke.

"I didn't think it would take you so long to find me, for I told Meecham where I was going."

Their hands slid along the coverlet toward each other, stopping just as they were within ames ace of meeting. "Yes, Meecham told me."

"Well, then, why didn't you come?" Something between doubt and a pout puckered her lips and tilted her chin up.

In spite of his fatigue Claymore felt the old urge to pounce assert itself. "You said you would not come here, if you recall. . . ."

"You know I didn't *mean* it," she challenged, and her lips began to tremble, till she pulled them together between her teeth.

"You had already peeled off on me once that day."

"What did you expect when you went ranting on about that horrid Gloria Golden in your sleep, and—*everything!*"

"What?" He let his hand inch forward and grabbed her fingers. They felt warm and soft. "What else did I do to give you so poor an opinion of me?"

"Nothing. You didn't do *anything*, Clay. That's just it."

"It's not that I didn't *want* to!" he defended himself, squashing her little fingers till they ached, and peering at her through the dim light of the only candle to determine whether they were discussing the same thing."

"It is certainly not that *I* didn't want you to. I am not so strange as that."

"You looked as if you didn't want me to. You looked so very young, frightened." She still looked young, but not, he thought, so very frightened. He brought out the diamond ring. "This is what delayed me so long the morning you left." He took it out of its plush box and slid it over her finger. It was still too big, so that the diamond slipped around to the underside of her hand, and she had to clench her fingers to keep it upright. She smiled, but did not go into raptures as though she had been craving it. He was rather glad.

"There, now we are *really* engaged," he said with quiet satisfaction. "And it's bigger than Wanda's, too."

"We are really married, Clay," she reminded him.

He scrutinized her pale face closely, and smiled softly to himself, before he raised her diamond-studded hand to his lips and kissed it. "Yes, you are *my wife*, and to hell with Homberly," he replied enigmatically.

"Oh, what has Rex to do with anything?"

"Nothing. Nothing at all." He put an arm around her shoulders, gently, and pulled her toward him. When he met with no resistance, but quite the contrary, felt her lean against him, he forgot he was half dead with fatigue, and said masterfully, "Now, Ellie, there will be no more of this dashing away from me, understand? I was wild with worry."

"Were you, Clay?" she asked happily. "I am so very sorry, and *you* must not talk about Gloria in your sleep."

"It was a *nightmare*," he explained, just that very moment visited with the marvelous inspiration. "I had a horrible nightmare that I was married to Gloria. I often get nightmares of that sort—witches chasing me, and houses burning down, and being married to someone I detest. That sort of thing."

"What a whisker," she jeered, and fell into a fit of giggles, more from nervousness than mirth.

"It's good to see you smile again, Ellie," he said, peering down at her happy face. She instantly turned serious, but the trick was already done. They were face to face, only inches apart, and in a second he was kissing her lips, fighting back the impulse to pounce.

"The shy one," he whispered into her ear, as she put both her arms around his neck and proceeded to tighten her grip.

"Oh, I think *you* are the shy one," she chided, as he nuzzled her ears, her neck, even her shoulder.

"Ellie," he said dangerously, and went on to attack her in a manner that gave her a much better impression of him, for it was clear the deceitful girl hadn't a shy bone in her whole body.

ALL AT $1.75!

Enduring romances that represent a rich reading experience.

BABE by Joan Smith	50023
THE ELSINGHAM PORTRAIT by Elizabeth Chater	50018
FRANKLIN'S FOLLY by Georgina Grey	50026
THE HIGHLAND BROOCH by Rebecca Danton	50022
A LADY OF FORTUNE by Blanche Chenier	50028
LADY HATHAWAY'S HOUSE PARTY by Jennie Gallant	50020
THE LORD AND THE GYPSY by Patricia Veryan	50024
THE LYDEARD BEAUTY by Audrey Blanshard	50016
THE MATCHMAKERS by Rebecca Baldwin	50017
A MISTRESS TO THE REGENT by Helen Tucker	50027
REGENCY GOLD by Marion Chesney	50002
WAGER FOR LOVE by Rachelle Edwards	50012

Buy them at your local bookstore or use this handy coupon for ordering.

COLUMBIA BOOK SERVICE (a CBS Publications Co.)
32275 Mally Road, P.O. Box FB, Madison Heights, MI 48071

Please send me the books I have checked above. Orders for less
than 5 books must include 75¢ for the first book and 25¢ for each
additional book to cover postage and handling. Orders for 5 books
or more postage is FREE. Send check or money order only.

Cost $_____   Name _____

Postage_____   Address _____

Sales tax*_____   City _____

Total $_____   State _____ Zip _____

*The government requires us to collect sales tax in all states except
AK, DE, MT, NH and OR.

This offer expires 1/31/81   8000-4